Grace
PERIOD

Publishing and Design Services: Melinda Martin, melindamartin.me
Editor: Hannah Bauman, btleditorial.com

ISBN: 978-1-7360834-1-3 (print), 978-1-7360834-2-0 (epub)

Ordering Information:

Special discounts are available on quantity purchases by corporations, associations, and others. For details, contact mlihome@outlook.com.

Grace
PERIOD

MARI-LYNNE INFANTINO

This story is for all persons who dare to stand against domestic violence, forging a new life for themselves and their families, breaking the abuse cycle.

Chapter 1

Tina

Tina unclenched her jaw, easing into a smile as her husband twirled her one last time, ending the dance with a flourish. Eager for a moment's rest after two fast-paced song sets, she stepped off the vinyl floor and onto the concrete.

"Jarrod," she said, "let's sit down and have a beer. It feels like my feet are ready to fall off."

Jarrod Oliver frowned. "We're just getting started. You'll be fine."

Tina's breath hitched, but she swallowed any additional comments she might have made. Making the most of the quick break, she rocked back and forth, soothing the aching soles of her feet.

The beat of the DJ's choice invited dancers back to the floor. Jarrod squeezed her hand, pulling her through the crowd of dancers, the continued crushing across her palm serving as a reminder to keep up the pace. Concentrating on the rhythm of the new song, Tina almost missed the shift in Jarrod's attention. She chanced a momentary glance in the direction he was looking and noticed the woman's faint smile, eyes seductively fastened on her husband's face.

What's one more woman with slim hips and small breasts? Tina thought. *No wonder he's strutting like a peacock. I'm his Raggedy Anne doll, only dragged around the floor out of habit.*

Distraught, she stumbled, sensing her husband's agitation through his hold on her hand. His displeasure jump-started that familiar dread in her heart.

No, Jarrod, please not tonight, she thought. *My fault, I should have paid attention, my fault.* She concentrated on the dance steps, trying to ignore the flirtation going on over her head. *Can't he keep his mind out of his pants for just this one short night?*

She stumbled again, as much from distraction as her tired feet. Jarrod pulled at her wrist, jerking her to a halt on the dance floor.

"What the hell is the matter with you?" Jarrod snapped. "Sit your fat ass down if you're that tired. I'll find myself a woman who wants to dance." He stalked away without so much as a backward glance.

Embarrassed, Tina collided with another couple. "I'm sorry," she said automatically, her eyes tracking Jarrod as he moved toward the woman she'd noticed earlier. *You'd think I'd learn by now. We should have just stayed home. All I wanted was one night out, and where does he take me? This low-life bar where every drug user in the city hangs out, including himself. I'm just his excuse to be here.* She scuttled her way off the dance floor.

Damn it! One night out for our anniversary. Jarrod had

promised to take her somewhere different, yet here they were. *I even dressed up, wore Momma's pearls.*

Why do I believe him? she wondered.

When they'd first arrived at the dive bar, Tina had spent thirty minutes in a dimly lit parking lot while he conducted his business. "I just have to meet up with someone," he'd said. "Just wait in the car."

When Jarrod had finally made his way to the car, she'd smelled the liquor on his breath, realizing he'd never had any intention of going anywhere else. Tina didn't know if it was worse to be embarrassed in front of the local addicts or upset because it was their anniversary.

Lost in her thoughts, Tina walked right into a wall.

"Señora Oliver, are you alright?"

Tina raised her head, recognizing the familiar voice of the man standing beside her. She ignored his outstretched hand, looking around for a chair or a hole to sink into, for a chance to slow the screaming in her brain. *Ray Ruiz.* Tina acknowledged the man's sudden appearance with apprehension. *What's he doing here?*

"Yes, I'm just dizzy," she mumbled. "Please go away." Tina lowered herself into the seat at a nearby table, hiding angry eyes with her long hair, remembering too late she should never attract undue attention.

Ignoring her words, Ruiz glanced at her flushed face before he spoke. "I watched you dance with Jarrod earlier, but he's moved on. His current dance partner appears to be quite beautiful."

Startled, Tina glanced across the room and saw Jarrod's arms around the woman he was staring at earlier. Tina gave a self-deprecating shrug. "Yes, she is." Drawing her dignity around her like a cloak, she hissed at the man. "Get away from me, Ruiz. Leave me alone. You'll only make everything worse. Don't let me keep you from your friends."

Ruiz smirked. "You aren't keeping me from anyone, señora. I have unfinished business with your husband, so I'll keep you company while we wait. I'm sure he'll be back momentarily. Care for a drink?" Ruiz waved his hand in the air to flag down the barmaid.

"Go away! Just go away." Tina squeezed her eyes tightly shut, willing him far away from her. Ruiz remained by her side, flicking away a piece of lint from his well-cut pants.

Resigned and quaking from the inevitable, she heard Jarrod's footsteps stomping swiftly toward her. Too late, she tried to rise from her seat, but Jarrod reached her first, pinning her hand to the table.

"I didn't do anything," she muttered mutinously, but her husband was glaring at the other man.

"What are you doing here, Ruiz?" Jarrod barked. "Aren't you supposed to be in San Francisco?"

Tina's eyes opened wide, sensing that a confrontation between Jarrod and Ruiz was imminent. *On purpose*, Tina realized. Ruiz was deliberately inviting Jarrod's jealousy.

She tried to pull her hand away from Jarrod's iron grip,

but it only served to bring his attention back to her. "I can't leave you alone for a minute before you're slutting it up with another man, huh?"

She stared straight ahead, knowing what he'd do to punish her, preparing her body for the assault. Instead, her husband turned back to the man still standing there.

"Ruiz, what do you want with my wife? Doesn't your dear faithful *esposa* give you enough attention?" Jarrod sneered at the other man in his fancy clothes, clearly forgetting his deadly speed, his expertise with weapons. "Excuse me while I remind my bitch not to speak with other men, especially you."

Yanking Tina to her feet, Jarrod grabbed her by the throat, snapping her string of pearls.

"Jarrod, stop!" she cried. *Not Momma's pearls.*

Her hands came up to protect her face, but his fist connected anyway. She fell sideways over the chair, abrading her cheek against the concrete. Still seeing stars, Tina scrambled to her knees on the floor, reaching for the pearls currently bouncing under feet and surrounding tables. Blood gushed from the open cut near her eye. As she swiped her hand across her face to wipe it away, Tina heard Ruiz's challenge.

"You want someone to hurt, *pendejo*, come on! I welcome the opportunity to put a few slices in your gut, but *un momento,* perhaps you'd like to trade your life for the payout money and gems you've managed to stash away." Ruiz's voice bristled with hostility. "Owen Donaldson is still waiting for his delivery. Did you think he wouldn't send someone to collect? You should have known that someone would be me."

Tina shuddered, watching the two men glare at each other. She knew who Donaldson was. A drug boss with contacts all over the city, he also smuggled gems into the United States from out of the country. Jarrod and Ruiz served as his front men. While Jarrod ensured the money drops for the drug deliveries, Ruiz was his enforcer for everything else.

An ugly, vicious man with scars covering parts of his face and neck, Donaldson had eyes of ice that stared at everything and missed nothing, including her. Tina knew this because every so often, Jarrod met with his employer at their apartment. Ruiz accompanied him from time to time as the boss man's second in command.

Jarrod hated Ruiz, and Ruiz hated Jarrod. Tina wasn't around Jarrod's work much, but he complained about Ruiz enough for her to get the picture. Jarrod tolerated Donaldson, believing himself to be smarter than both men, but then again, Jarrod almost always thought he was more intelligent than most people. He wasn't.

Needing to see clearly, Tina wiped the blood away from her eye once more, smearing it all over her face. She, like the crowds surrounding her, was mesmerized by the drama in the room.

"You want your money? You'd better run home to Momma. Maybe there's a payout between her legs, Ruiz, or just another man amusing himself. I certainly found her entertaining."

The excitement in Jarrod's voice disgusted Tina. She knew

her husband was already beyond reason, spoiling for a fight. Oddly, she could only be thankful he'd be hitting someone else tonight. He wasn't smart at all; he was an arrogant bully.

"Bar fight, bar fight!"

She heard the loud chants of the crowd surrounding her, many of them taking bets on who would win. Ignoring the hands of the people trying to help her up, Tina managed to stand on her own. She waited for the first move, observing both men through her rapidly swelling eye. Jarrod lunged first, his massive fist glancing off the jaw of the fast-moving man, then quickly followed through with an uppercut that snapped his head back.

Ruiz responded, knocking Jarrod back with several blows to his face, stomach, and ribs. Tina's husband was lying on the floor. Tables flew across the room, opening space for the two fighters. Spectators' screams mixed with excited voices, all hungry for blood.

Ruiz stepped back, baiting Jarrod with scorn. "Get up, Oliver, or are you only able to hit women?"

Tina swallowed hard, knowing the words raised a red flag to Jarrod's pride. Jarrod was a huge man. Standing at six feet, four inches, and broad through the shoulders and chest, he towered over people, scaring them into submission. Other than herself, he seldom lashed out with his fists, preferring his handgun and physical presence to intimidate. With the aid of a chair someone kicked in his direction, Jarrod stood.

Tina stood quietly, watching her husband's eyes sweep the

room, searching for her. She ignored her aching head, and she could feel the burning of the raw scrape on her cheek. When Jarrod's eyes landed on hers, he snarled, and his fists tightened. Tina's stomach flipped nervously as Jarrod turned his attention back to Ruiz.

Belligerent as a rodeo bull, Jarrod moved forward, fists swinging at Ruiz, who merely stepped aside and laughed when Jarrod lost his balance. Her husband tripped headlong into the jeering crowd. They shoved him back toward his opponent, and Tina didn't need to be a mind reader to know Jarrod's humiliation was enormous.

"You're nothing but words, Oliver," Ruiz taunted. "Nothing but a pretty face for women to admire. One more chance. Where's the money and Donaldson's packet?"

Jarrod Oliver straightened up, slowly catching his breath. Sensing his frustration, Tina stared at the sweat rolling off her husband's body, suddenly realizing that he might lose this fight.

Regaining his confidence as he strutted before the crowd, Jarrod growled out a response. "His money? Donaldson? I thought it was *our* money, Ruiz, the payout for work we both completed. Everything we work for turns to gold for him. I've had enough of that. I decided it's my money now. I deliver the stuff, I collect the payoff. Donaldson's nothing but a fat old man, and it's about time someone took over his clientele instead of just his deliveries. I'll handle him right after I finish you off."

"Loco! You're crazy. You think you're the man to kill Donaldson?" Ruiz shook his head. "If anyone, that would be my job, though why I would, makes no sense—yet. Come on, don't drag this out. You've worked with me long enough to know I'd rather just get the packet back to Donaldson so I can go home. Sonia may be a whore, but she serves her purpose well." Ruiz laughed the cold amusement of a murderer, and Tina swallowed hard. "Where's your weapon? You want to take care of Donaldson, but you don't even carry your weapon?"

Tina sucked in her breath, watching in silence as Jarrod reached for the Ruger handgun he habitually carried with him. Tina knew it was locked away in the car for only one reason. Her husband had promised her one thing: a trouble-free night for their anniversary. But not here! They weren't supposed to be here!

Tina caught the dirty look he cast in her direction, blaming her again. He looked around at the crowd of people waiting to see what he would do. He found the bouncers hanging back at the far end of the room. Jarrod Oliver's reputation did not allow him to back down from a fight.

Clamping her hand over her mouth, Tina stifled a scream as she caught a glimpse of a bright flash of steel in Ruiz's hand.

"*Basta!*" Ruiz scorned. "You're not brave enough to kill Donaldson or me. Again, your words deceive you. Meanwhile, you can dance with *El Diablo* tonight."

"Fuck you, Ruiz!"

Ruiz stood ready as Jarrod charged once more, scoring

with a head butt into Ruiz's flat belly, knocking him sideways and down. Both men scrambled up off the floor, Jarrod's fist connecting again. Ruiz grabbed Jarrod's torso, and they both crashed together, grappling for the knife. Tina barely saw it slide first into Jarrod's ribs and then deep into his chest, the crimson blood staining the blue silk shirt she had ironed with such anticipation earlier that day.

Blood gurgling out the corners of his mouth, Jarrod sank to his knees, staggering toward a horrified Tina who found herself abandoned by the crowds. His dead weight collapsed on her, slamming her back once more onto the concrete floor. Her head cracked against the hard surface. Bouncers, reluctant to come between Ruiz or Jarrod earlier, pushed the crowd of faceless people aside.

Through ringing ears, Tina could hear screaming, the whine of police sirens, and a woman screaming, "You killed him!"

Struggling to get free from under Jarrod's limp and lifeless body, Tina's hands slid beneath him in the growing pool of blood. She recoiled as Jarrod's murderer spit on his face.

Coldly and calmly, Ruiz stated, "I warned him once before. Do not underestimate me, ever." Barely leaning down, he directed a low-voiced threat at Tina. "Now it is you who owes Donaldson, Señora Oliver. I'll be back to collect it. But soon, it will all be mine. What's mine, I keep."

Ruiz melted into the horde of strangers as hot tears raced down Tina's cheeks.

Chapter 2

Tina

Absentmindedly dumping sugar in her hot chocolate, Tina dragged her stir stick through the paper cup, watching the cream swirl around and around until the white foam dissolved in a sea of gray-brown liquid. Spotting an empty table toward the rear of the coffee shop, she placed a plastic lid on the paper cup and shifted the two backpacks over her shoulder. Grabbing the cup and her belongings, Tina reached the table and gingerly lowered herself into one of the chairs.

Easing her burdens onto the second chair, she pulled it closer to her side. Slowly, Tina lifted her legs on top of the packs, resting her body while making sure they stayed secure in her sight. One held a bare minimum of her clothing and the other, well, the other carried items of more value.

She pulled a rubber band from the pocket of her Levi's to tie her hair back, accidentally brushing her hand against her cheek. She flinched. Bunching her hair up in a messy ponytail, the aching woman hooked the stray ends behind her ears. It was always falling in her face.

Tina removed the lid to the hot chocolate and took a sip, making a face from the cloying sweetness passing over her tongue and down her throat. *Oh, God, that's nasty. Did I put sugar in this?*

The coffee shop window revealed the bus stop she'd arrived at down the street. Shifting her body on the cheap plastic chair, Tina flexed her back and shoulders, trying to ease the ache. Emeryville was almost 400 miles from Los Angeles, and nine hours by bus. Tina was exhausted from the long ride, and her butt hurt from sitting on the covered sponge rubber that had flattened in so many places. Tina was confident the train station was close. She'd read the direction signs but wanted to make sure nobody was following her.

Closing her eyes for just a moment, Tina saw again the angry eyes and sweaty face of Ruiz, yanking her arm, trying to pull her from Jarrod's car as she parked it in the carport of her apartment building. Quickly, she startled herself awake, looking around the coffee shop.

Don't fall asleep, Tina, she scolded herself. She still couldn't get over the frightening few minutes when Ruiz had appeared almost out of nowhere the day before. She could still hear the flat, deadly tone of his voice.

"The police are already looking for me, señora, but I'm not going to prison for murdering that bastard you called your husband. You're going to hand over those diamonds and the money. Don't even think about going to the police because Donaldson has eyes everywhere and I have many ways to murder a scared rabbit like you."

Tina sat up straight in the chair and picked up her cup. *If it wasn't for those two men that came toward us, I'd probably be dead by now.* Two men—people she might have assumed lived in the same complex—had shown up at that moment. One had gone after Ruiz, though she hadn't seen any ID or indications they were cops. *They looked as evil as Ruiz.* She'd started screaming she wanted a policewoman as a witness, but the second man didn't call anyone. Instead, he took off in the unmarked car. *Was he a straight cop or one of the crooked ones that Donaldson paid?*

A helicopter circling above the roofs of old run-down buildings in the skid row section of Los Angeles made her nervous. *No need to be concerned. Cops and helicopters regularly patrol these neighborhoods.* What street was she on, anyway? There was traffic everywhere, and homeless people were sitting on every corner.

Scowling, Tina considered her circumstances. *I'm going to turn into one of those people with a cardboard sign. 'Will work for food.'* She imagined her life filthy and begging, standing under the shelter of a bus stop. She shook off the thought with firm resolve.

Tina took another sip of her drink and gagged, disgusted that she'd ruined a perfectly good cup of hot chocolate because she hadn't been paying attention. Swallowing hard against the sharp pain in her side, Tina grabbed the packs once again to stand in line, ordering a cup of coffee and a slice of lemon cake.

As Tina placed her order, she saw the server do a double-take when she glanced at Tina's face. She turned back around and put a slice of cake on a dish and shoved it toward her.

Tina bit back a sigh. She shouldn't have pulled her hair back; it showed off her bruises too easily.

Furtively glancing toward her manager, the server shook some ice cubes in a plastic bag and poured Tina's coffee. "The charge is $5.05 for the coffee and cake," she said, "but the ice is free."

"Thank you very much," Tina mumbled gratefully.

The employee opened her mouth to say more, but her boss was glaring at them both. She shrugged and waited on the next customer. Tina flashed a crooked smile and sat back down, pressing the numbing ice pack against her cheek.

After finishing her coffee and cake, Tina was ready to move on. She pulled a pen and a $5.00 bill out of the backpack. Folding the money inside a torn piece of napkin, she scribbled *thanks* across the top, dropping it in the tip box by the cash register as she left.

It's only a short distance to the train. I can do this. Wary of passers-by, Tina walked the few long city-blocks to Union Station Los Angeles. Eyes shifting right and left, she continued moving forward, in the direction of the train station, pacing the sidewalks in circles at red signal lights, nervous of losing her backpacks to thieves. Finally, though, Tina made it to Union Station, and without any incidents.

Inside the vast transportation hub, she wandered for a bit,

panicked by the large numbers of people scurrying around her. *Breathe,* she told herself. Tina noted the security lines, then ducked into a women's restroom.

She sank onto the toilet seat of an empty stall. Opening one bag, Tina withdrew $250 from several stacks of bills tightly banded in a zipped section of the pack, quickly stuffing the money in her jeans pocket along with her driver's license. Tina set her lips in a thin line, thinking of the choices she had made.

I need the money. The police don't, she repeated to herself for the thousandth time. *It's mine now. Jarrod can't spend it, and Ruiz will kill me even if I give it to him. Donaldson won't want any loose ends hanging around.*

Tina pulled her old cell phone from a side pocket of the lighter backpack. She'd erased her personal information and turned off both the navigation and location settings. But was it enough? On a television show she'd seen, the police seemed to get a lot of information by going through your cell phone service. Tina didn't know much about the internal operation of cell phones other than how to take pictures and use the standard applications that came with it. Better not to take any chances. Before she could change her mind, Tina dropped it in the toilet and flushed it.

I'm doing what's necessary to stay alive, she reminded herself. She shook her head once, trying to calm her nerves. If only she could shake off this headache too. The night Jarrod died, the emergency technicians who'd arrived at the bar told her she had a concussion. They tried to force her to go to the emergency center, but she refused. She'd survived countless head injuries without the benefit of doctors. Instead, Tina had ended up at the police station, held for hours before they released her to deal with the coroner's office. The police asked her the same questions about Jarrod over and over again. Tina's only record was a DUI when she was nineteen. So long ago. How could she make the police understand the dread of living with a drug dealer, the callous way Jarrod treated her, abused her, his possession. A possession he barely tolerated but wouldn't let go.

He's dead. I loved him, then, I hated him. He's dead. HE'S DEAD! screamed her brain.

"Please keep me safe, God," Tina whispered, hoping He was listening for once. "Let me go home, where nothing changes."

Change. Wasn't that why she hooked up with Jarrod all those years ago? She'd been bored, challenging herself by dating the bad-boys, searching for adventure in her life. *Adventure is overrated. Look where it got me.*

Tina opened her eyes, staring at the graffiti-covered partition walls surrounding the toilet. The lock was threadbare, barely keeping the stall door closed. *Yes, some things never change,* she thought. *Maybe it's better that way.*

Unzipping her blue jeans, she reached behind her and pulled the pistol from the built-in holster of her spandex shorts. Holding it nervously in both hands, she shuddered. *I hate this, I hate this, I feel like a criminal.* She hated touching this gun, but even worse now, she was afraid to be without it.

Please God, I hope I don't ever have to use it.

Slowly, Tina disarmed it, separating the magazine and cartridges, placing them in separate locations in one pack. She took apart the gun, separating the slide and frame, and placed it in the other pack, wrapping it with her clothes. Tina zipped her jeans, then checked her pockets. That's where her concealed carry permit was, in case she was stopped in the security line.

Standing resolved and ready, she looked down into the toilet bowl, flushing once more any evidence of the phone's existence, and walked out.

Checking metro rail departures, Tina found a train bound for her destination and purchased a ticket. Securely strapped on her back were the pitiful few belongings she took from the apartment. Tina glanced down, making sure the other back-pack was cinched closed and attached firmly to her chest, then she collapsed on one of the long benches.

I'm going home. I'm going home, she repeated in her mind like a worn-out mantra.

Wrapping a hand tightly around one of the shoulder straps, Tina blew out a short sigh of relief.

I'm going home to Sammy. I hope she lets me stay.

Chapter 3

Tina

Facing the wall, the TV remote still gripped tightly in her fist, Tina woke, disoriented and a bit surprised to find herself lying in a strange bed. Slowly, she raised her head, remembering where she was.

Sleepy eyes darted around the simple bedroom on the third floor, revealing the mahogany four-drawer dresser where she'd shoved all her possessions the night she'd arrived at Sammy's. Gazing further, she located her sneakers, spotting her dirty pair of socks balled up next to them on an old multi-colored rag rug. Yawning, Tina snuggled back down under the warm quilt covering the twin bed that used to belong to her cousin Sara.

Squeezing her eyes shut, Tina considered keeping them closed. Maybe if she left them closed and stuck her head under the bed covers, everything else would go away.

She tried it. It didn't work.

Grace Christina Oliver, or *Teensy* as Tina was often referred to by family, groaned. She was anything but teensy as she used to be as a child. *Momma used to say I shouldn't care about that old nickname because my heart is gigantic and it's the heart that carries the truth.* Although Tina's heart was more apt to get her in trouble.

"Trouble," Momma had been fond of reminding her, "240 pounds of Jarrod trouble squeezing your brains like a dishrag in the spin cycle of the wash."

Tina rolled over and stared out the small window in the far corner of the attic bedroom. The pre-dawn sky greeted her. She sighed, relieved that the night was finally over.

Coward.

Blinking the sleep from her eyes, Tina sat on the edge of the bed, her breath caching at the sharp pain still jabbing her ribs. She stood, stretching carefully. She wandered into the bathroom and stared in the antique oval mirror hanging over the small vanity. Tina made a face at her reflection.

Could I look any worse? There she stood, all five foot nine inches of battered glory, with long, straight brown hair and eyes the color of cinnamon. She winced at her face, still tender to the touch, relieved to find the swelling almost gone. The bruises on her cheek were fading to purple and yellow now. *Whew! A little better*, she thought as she leaned closer to the mirror, examining her slightly crooked nose and tiny dimple at the corner of her mouth.

"Well, at least my teeth are still in place," she muttered as she grabbed the toothpaste.

Shuffling back to the dresser, Tina reached into the top drawer, grabbing panties and a misshapen bra. She dressed, pulling up her frayed blue jeans and shrugging into an old green t-shirt. Crouching down to lace up her old pair of Van's sneakers, her eyes strayed toward the bottom drawer of the dresser.

Almost against her will, she opened the drawer and pulled out the old crocheted afghan folded neatly in layers of tissue. It was one of the very few things she had taken with her from the apartment, a gift from her Grandma Gable to Momma, now passed down to her. With shaky hands, Tina unwrapped the slightly less than $50,000 she'd hidden in its folds. It wasn't a great hiding spot, but she hadn't thought of anything better yet.

Then, Tina lifted out the old wooden yellow box Momma gave her. She held it for a while, letting her fingers stroke the coarse grain of the wood, much as she would stroke her fingers over Momma's face when she was a little girl. Tina sighed and unlocked it with the key pulled from her jeans pocket. She permitted herself a moment to peer inside.

Now what? she thought.

Carrying the box, Tina walked back the few steps to the bed, lowering her body on the mattress. Her fingers caressed the earrings her mother left her and a silver bracelet she'd purchased with her first paycheck. Sadly, she looked at the pitiful few pearls she'd managed to rescue from the floor of the bar that fateful night.

"Momma, maybe there are enough left to create a bracelet," she whispered.

Moving the jewelry aside, Tina removed the false bottom

and gazed at the diamonds winking at her. Just as quickly, she snapped the box closed. Confusion and anger flitted across her face. When she stood again, she confirmed her decision.

They're mine. I might need them. Still, her shoulders sagged as she shoved the box back in its place in the bottom drawer. She folded the afghan up again, then placed it in the drawer and smoothed it over the box.

Then, she tried to put it out of her mind.

Gripping the curved railing, Tina made her way downstairs, taking a few minutes to look at family pictures hanging on the wall at various floor levels. Here were framed photos of Grandma and Grandpa Gable with Aunt Sammy, Aunt Susan, and her Momma Sharon when they were little girls. She smiled at Aunt Sammy, Uncle Dan, and their kids splashing in the shallow surf of Dana Point.

Tina leaned forward, touching a family portrait of Aunt Susan and Uncle Ben and their five children. She missed Uncle Ben so much. She wished once more he were *her* dad. Would he ever understand the choices she'd made?

Tina paused to stare at the framed photo of herself at twelve years old, smiling into the eyes of her Momma. Sharon had been the oldest daughter, the family rebel. *Am I very much like her?* Tina mused.

She squared her shoulders and marched down the rest of the steps to the large and airy kitchen in her aunt's bed and breakfast inn. Butcher block counters were lined above and below with cupboards. A large scarred pine table sat squarely in the middle of the floor. Plugging in the grinder, Tina took a deep breath, enjoying the rich aroma of the coffee beans inviting her to start a pot brewing. She had the daily morning routine down pat now, the simple but essential tasks required to begin a day of innkeeping.

Waiting patiently for her coffee, Tina stepped outdoors to enjoy the chilly sunrise illuminating the side garden full of herbs, citrus trees, and fresh vegetables.

"Thank you," Tina briefly whispered to the heavens. "Thank you for bringing me here safely." For a moment more, she delighted in the caress of the early morning breeze, then quietly walked back inside.

Absentmindedly, Tina sliced two pieces of homemade bread and popped them into the toaster. Humming a bit out of tune, Tina opened the refrigerator spotting a jar of strawberry jam. *Yum,* she thought as she reached for the jar. She uncapped the lid and scooped out a bit of the sticky fruit spread with a nearby butter knife. Too hungry to wait for the toast, she slipped it between her waiting lips, shamelessly licking the jam dripping down her lips.

"Glad nobody's up yet," she said aloud.

"I am!" growled her aunt, and Tina whirled around. Sammy Cooper raised one eyebrow and cocked her hand on an ample hip. "I was thinking of that very bite, and now it's all over your mouth."

Startled, Tina backed against the cabinets. "I'm sorry, Sammy! I wouldn't have taken it if I'd known you wanted it.

Oh, here, maybe we can scrape some more out of the jar? I'm sorry."

"Teensy, for sweet pity's sake, it's okay! I was only teasing you. It's all right honey!" Sammy leaned forward as if to reassure Tina, then smiled at her instead. "It's all right, no need to apologize."

Although Tina quickly recovered, her fingers did not readily release their grip on the butter knife, and she watched closely as Sammy walked to the coffee station.

"Coffee's ready," Sammy said, voice light. "Just what we need, isn't it? A nice strong cup of java with lots of sugar."

"Oh, Sammy," Tina said, relaxing a bit, "sugar should be your middle name."

Tina's aunt responded with a low laugh, "Well, missy, sugar is one of the four basic food groups to my way of thinking! Come on over to the table before we get busy and let's have ourselves a cuppa. I think there might be enough of that jam for one more piece of toast, don't you?"

Sammy poured two oversized cups of coffee into brightly colored mugs, pausing to ask, "Cream with one sugar, right?"

Nodding yes, Tina reached again for the bread loaf, her quivering lips lifting into a tentative smile. Tina concentrated on the toaster this time, glancing sideways to watch her aunt as she added cream and sugar for Tina and an extra spoon of sugar to her own cup.

Sammy padded over to the table, patted the cushion on the long bench seat, and smiled again. "Come on, sit down with me for a while. We'll figure out today's work schedule."

Sammy continued her one-sided conversation in a matter-of-fact voice. "Your bruises are fading. The purple's not as noticeable, always a good sign. Go slow this week while your face heals a bit more, then we'll see about increasing your workload."

"I can do more now, Sammy," Tina said. "I'm strong enough. I'll keep out of sight of the guests till my face heals, but I promise I can do more." She bit her lip, hoping against hope that Sammy wouldn't send her away. Where would she go?

"Tina, stop worrying. We'll take it slow for a few more days and work together till you get a little stronger, okay?" Sammy's voice was gentle. "We've got three guestrooms still occupied from the weekend. Two couples are leaving today, so we'll need to deep clean and prep those rooms after checkout, but the Dennisons are staying on until tomorrow, Tuesday," her aunt explained. "We'll tackle the baking on Wednesday, then we're free to relax till Thursday evening when Mr. and Mrs. Howitzer arrive for a four-day weekend. An additional couple and a single will be here Friday and Saturday night. Not too bad so far this year, and it's only the beginning of March."

The toast popped up, and Tina tried not to jump at the sound. Buttering another slice for Sammy, she balanced all three pieces on a plate with the almost empty jar of jam, then joined her aunt at the table.

"I never realized how much work went into maintaining a bed and breakfast inn," Tina said. "It's hard to keep up. Now that Sara and her husband moved to Arizona, how have you been managing it all on your own?" Tina held her breath, fearing that her aunt wouldn't need her, when she wanted so badly to stay.

"I hire assistants, Teensy," Sammy said. "Hotel and culinary students like interning here, especially during the summer months. But I've wanted to hire you for years. Now that you're free to join me, I get to have my way!"

Sammy flashed a mischievous smile, and Tina couldn't help but smile back in relief.

"Free," Tina echoed. "What a way to put it." She touched the swelling just below her eye and cheekbone areas. "But I'm here at last."

Sammy put a hand on Tina's. "That you are, Teensy, and I'm so happy you are."

Tina sucked in a breath and looked down at the table. "Auntie Sammy, I've meant to ask…Can you please try to call me Tina, at least in front of the guests? After almost thirty years, it's hard to drop a nickname, but please?" Tina took a bite of the toast, savoring the last taste of strawberry. "Thirty, not so old," she mused, "but physically, it feels like a wave knocked me over and spat me out on that shore." Tina pointed a finger in the direction of the ocean just down the hill. She put her chin on her hand in defeat and sighed. "What am I going to do from now on?"

"You can't change who you were," Sammy said slowly. "You can only accept that part of your life is over. He's out of your life, Teensy. I'm not going to tell you I'm sorry he's dead, but I am sad for the way it happened. Jarrod used you as his punching bag for years till someone else decided it was his turn to be the bag."

Closing her eyes, Tina willed the tears to go away. If she was honest, she was glad Jarrod was gone, but she didn't even know who she was anymore.

"What you can do for now is put one foot forward in front of the other and step," Sammy said. "Each day, one more step, okay? Now, let's take a look at next week's menus Teens—Tina, and divide up the chores, shall we?"

Chapter 4

Tina

Tina glanced out the window of the rear guest room at springtime flowers just beginning to bloom along the walkways. March in California, 65 degrees. She loved this view.

Beyond the cement block property walls and the cliff below, she could see the sailboats racing the wind outside the small stone-lined marina that hugged the shore. Visitors were fond of searching for the blue whales migrating to Mexico at this time of year. Sailors eagerly rode the currents, hoping for a glance at the majestic mammals. Displays beckoned from colorful marina storefronts advertising souvenirs and open-air restaurants. Cyclists and skateboarders rode swiftly alongside the access roads, never heeding the cars driving toward them. Dana Point, California, seaside city, a mix of the old and modern.

Leaning back down over the queen-sized mattress, Tina made quick work of stripping the sheets off the bed, dropping them in the laundry basket. She gathered the clean white fitted sheet in her hands but paid more attention to the flowers outside the window.

Gable House was a three-story English manor home that Tina's grandfather built for her grandmother in the Fabulous Forties. The home received its name from her maternal grandfather, Samuel Gable. Originally five bedrooms when it passed down to Sammy and her late husband Dan, they'd raised their three children in cheery spaciousness.

Years later and needing a new source of income, Sammy and Dan had turned Gable House into a bed and breakfast inn, updating and adding additional bedrooms and bathrooms to the second floor for guests. Tina thought it was one of the most beautiful homes in Dana Point.

She loved her aunt Sammy and this house. She'd stayed every summer so that Momma wouldn't have to pay for babysitters, enjoying the fresh air and freedom of a house with a yard. Sometimes Tina would hide in the attic among the old furniture, curled up on a dusty sofa reading or staring out the high attic windows.

She cocked her head sideways, giving some consideration to the storage room. *There are a lot of hiding places up there.*

Could she stay? Or should she leave? Deep in thought, Tina jumped as Sammy opened the door of the bedroom and peered in the room. Tina looked down at the bed and realized she should have finished with this room about twenty minutes ago.

"Sammy, I was just thinking about every summer I spent here. I love this home," Tina said. "I used to sit on the stairs and watch everybody. This was David's room. He had his sports junk hanging all over and those stinky socks of his ... I remember how you would yell up the stairs, 'Clean your room and close your door! I can smell your gym socks from here! I'm going to come up there and whoop you if you don't get to it!'"

Sammy laughed and gave the memory a little push. "Yep, and did you ever notice him jump in fear? Not my son! He always kicked his stuff under the bed, yelling, 'I'm done!'"

Sammy gently took the fitted sheet from Tina's trembling fingers and spread it over the bed. "You take that side, and we'll finish together."

"Sometimes I wonder why Momma never let you and Uncle Dan adopt me, Sammy," Tina said. "I heard you arguing with her once about it."

"Well, Teensy, your momma loved you so much. You were her piece of heaven. I don't know if she ever told you, but Sharon ran away from home when she was seventeen, hooking up with a tattoo artist who took his business on the road. I'm still not sure if he was your father or not but they lived together for about ten years before you were born. I don't think it matters anymore unless you feel the need to know." Sammy stopped working long enough to ask, "Does it matter to you? If so, I have some information about him, which you can have if you need it. She was always a free spirit, I didn't know whether it was relevant."

Tina hadn't thought of her father in years. Uncle Ben and Uncle Dan were just fine for her.

"Your momma wasn't one to settle down too much,"

Sammy continued. "I think you must have been around six years old when she brought you back here. She was going to make a new start, she said, and raise you right. She tried hard to fit back in, even got a job at one of the local hotels bartending, but Sharon couldn't make it stick after so many years away, so she packed up again and took you with her."

Tina watched her aunt's hands competently smooth and brush against the newly made bed, making sure the pillows were plumped high and full under the comforter. Sammy reached up to place the smaller decorative ones along the headboard. The bedroom and bath now sparkling clean, Tina rolled the cart with its cleaning supplies across the hardwood floor and out the door.

Smiling a bit ruefully, she responded, "Yeah, Momma bounced us around a lot back then."

Tina and Sammy made their way over to the next bedroom, working now in tandem to get the rooms freshly prepared for incoming guests.

Tina stopped for a second to look over at her aunt. "Funny! What I remember most about those years is emptying the trash each day."

Sammy chuckled. "The trash?"

"Momma used these flimsy plastic bags from the convenience stores for liquor and fast foods," Tina explained. "She'd pull out the liquor bottle for her and peanut butter crackers for me. Those were our treats. She'd wad the empty bag next to all the others on the side of the refrigerator. Every morning I'd grab an empty bag and fill it up again with empty containers of milk or booze, candy wrappers, Top Ramen packets, or empty Kraft macaroni and cheese boxes. Then I'd wake her up to get ready for work. The school was just around the corner, so I'd drop the trash in the dumpster on the way."

If her mother stayed home from work because her head hurt, they'd sing and laugh and cuddle up in front of the tv. Momma almost always ran low on money before the rent was due. Sometimes the electricity would be turned off, and when it did, they colored by candlelight from an endless stack of Scooby-Doo or Barbie coloring books with huge boxes of sixty-four crayons. Momma always made it fun wherever they lived, but it was Gable House that defined security during Tina's childhood.

Tina snuck a peek at her aunt, wanting to confide her latest secrets but so afraid she'd be told to leave. Could she make a new life here as an adult? She wondered if she should find somewhere else to live, somewhere where Ruiz could never find her. Startled at the turn her thoughts had taken her, she realized that never once had she considered her aunt's safety by being here. Selfishly, she kept those thoughts to herself.

"Sammy, did you mean it when you said I could work here at the inn? If you still want me, I'd like to stay with you." Tina held her breath until her aunt responded by hugging her close.

"Of course I want you to stay, Tina! It's always been what I want, but are you sure it's the right thing for you? Let's give it a trial run till after the summer." Sammy smiled one of her big light-up-your-eyes smiles. "You work in the bedroom while I go clean the bathroom."

Tina industriously applied her mind to the task at hand, slipping the sheets and pillowcases in place, imitating Sammy's way of brushing her hand along the comforter, making sure everything looked professional. She wiped the dust away from the bedside tables and dresser, finally turning on the vacuum cleaner to finish.

Time flew by while they completed all the upstairs chores. Downstairs, the laundry service came with a fresh batch, hauling the dirty laundry away. After a quick look at Tina, the serviceman handed the weekly work ticket to Sammy, driving off down the road.

"Tina! I think he was a little shy around you." Sammy laughed, following her niece into the library.

"Nah, he's probably just wondering who the new chick is." Tina picked up the used books from the tables and sofa, automatically reading the titles before placing them back on the shelves. Gazing out the library window, she watched the hummingbirds gather under the eaves, sipping from their feeders.

Chapter 5

Ruiz

Bloodshot brown eyes stared back at Ray Ruiz from the wavy glass in the bathroom mirror, reminding him of his overnight drinking spree. He scratched at the scruff of his five-day-old beard.

I've looked worse, he thought, *but dammit, I hate being filthy! I need to leave this place. Hiding from the police won't get the job done. Owen will find me faster than the cops, and he'll order one of his flunkies to kill me if I don't find that woman and the diamonds first.*

The enforcer stepped into the tiny shower cubicle, turning the water on high and making quick use of the small cubes of soap and shampoo supplied by the motel. Before the water ran completely cold, Ruiz soaped his hair, watching the dirt sluice down the drain. He kept his eyes trained downward, a habit he'd picked up from a few years of community jail time.

The shower reminded him of the dirty bathtub he used to share with his brothers as a kid. It was rarely scrubbed, the small room always smelling like the dirty diapers overflowing in the bathroom trash. Pulling his head free from the water and his thoughts, Ruiz ran the washrag over his face and ears, turned the water off, and stepped out on the towel mat, shaking the excess water from his body like a dog.

He dressed, quickly stepping into the now clean underwear he had washed by hand in the same sink, shivering at the slight dampness as they slid over his skin. He was still wearing the same filthy pants and shirt he'd been wearing this entire week.

Ruiz sat down on the bed. *Hell, what a mess,* he thought. *The police should've backed off by now. They've checked my home, Oliver's home. It should be safe enough to travel if I stay off the main streets.* Before he went any further, he needed some more clothes. *And then I'm going back to Oliver's place to look for some clues to see where his wife ran to. Surely she has family somewhere close by.*

Ruiz felt better now that he had a plan. He checked the contents on the bedside table and his wallet, counting the remainder of the $2000 he started out with. He was down $712 on the motel bill, food, and beer. *Can't use the credit cards, cops can track you anywhere.*

He realigned his day in order of importance. *Get into Oliver's house. I can't meet with Owen until I find Oliver's widow.*

He stood up and squashed a cockroach under his shoe, then glanced over at the spider spinning her web in the right-hand corner of the ceiling. He shuddered. *And I gotta find another motel somewhere out of the main drag areas. This one sucks!*

Satisfied with his decisions, Ray tucked his gun in the

shoulder holster under his leather jacket, and his knife in the holster on his belt. He walked a few blocks west to a small motorcycle shop owned by an old friend and his brother. For a hefty monthly fee paid in cash, Ruiz kept his old Harley parked there.

Fernando wasn't there, but his brother Jorge bent over the engine of a Street Rod scratching his ass. Ruiz nodded briefly, acknowledging his presence. He continued walking toward the back of the building where his bike was waiting but darted into the office where Fernando kept his paperwork and files. He looked around at the grease-stained repair books and the dirt on the office walls, thinking the place probably hadn't been cleaned since Fernando first opened the shop. Ray pulled out the file drawer where Fernando kept his cash box. Not much there, a few twenties. He picked up the cash and closed the drawer quietly, turning to leave. His hair stood up on the back of his neck when he found Jorge staring at him from the doorway with a pistol pointed right at his chest.

"Good thing we don't keep a lot of money in there any-more. Whether it's a good thing for you or me, I don't know. Drop the money, Ruiz. You got two minutes to get to your bike and get the hell out of my shop, and don't come back. Thank my brother and your friendship that I don't shoot you right now."

Ruiz stared at Jorge, deciding it wasn't worth going for his gun. He already had a few murders hanging over his head and didn't need to bring the police back around. *Besides, Fernando would be one more person to deal with if I kill his brother,* he thought. After a few seconds, Ruiz shrugged.

"Habit. It was only a few twenties, Jorge; you probably need it more than I do. Plus, I'll pay you the money I owe for the parking space since you don't have much in the drawer. *¿Sí?*" Jorge nodded a quick yes, and Ruiz pulled out his wallet and dropped $250 on the battered steel desk. "I don't want to leave owing any debt." He grinned and sauntered past Jorge.

"You've got ninety seconds left, Ruiz."

"Consider me gone, old friend."

"You're not my friend. Consider yourself lucky that your bad karma hasn't caught up with you yet." Jorge kept his gun aimed on the thief.

Ruiz lifted his hands in the air and swung a leg over his old HOG, kicked it over, and drove out the shop. *Asshole might have shot me,* he thought, then chuckled. *What's that he said? Karma? Karma, yeah right! More like making your own luck, I'll watch my own back and get you before you get me!*

He drove the Harley in the general direction of Oliver's apartment, keeping an eye out for cops or anybody that remotely looked like one. He found a space in the back row of the complex away from the street. It was only around 10:00 A.M., and with a bit of luck, most people would be at work. He spotted an old lady getting into her car as he walked by the carports, but since she didn't seem to take any more than a casual glance at a stranger, he continued making his way to Oliver's home.

He walked around the building, checking to ensure nothing looked out of place or that there were any cops in the vicinity. He knew Owen would've already had the place turned upside down looking for those diamonds. Additionally, the police had been here because there was the standard yellow banner around the building, but really, what was the reason for it? Oliver hadn't died here and of all people, he should know. It took a brief minute to break the lock, then Ruiz slipped inside, certain that nobody noticed him.

It was plain stupid of me to kill Oliver in front of witnesses. Big mistake. I should have waited outside, but it was too tempting to gut him in front of the wife.

Standing quietly in the entryway, he glanced around the small space, making sure the apartment was empty before stepping into the kitchen to ransack the drawers.

"What a clean freak," Ruiz muttered. No smudges on the cupboards, no dishes in the sink. The overall cleanliness of the home could still be seen through the disordered movement of furniture and drawers. He tipped the three drawers upside down in search of an address book or letters, anything that would leave a clue to where Tina went.

In the third drawer, he found an old black and white photo of two girls and a baby held in the arms of a woman. They were posing in front of a house. He turned the photo over, barely able to read the faded pencil writing on the back: 1957, Grandma, Momma, Aunt Susan, Aunt Sammy.

Ruiz pocketed the photo and searched for the mail, finding it in the dining room area. *Nothing but bills,* he thought in disgust. No wonder Oliver was anxious to make a score.

Ruiz left the kitchen and walked to the bedroom, pulling out the drawers of the cheap dresser on the right. *Nothing left in this one. It must belong to Oliver's wife. I know she's gone.*

He stepped around the bed to a taller dresser and paydirt! He opened the first drawer— underwear. He slid his hand around the drawer, finding nothing.

Ruiz hesitated. *I refuse to wear another man's underwear.* He slammed the drawer shut. The second and third drawer held two pairs of jeans and a bunch of old colored tees. Desperately in need of clean clothes, Ruiz dropped his pants and shirt right there on the floor and tried on the jeans.

Just as he thought, they were baggy and way too long, at least two sizes bigger than he was, but he could make it work till he got to a Walmart or Target or someplace like that. He left a pair of jeans on and rolled up the cuffs. Disgusted that he had to wear the clothes of the man he killed, Ruiz unbuttoned his shirt and pulled on a blue t-shirt with a Corona logo.

Ruiz opened another drawer and found some clean socks. He breathed a sigh of relief. He really hated wearing dirty socks. Sitting on the side of the bed, Ruiz pulled on the clean socks, retied his shoes, and instantly felt better. He chuckled.

Damn! Saved some money thanks to you, Oliver. Grabbing a few more t-shirts, socks and the other pair of jeans, Ruiz shoved them in an old grocery bag he'd seen in the kitchen.

Stop! He stared down at the clean clothes he was wearing.

Idiot! You almost forgot that photo and your wallet and keys. Backtracking to his pile of dirty clothes, Ruiz fastened his own belt around his waist, adding the additional items in the pockets of his second-hand clothing.

Next, Ruiz spotted the closet. There was the old beat-up jacket he'd seen Oliver wear before. He went through the pockets and found $30, shoving the bills in his jeans. *What's that up there?* Ruiz reached up and found an old cardboard box full of receipts, tax papers, plus—jackpot!—more photos.

Is that the same house? he wondered. It looked updated, only now there was a sign hanging off to the side, but it was unreadable in the photo. Maybe he could read it with a magnifier. *Now we're getting somewhere.* He spotted a generic canvas holder in the corner of the closet that his wife Sonia had used to distribute money payout transactions.

Oh, Mrs. Oliver, you lied to me! $50,000 missing, half of that was mine, plus the diamonds for Donaldson. You're mine now, bitch, as much mine as that whore wife of mine was.

Four days ago, he'd shot Sonia right between the eyes. *Hell! The woman had to be the most unfaithful bitch there ever was.* He thought about the tricks she turned, many at Owen's request. That was business. But sleeping with Oliver? How long had that been going on? *And the wife-beating bastard didn't even care for her. At least I didn't beat her! She didn't feel a thing with a bullet.*

He'd known just where his wife would run. Stupid cops were so predictable, she would never stay in a shelter with a bunch of women when she could be out turning tricks for her fix. It would have been better if he'd been able to stay in the abandoned apartment overlooking his sister-in-law's house, but that location was too hot now.

I'll find you Tina Oliver, and as soon as I get my money and those diamonds, you can rot in hell with Sonia. He shook his head. *Karma, what a crock.*

Ruiz wandered around the apartment for a few more minutes, making sure there was nothing left that he wanted. He slipped back out the door with the grocery bag of clothes thinking no one was the wiser and headed for the nearest Target.

Ruiz was in such a hurry that he never noticed the old woman he had passed earlier, now sitting quietly in her car, watchful as he drove out of the apartment complex. He never saw her pick up her cell phone to call the police and report a stranger.

Ruiz missed the cops by less than ten minutes.

Chapter 6

Sammy

Sammy's body was wedged half in and half out of the old kitchen cabinet. Grumbling to herself, she wiggled the upper part of her body further into the cupboard. Reaching with the tips of her fingers as far as she could go, she cursed all cabinetmakers.

Why in the world do they make corner cupboards so deep and wide? If I were taller, I could grab this godforsaken pan! Sammy thought. *It should be up in the top cabinets for easier access.*

She stretched out further, sucking in her breath to make one last attempt. "I just need to . . . reach it with my fingers a little bit more . . . gotcha!" She pulled back on the springform pan, and it fell, clanging against the other kitchenware in its way on the shelf. "Crumbs!" Sammy reached forward one more time. "Caught ya."

Now that she was on the floor, how in the world was she going to get up?

Gripping the pan again, Sammy twisted, shimmied, and inched her way backward until she could maneuver her shoulders out of the cupboard, banging her head on the cabinet frame. Sammy sat on the cold tile floor, rubbing her head. *Ouch! Man, that hurts!* She heaved a deep breath, and took a quick peek, hoping nobody else was around to see her inch her way up off the floor. *Was that the bell?*

Twisting her body sideways, she grabbed the edge of the cupboard door, pulling herself up to a half-standing position, rear end first. She maneuvered the rest of her torso into an upright position and flexed her knees. "What possessed me to get on the floor? I should have just asked Tina to get it," she muttered. Disgusted, she grabbed the offending pan off the floor and tossed it on the counter.

"Um, excuse me, you need some help in here?"

Sammy squealed like a little girl and jumped, slamming her knee into the cupboard she'd just extricated herself from. "Damn, damn, double damn!"

"Whoa, steady there, I didn't mean to scare you."

Whirling around, Sammy gazed up into a pair of concerned brown eyes and groaned aloud. Male eyes. *It figures. Men always show up at my most unflattering moments.* Feeling a flush of embarrassment, she thought ruefully of how she must look in her old blouse stained with blueberry juice, then shrugged.

"That's ok. I wasn't expecting company. You just caught me in a very awkward moment." Sammy gave an annoyed look at the kitchen cupboard but summoned up her innkeeper smile. "My darn knees just don't work as well as they used to. I practically had to crawl in that cabinet to find that pan."

"Aw, not to worry, I'm in the same boat." The man tapped the cane he was leaning on against the floor, bringing attention to the knee brace wrapped around his left knee. "I was going to ask if you were hiding from your guests, but I don't see anyone else around. Are you Mrs. Samantha Cooper?" A smile accompanied the gentleman's question. "I'm looking for the innkeeper. I rang the bell at the registration desk out front, though you probably didn't hear it. Then I heard the pans clanking together and something fall, so I thought maybe someone needed help in here. My timing stinks, doesn't it?"

At a loss for words, Sammy took stock of the tall, older and—*oh wow*—good-looking man with the rangy build who was currently smiling at her. Something clicked in her mind, or could that just be her heart restarting? She cocked her head to the side and smiled ruefully.

"You've found me in all my glory," Sammy said. "I'm not expecting any guests until tomorrow, but may I help you?"

"I sure hope so," he replied. "I'm Matthew Phillips—Matt. I'm here early, hoping you can extend my upcoming Friday reservation into a two-week stay beginning today. I didn't expect to drive down to Orange County this early nor stay so long. It was supposed to be a weekend trip to check on Dad, but the doctor decided he needed an earlier surgery, which is why I'm here two days early. I hate hotels. Would you, by any possible chance, have that room available now? Please tell me yes."

She smiled. "The answer is yes. Let's start over. Sammy

Cooper here, but please, just call me Sammy." She wiped her hand on her slacks and held it out to shake, taking a closer look at the man standing next to her. Matthew Phillips was tall and about her age, with silver-streaked brown hair and a mustache, a straight back, and—*oh be still my heart!*

He grinned. "Sammy it is. I have to tell you, I know just how your knees feel." Matt tapped his knee with the cane. "Football injury at my age." He rolled his eyes. "I was standing on the sidelines at a high school football game with an old friend and got run over by an over-zealous linebacker leaping for the ball. Not a pretty sight, I can assure you." He paused, then added, "I'm ready to sign on the dotted line if you have that room available?"

Sammy straightened her shoulders and marshaled her thoughts back to business as usual. "Certainly! I'll require your ID and credit card. I may have to juggle your room a few times if you require one of the larger suites. During the winter months, we usually book just one or two guests during week-days. However, weekends are almost always full." She glanced at his knee brace again, then added, "There *is* a room on the second floor available the entire time…if you don't mind a smaller bedroom and bath, although perhaps not with your knee injury. It's not handicap accessible."

"The second floor is fine," he responded. "The exercise up and down the stairs will be good for me. I need to flex the knee more anyway."

Sammy smiled, then blushed as Matt continued to look at

her. Sammy felt like a cookie waiting to be nibbled. It made her stomach flip-flop inside. Matt looked away but not before Sammy saw his ears turning red.

They were just leaving the kitchen when Sammy heard Matt's stomach grumble, and she noticed him looking at the coffee pot still warming on the burner.

"Are those rolls still warm?" Matt asked, pointing toward the tray of cinnamon rolls covered with creamy white frosting. "I'm famished, and they smell fantastic! Please? A cup of coffee and a roll, ma'am?" He clasped his hands together in a prayerful position and stared hard at the rolls, swiveling his neck back to look at Sammy.

She laughed. "Sure, have a seat at the table while I grab a plate and a cup for you. I'm afraid you caught us unprepared, but mid-week, we generally have few, if any, guests."

Sammy looked down again at her stained baking blouse and shook off any lingering embarrassment. He'd already seen her in it. *No point in trying to doll myself up now.*

"Wednesday is the day we get our baking started for the weekend," she explained. "There will be plenty of fresh bread and pastries ready for you tomorrow morning. I'm pleased you'll be staying with us."

She looked up as Tina pulled open the back door of the kitchen entrance. "Sammy, I'm sorry it took me so long! I was out in the side garden picking some lemons and scratched my thumb on a thorn, darn it. That sticker went clear through the skin. Now I have one more thing to add to my list of injuries. Then I thought you might let me make a few loaves of rosemary bread, so I gathered some herbs as well. Do you need anything?" Tina emptied her hands of the four Meyer lemons and sprigs of fresh rosemary on the kitchen counter and spun around, effectively halting her feet almost as fast as her rapid-fire sentences. "Oh, excuse me! I didn't know someone was here."

Sammy caught Tina glancing down at her old blue jeans and filthy hands from grubbing in the garden. The younger woman hunched her shoulders forward and hid her still swollen face behind her hair.

Sammy tried to make the introduction casual and light-hearted. "Matt, this is my niece and assistant, Tina Oliver. Tina, this is Mr. Phillips, who arrived early for his reservation. Mr. Phillips will be staying with us for a few weeks while his father recuperates from surgery at St. Mark's. We're going to place him in the Emerald Room after his hunger is satisfied with one of those fat cinnamon rolls you made this morning."

At Tina's brief nod, Sammy's voice took on the demeanor of the experienced innkeeper that she was. "Mr. Phillips, er, Matt, I think you'll enjoy the Emerald Room. Although the bedroom is smaller, as I mentioned, it has a lovely view of the marina and the access road down to the beach area. Tina, will you run upstairs and make sure that the room is ready for occupancy? Then we'll meet you out in registration."

Tina nodded again, her eyes wide. Sammy quickly brought Matt's attention back to his hunger, allowing Tina to make a fast and unnoticed exit.

"Matt, wait till you try this roll!" Sammy exclaimed as she poured two cups of coffee and plated a cinnamon roll for him. "The first time I ate one of Tina's cinnamon rolls, I licked the frosting from my fingers, it was that good. After you have a bite to eat, I'll enter the rest of your identification info into the computer. We'll complete the extended stay dates and get your signature."

Setting the coffee and pastry in front of her guest, Sammy leaned back against the kitchen cabinet. She sipped her coffee and watched him enjoy the cinnamon roll, gulping coffee in between bites.

Funny, she thought. *I haven't felt this comfortable with a man since Dan died.* She wasn't sure what it was about Matt, but something in his demeanor put her at ease.

She was startled out of her wool-gathering when she heard him ask, "Have you always been called Sammy?"

"Oh, Sammy is my family nickname." She shrugged. "Our family tends to brand you that way. This home and the surrounding gardens have been in our family for almost seventy-five years." Sammy laughed, then added, "My father wanted a boy so bad, but my mother told him that three children were enough, never mind trying for a fourth. So he never did get his son to pass on the family name of Samuel William Jonathan Gable. When I was born, the youngest of three girls, he named me Samantha, which was as close to Samuel as Momma would let him get. He always called me Sammy, and that's who I've been ever since."

Sammy stood up straighter, deciding she'd been chatty enough for the first morning's acquaintance. She enveloped herself in the more professional image of Mrs. Cooper, deciding it would keep the man out of her mind if she just thought about him as a short-term guest. She watched him stand and flex his knee a bit.

"Well, the name suits you," Matt said as they walked toward the registration desk, "but I do love the name Samantha as well. Thank you for the coffee and roll. It was delicious. I'm looking forward to some of those other bakery items you'll be making." Reaching the small registration area, Matt pulled out his driver's license and credit card.

Sammy typed in the additional information, listing his home address in Los Angeles County. She printed the newly-completed registration form, including the inn rules and regulations.

Glancing up to hand him the finished form, Sammy blushed once more as she noticed he was eyeing her as a man who likes what he sees. She handed him a small set of keys, trying to gather her thoughts.

"The salon's just through that door on my right," Sammy said. "There's a library with French doors that lead to the gardens. The dining area is to my left and situated close by the kitchen. We lock the house in the evening at 9:00. You will need to use the house key and the passcode listed on your registration form if you come in after that time. The other key is for your room."

Tina's mind worked overtime as she waited for Sammy to finish registering their new guest. *Check out the Emerald Room? Sammy and I just did that this morning when we went over all the upcoming reservations. Jeezalu, I think Sammy's cheeks are a bit pinker than usual.*

Tina waited silently by the stairs and gave a quick nod to her aunt that the room was ready.

With a final sweet smile, Sammy added, "I enjoyed our conversation, Matt. Welcome to Gable House. Tina will help you with your bags and show you your room."

Tina snickered to herself as she watched her aunt move briskly out of the room, then the younger woman moved forward to show Mr. Phillips to his room.

"Mrs. Oliver," Matt turned his attention toward the younger woman. "May I call you Tina as your aunt does? It looks like we can forgo the formalities after this morning's introduction."

Tina clutched at her wedding ring, almost the only thing besides her mom's pearls never pawned. "Tina is fine," she said quickly. "Will you come this way?"

"My luggage is still in the car. I just need a minute to grab my suitcases."

Tina hesitated, her heart starting to pound, but after a quick glance outside the front entrance, she squared her shoulders and walked out to the parking area with their guest. She took only a brief moment to glance at the street just beyond the private parking lot. She shivered, imagining Ruiz somewhere around waiting for a chance to pounce. *No, he can't find me here. I was so careful.*

Quickly, she pulled her mind back to the work at hand, offering her help when Mr. Phillips pulled his large suitcase and overnight bag out of the sleek sedan.

"Thanks! This cane makes holding on to everything at once a bit awkward. I won't have much time to relax today as my dad is already in surgery, but I'm happy your aunt can accommodate me early."

Tina knew the guest's natural smile and words were meant to put her at ease, and she tried to relax as they made their way up the winding staircase.

"Here is your room. I wish we had an elevator. It would be easier on your leg," she said, stopping at the last bedroom to the right on the second floor. "There are five bedrooms on this floor. Yours is at the very end of the hall."

Tina stepped inside the Emerald Room and waited for him to join her. She glanced at their guest, then back at the room. Tina enjoyed the room's vivid colors with its splashes of emerald, lavender, and creams, copper bathroom fixtures and the strong rolltop desk just waiting for someone's use.

"Your bathroom is just beyond that door there," she continued, pointing. "Everything is ready for you." She placed his suitcase and overnight bag on the luggage rack, then pulled open the drapes, stepping back quickly so he could get a view of the marina.

"This room will be perfect," Matt said. "I noticed the photographs coming up the stairs. There's a family photo with Sammy's picture. Will I be meeting her husband later?"

"No, he's not available, but I'm sure my aunt can tell you anything you'd like to know."

She frowned. Ten years of struggle with Jarrod didn't leave her comfortable conversing with men, and Tina wasn't about to divulge that her uncle had passed away four years ago.

"If you don't require anything else, I'll leave you to get settled. Welcome to Gable House. If you need anything further, Sammy and I will be pleased to assist you." Finishing her terse speech, Tina turned and scrambled back down the stairs.

That man was fishing for information, Tina thought as her long legs took her swiftly back down the stairs. *I need to be careful.*

Chapter 7

Sammy

Sammy replayed the conversation with Matthew Phillips in her head as she waited for one of the Windows applications to open on the computer.

How can I be so foolish, practically leering at the man? I'm fifty-six years old, not twenty-five. Oh, God, I didn't even put on any makeup today, and that stained blouse! She groaned.

With a quick look around to make sure the coast was clear, Sammy opened the top right-hand drawer of the desk and fished around for the small mirror and lipstick she kept there for emergencies. *Yeah, right, emergencies like tweezing a hag-hair from my chin or a stray eyebrow.* She sighed. *Impossible fantasy, trying to look young.*

Sammy scrutinized her face in the small 3x5 silver mirror, staring at the minuscule wrinkles around her eyes and mouth that were trying to create a permanent crease. *It could be worse, I suppose. I could have had a wart on the side of my nose like my great aunt.* Laughing at her vanity, Sammy batted her grass-green eyes in the mirror, patting the springy auburn curls liberally sprinkled with gray. She glanced up to find Tina standing almost in front of her with a grin on her face.

"Good grief, girl!" Sammy blushed, clicking the mirror closed. "How long have you been standing there?"

Tina giggled. "Why Auntie Sammy," she drawled, "is that lipstick I see? I wonder why?"

Sammy squinted her eyes in mock annoyance. "Why Ms. Tina, is that sarcasm I hear? For your information, smarty britches, I'm not too old to enjoy a handsome man. He certainly qualifies, don't you agree?"

It was fun to banter with Tina. She'd missed that over the years.

"Uh huh, sure," Tina said. "He noticed your family photo with Uncle Dan. I just told Mr. Phillips he wasn't available and to talk to you if he had any questions. Was that okay?"

Sammy nodded. It wasn't her favorite topic, but she'd tell Matt the truth if he brought it up with her.

"Well, I'll be in the kitchen where my extreme youth is protected from your flirtatious ways. I'm going to get that bread started, okay?"

Shoving the mirror back into the drawer, Sammy almost slammed her hand in with it. "Sure, honey. Do you need any help?"

"Nah, flour, yeast, etcetera. I'll tape the recipe to the cupboard so I don't screw it up." With a cheeky grin, Tina pointed at a non-existent smudge in her aunt's lipstick as she departed for the kitchen with a wisecrack. "Missed a spot."

"Brat! Give me fifteen minutes. I'll meet you there. Oh,

Lord, here he comes again." Sammy looked across the room from the small registration area and watched Matt descend the staircase.

"I'm relieved to be settled," he said, approaching the desk.

"I'm glad to hear it," Sammy replied, using her best inn-keeper smile.

"The room is perfect. The view to the marina is breathtaking!"

"I agree. I've always loved living by the ocean and watching the boats move in and out of the harbor." Sammy moved a few forms around the desk, suddenly feeling shy. "Is there anything else I can get you? Would you like a map of the city?"

"No, I'm familiar with this area. Dad doesn't live too far from here. Speaking of Dad, I better get over to the hospital and check on him. He should be out of surgery by now. I took a few weeks personal leave to be near him while he recovers, so I'll be in and out of the inn quite a bit over the next few weeks."

Sammy nodded. "No problem. We'll be here to assist you whenever you need it. Though hopefully the next time you find me, I won't be stuck in those dang kitchen cupboards."

Matt chuckled. "By the way, your brother-in-law Ben and I are friends. He's the one who recommended I come here. Perhaps we can chat a bit more when we both have more time."

"Oh, sure," Sammy said. But she was actually surprised. He knew Ben?

"Well, I'm off for the hospital. I'll see you soon, Sammy."

She said a quick goodbye as Matt left. Pushing their conversation firmly to the back of her mind, Sammy headed into the kitchen.

"Teensy..." she started to ask a question but stopped and stood quietly just inside the door.

She could hear Tina's one-sided conversation as she began preparations for the rosemary bread, adding the yeast in the warm water and the flour and salt, mixing it to form the sticky ball of dough.

"Never happy with me, though he sure liked my cooking well enough," Tina muttered. "Enough to keep me in the kitchen all the time. I guess that's where I belong all right, here in the kitchen."

Sammy let Tina rage, not sure if it was smarter to keep quiet or let her know she was there. What in the world caused this mood change in her niece?

Tina pulled out the baking bowls from the cupboards and dropped them down carelessly on the counter. Sammy winced. Reaching into the pantry for baking powder and sugar to make cranberry muffins, Tina also found an open box of rice crackers. She crammed several in her mouth, almost choking.

"No, never fast enough, never pretty enough, never thin enough for Jarrod," she shouted out loud, slamming cupboards and kitchen drawers.

Alright, enough is enough, Sammy decided.

"Teensy, what in the world is the matter with you?" Sammy demanded.

Tina whirled away from the counter, big eyes staring around at the mess she'd made. The flour was spilling out of its bag. She'd poured too much in the bowl, the measuring cup was lying on its side, and extra yeast packets were on the floor for the bread dough she had started. Smashed crackers were all over the counter. Tina's knees buckled, long legs losing their battle with gravity. She slid to the floor, keening her sorrow.

Sammy's heart ached as she watched her niece finally releasing her emotions. Tina had seemed so stoic, refusing to talk about her life, her trauma.

"Sammy, Sammy, what did I do wrong?" Tina cried. "I was thinking about Jarrod and why he was never happy with me. Nothing I ever did was right. I tried *so* hard." Her voice broke on the last two words.

For the second time that day, Sammy lowered her body to the floor, arranging her back against a cupboard. She sat this way for a few minutes, watchful, but not touching Tina in her distress. She swallowed hard, praying for the right words.

"Oh, baby, Teensy—Tina, look at me." Sammy paused until Tina looked up. "I love you. I've always loved you and I'm here for you. I promise to listen if you want to talk to me. We've all been praying for you." Sammy hated to see the pain in Tina's eyes. She felt so hopeless not knowing the best way to help her niece.

Tina closed her eyes and took deep, jagged breaths. Wiping her eyes on her sleeve, she began haltingly, "Jarrod was obsessed with me. I didn't know how bad it was at first. I was flattered that he loved me so much. Once we were married, he demanded my complete attention, so much that it exhausted me. Every time I tried to get away to visit, he would get so angry and accuse me of meeting a man. It scared me. Everything got so much worse when we moved up to Emeryville. You were all so far away."

Tina glanced toward her aunt, her lips quivering.

Sammy answered slowly and carefully. "I'm so sorry that we didn't do more to help you. We had our suspicions that Jarrod was an abuser when you started to withdraw from us."

Not long after Jarrod and Tina had moved away, Tina was still working and only coming home once-in-awhile for the holidays. Sharon, Tina's mother, had packed up her bags and moved to be closer with Tina.

"Then your mom got sick…" Sammy said. She knew her niece had spent every free moment taking care of Sharon. "Sharon noticed the change in you. Quiet as a mouse, bruised, never discussing your marriage or Jarrod. Just as the illness was changing her life, there was an even faster change in you. So she called a family meeting and we flew up there to see her; me and Dan, and Susan and Ben."

Tina was quiet, just watching Sammy. How much should she share with her niece? Sammy didn't know, but Tina's curious eyes told her to continue.

"Sharon told us she begged you to leave him, but you wouldn't budge. We saw an attorney, only to learn there wasn't anything we could do unless you were willing to prosecute him." Sammy pressed on. "We wanted to take you home. We should have fought harder, Tina. I'm so sorry, baby. He made you believe the problem was you. You weren't." The older woman stopped speaking and reached out now to hold Tina's hand in hers, feeling Tina's body quake with her emotions. Sammy couldn't possibly imagine how she'd survived the abuse for so many years.

She waited quietly, hoping Tina would confide in her, but her niece remained mute. Finally, Tina threw herself in her aunt's ample arms, curling her body closer like the child she once was. Sammy held her close, sitting on the floor for a long while, until Tina's tension lessened.

Cracker crumbs in the corners of her mouth, Tina hic-cupped the last of her tears away and gave a consenting nod. "Okay, okay, I'll be ok. I'll make this okay. I'm sorry, Sammy, I'm so sorry. Look what I did, look at this mess I made!"

Sammy gave an inward sigh of relief but otherwise re-mained still, willing to hold her niece all day if she needed arms wrapped around her. She prayed Tina was really listening.

"We'll make it okay together, baby. No more saying *I'm sorry*, Tina, alright? When used too often, apologies tend to lose their meaning." Sammy gave Tina an extra squeeze and released her with a shaky smile. "I will say this, though. You'd better reach down to that fourth shelf in the pantry and let's hope there's another box of crackers hiding in there to accom-pany the brie plate for this weekend." Sammy laughed, and Tina gave her a wry smile. "Let's get started, woman. Bread and cakes don't make themselves. Now you stand up first, so you can pull me up off this floor."

Once standing, Sammy placed a hand on her hip and winked at her niece.

"Want to know a secret? I used to make a huge pot of mashed potatoes swimming with butter whenever I was angry at your uncle. I'd use the masher and pretend it was his head. By the time I ate my way through half the pot, I had realized it was hurting me more than him. Darn calories love my hips. But then again, so did your uncle. You don't have to be a tiny little thing to please a man." Sammy put her hands on her well-rounded hips and did a sassy little wiggle. She grinned. "Mashed potatoes are still my favorite comfort food. Want some?"

Tina stared at her aunt while drinking a glass of water, giving herself the hiccups. She started to laugh. She laughed through her tears, then squared her shoulders, pushing herself away from the counter. She slipped her arms around her aunt once more and hugged her tight.

"Oh, my God, I haven't laughed in what seems like forever. I keep thinking of Uncle Dan with a mashed potato head!" Tina wiped at her eyes. "You know what Momma used to tell me when I'd take the liquor bottle from her and ask her to stop drinking? 'You are so right tonight, though you've been wrong for so long.' Aunt Sammy, I'm awfully tired of being the little girl in the corner. But I've forgotten how to fight. I used to stand up for myself, you know. I'm so afraid, though

I'm the one still alive!"

Sammy smiled at Tina. Maybe she had been listening to Sammy after all.

"Jarrod can't hurt us anymore," Tina continued, "And neither will Ruiz. I won't let him. I'm going to make it okay. Where do you keep the cranberries, Sammy? I'll get the muffins started. I don't think I'm hungry for mashed potatoes this early in the day."

Sammy stared at her niece. "Who is Ruiz, Tina? What needs to be okay?"

Tina didn't answer.

Sammy felt like pounding her head against a wall. Normally she kept her mouth closed when it came to the subject of Tina's husband, Jarrod. But damn it, he deserved his fate. No one could ever accuse her of being a hypocrite.

The more Sammy chewed on her thoughts, the angrier she became. That useless piece of garbage Tina married almost ruined her life with his abuse and selfishness, changing her into a frightened tit-mouse. As it was now, she was afraid to take a step out of the yard. *And who is Ruiz?* Sammy wondered.

Something was still terribly wrong. Tina had arrived late in the evening at Gable House only a week ago. The inn had been locked and Sammy was relaxing in her room until there was a knock on the door. Throwing her robe on, she'd checked through the security door. A taxi was pulling out of the driveway.

Her niece stood in the door entrance, pale, black and

blue from bruising, exhaustion painting dark circles under her eyes where the bruises missed. She'd arrived clutching two backpacks as though the devil himself wanted them. Sammy opened her arms and welcomed her in. She held Tina's trembling body and listened as she cried out her story of her husband's murder and the police interrogation of what she knew of his drug dealing. Sammy remembered how Tina sat on the table bench while Sammy made her a cup of tea, the girl consuming it as though her throat were parched.

Tina didn't say much more that night she arrived. She just kept pleading with her aunt over and over, asking if she could stay at Gable House. Sammy recalled Tina seemed subdued and fearful of being kicked out. Well, of course, she was welcome.

Now, as Sammy pieced all her thoughts together since that day, something still seemed off. It was as if a piece of Tina's story was missing. *It's difficult to trust when your gut tells you something is wrong.* Sammy would have to be patient and watchful until Tina was ready to confide in her, but how long should she wait?

Maybe Ben can coax her, Sammy thought. Tina used to turn to Ben as a surrogate father when she was young, following him around like a puppy dog, content to be in his shadow. Susan and Ben had welcomed Tina home the day after she arrived. Tina hugged them tight, but again, barely said a word. As usual, her sister Susan barely let Ben open his mouth.

"I'll come back later when Tina is ready to open up to

all of us," he'd said. "In the meantime, let me consider some options." Ben had agreed with Sammy's assessment.

Rousing from her thoughts, Sammy reconsidered that whatever Tina was worried about, she just needed time to come to terms with it. *Well, we'll all do our best to help her till she climbs out of her shell and shares what happened. Today was a good start. But who is Ruiz?*

Chapter 8

Tina

T ina sat on the thick grass carpet in the back yard, soaking up the sun and enjoying the warmth on her face and arms. After a busy morning serving breakfast to the Gable House guests, she needed a moment to herself. She gazed at the beauty all around her and not for the first time, was grateful for the serenity of her aunt's home.

The garden gate squeaked open, then closed. Tina glanced up quickly, relaxing when she saw it was only Miguel Salas, landscaper extraordinaire and a new-found friend.

She watched closely as Miguel looked around him, as if to make sure the flowers and shrubbery were as perfect as he'd left them. She smiled, knowing the pride he took in the sweet scents of the lavender, roses, honeysuckle, and gardenias perfuming the open air. Their response to his care was the beautiful color they provided. It was Miguel's *jardín*, she had heard him say, even if it was Sammy's backyard.

"*Buenos días mis pequeñas flores*," he called out to his roses. "How was your week? Did you grow for me?"

Like a well-satisfied lion, Miguel surveyed his domain.

Gable Gardens were among the loveliest in the county. The few acres of land connected to Gable's Bed and Breakfast Inn were his pride and joy. In the spring, the green and white gazebo was wrapped in trailing vines of violet and varicolored trumpet lilies, beckoning guests to be tranquil, if only for a few moments. The arbors tucked away in the corners of the garden held small curved benches next to water features that gurgled and sang to visitors and birds alike. Small patches of green lawn allowed children to romp and adults to spread out a blanket for picnics and an afternoon of reading or a snooze.

But not on Tuesdays. Tuesdays belonged to Miguel and his pruning shears and mower and edger. Tuesdays belonged to new plantings and weeding.

Tina jumped up from her beautiful patch of green and walked toward the man. "Hello, Miguel. I was just taking a break for a few minutes. Your subjects look beautiful as usual today, though I thought I spotted a weed a while ago trying to make its way up through the rose garden."

"*Hola, chica! ¿Cómo estas hoy?* What? Weeds? They wouldn't dare!"

Tina knew he was waiting for her to respond to him in Spanish as she had mentioned she wanted to improve her knowledge of his native language. She'd learned some in school years ago and practicing with Miguel was a good exercise for her brain.

She replied slowly in Spanish, "*Estoy mejor amigo. Pienso que la casa y el trabajo es son buenos para me, Miguel.* The work

68

keeps me busy, and I love being here with Sammy. I enjoy stepping outside to watch the sunrise in the early morning. It is so peaceful."

"*Bueno,* your Spanish is getting better! I'm glad you're practicing," Miguel replied. "And I'm happy you're feeling better. I know how much work it takes to keep the big house in great shape." Miguel grinned at the flower beds all around them. "Look at my beautiful flowers, Tina, almost as beautiful as you."

Miguel watched Tina out of the corner of his eye as she snorted inelegantly, laughing out loud and shaking her head before she commented, "Seriously, old man? Before or after the bruises faded?"

"You wound me! I'm older, but *viejo?* Nah," he replied with a grin.

For a few minutes Tina watched him pulling the few weeds threatening his flowerbeds. Miguel's hands kept up a steady pace, strong and patient.

Dressed warmly for ocean breezes, Miguel wore a soft blue and black checked flannel shirt that appeared shiny and smooth from many washes. His face was leathery from too much sun, but his eyes were sharp, and his body well-muscled from the constant outdoor exercise required to maintain the landscaping work he loved. Pausing a moment, Miguel stretched and stood tall, acting as though he just noticed Tina still standing there.

Tina thought of how his deep brown eyes were kind and

welcoming. It gave her the courage to ask the question on the tip of her tongue.

"Miguel, my half-day off is supposed to be Mondays," she started, "but I could ask Sammy for Tuesdays a few times a month. If she agrees, would you teach me about the different flowers and plants and how to care for them? I could be a help to you weeding the garden, and it would be good exercise for me, too."

"So then, are you saying I need help or do you really want to learn?" Miguel frowned. "Taking care of the garden is my job, Tina. I don't need any help."

"No! That's not what I meant at all, Miguel, please don't think that! I want to be useful, and I love to be outside in the sunshine and the garden. I really would like to learn about their care." She swallowed hard. "I mean to learn if you will teach me. Please? I won't get in the way."

Miguel shot her a piercing glance from under the brim of the baseball cap he was seldom without, chewing on her words for a minute. Tina bit her bottom lip. *Oh, I hope I didn't offend him,* she thought.

"Well, if you're serious," Miguel finally said, "and your aunt doesn't object, I'd welcome your company maybe once or twice a month. We could see how it goes. Only for a few hours, though, *tu comprendes?*" Even with his stern tone, Tina didn't miss Miguel's small smile.

"Yes, Miguel, thank you!" Grinning, she turned and headed back toward the house. But she stopped and spun around. "Until next Tuesday then, Miguel. Adios!"

Chapter 9

Ruiz

Ruiz leaned back on the seat of his Harley. Currently parked in between a truck and a beat-up Ford Explorer, it was barely noticeable in the Dana Point Harbor parking lot. From behind his sunglasses, Ruiz surveyed the back property line of the bed and breakfast inn with high-powered binoculars. Orange trees just inside the concrete wall separated the private property from the steep hill leading down to the harbor connector road.

He'd made mistakes with the Olivers. Threatening the wife had only made her run. The money was needed, but worse, Owen was holding him personally responsible for the return of the diamonds. The boss wasn't giving him much more time to take care of the situation on his own.

Both cops and detectives were searching for him. The increased need for caution slowed him down, but now Ruiz was wanted for two murders. He thought of Sonia's death with some regret.

Donaldson often used Sonia as part of the client delivery thank you process. Owen had clientele you couldn't get close to. Sometimes it was easier to use a woman for delivery. Following Sonia's pickup of the diamond packet, Oliver had been waiting in the wings for the delivery handoff. *Double-crossing bastard,* Ruiz thought.

He'd also shot that idiot off-duty policeman Donaldson kept on the payroll at the bar. All that cop needed to do was patrol outside, warning the bar manager of any additional police called to the club for violence. Ruiz shook his head in disgust. *Man can't keep up to his end of the employment agreement?* Ruiz thought. *He deserved to be shot.*

Ruiz sighed and looked through the binoculars again. It hadn't been that hard to find Tina. Oliver had bragged several times about his wife's wealthy relatives and how he was going to make sure that he got plenty of money from that association. *Bah! What a crock! It's a good thing I wasted Oliver.* He'd saved the little widow from a lifetime of getting her brains knocked around and probably a case of syphilis. Ruiz chuckled. If anything, she should be thanking him.

He was positive she was living in that big old house on the hill. *You are not very smart, little widow woman. You left a bread crumb trail to your hiding place. The problem isn't where you are but how to access it.*

Ray learned more from that short trip to their apartment than anything Oliver had ever disclosed. After leaving the apartment, he'd purchased a magnifier and was able to make out most of the signage on the photo he took. *Ga* and **Inn** were visible, so it hadn't been too difficult to put two and two together with the help of a little Google research and picture comparison of the house. Finding an address on the internet was even simpler but traveling the distance south was an annoyance he hadn't expected.

Unfortunately, after a week of surveillance, he'd only caught one glimpse of Tina Oliver with the aunt. If she didn't start coming out of that fortress soon, Ruiz was going to have to lure her out. He'd attempted to get in the house a few times through stealth, but security cameras strategically placed around the property seemed to provide a view into every corner of the yard and entryway. Concrete block walls surrounded the property. Getting to Tina in her fortress of solitude was going to require a bit more finesse.

His second try was no better. He'd wandered into the house only to get as far as the front lobby with a prepared story about how he and his wife—that dead *puta!*—were going to be celebrating their anniversary soon, and he was hoping to take a tour of the house and gardens. He was stopped cold by the redhead at the registration desk, who provided him with a brochure and website address. He could still hear her voice in his head. *Due to the security of our guests, tours are not provided. However, information is available… blah blah blah.* He should have shut her up, but there had been several other people hanging around inside at the time. He hadn't gotten so much as a glimpse of Oliver's wife.

He had noticed the wide staircase leading up to the bedrooms and a doorway leading into the back rooms which he surmised was a kitchen area. Outside in the front parking area, he had wandered to the side gate leading to the back garden. The tall gates were locked. Ruiz had to make do with the virtual tour of the inn online, not nearly good enough.

He couldn't keep hanging around here expecting a miracle. Ruiz was going to have to use other eyes and ears. There was one other person who Ruiz knew he could recruit to keep an eye on the house. Angela would do it. She lived on the other side of the harbor, and he would make sure she had no choice.

He opened the saddlebag attached of the Harley and checked to make sure he'd safely stashed the small bag of off-white rocks. Handling Angela would be a simple matter. Give her the crack, she was yours for the taking. She'd do whatever he told her.

Tina Oliver must have the money and diamonds. If the police had taken possession, Donaldson would know by now. I might have to kill that woman to get it. Ruiz had no other choice. Owen Donaldson was breathing down his neck. His boss didn't trust anyone and got rid of those who double-crossed him.

Ruiz tucked his binoculars into the saddlebag. He leaned forward over the tank of the Harley, turned the engine over, and roared down the street. "Little *gatita,* you didn't run far enough," he muttered. "There's more than one way to skin a cat."

Chapter 10

Sammy

S ammy was a dusting whirlwind. Every other day, during the mid-morning quiet, she dusted or polished her way through the main living areas and empty bedrooms, enjoying the solitude. She looked out the bay window of the grand salon at the harbor, counting row after row of the tall masts of the sailboats. There were four times as many boats in the harbor as she could see riding the ocean waves, but it still excited her.

Sammy dragged her thoughts back to the present and thought of Tina. She seemed healthier every day, yet the smiles came slowly. As she stepped out the side door to pick some fresh flowers, Sammy found her niece reading in the garden. This morning she was sure she'd managed to convince her niece to go out and explore the changes down the hill.

"I thought you were going to go to the harbor!"

"No, it's more peaceful here on the grass with the sun on my face and this book from your library. Come on, Sammy, sit down with me for a few minutes. Aren't we lucky we live here?"

"Well, it *is* gorgeous outside," Sammy conceded. "I can feel the ocean breeze." Sammy slipped off her shoes and sat on a small bench near the blanket Tina had laid across the beautiful green grass. "Your Uncle Dan and I always dreamed of taking a sailing trip around the world when we got to this age. When the kids were younger, there were always bills to pay." *Now it's too late,* Sammy thought.

"What made you decide to open a bed and breakfast?" Tina asked. "I wasn't around then."

"Actually, it was your Uncle Dan's idea. He got laid off from his engineering job one year right after Christmas. He hated to tell me, and he walked around the house so defeated. For a week, we walked around shell-shocked, trying to figure out what to do as the job market was tight for his profession. New Year's Eve came around, and we decided to stay home in front of the fireplace, watching old movies. But we didn't. Instead we wandered into the library and opened up the old photo albums.

"One of these days I'd love to look at those again. I used to stare at them for hours when I was a kid," Tina responded.

Sammy smiled. "Your grandfather had all these old black and white photos of the land and the various phases Gable House went through while being built. There were two generations of children playing in the big yard and photos of the brand-new garden. We sat there looking at photos until midnight, and I remember I said to your uncle, 'I sure hope we can hold onto this house long enough for another generation. We'll be having grandchildren someday.'"

If Sammy closed her eyes, she could see the way Dan had

scratched his ear when she said that. He was always scratching his ear while he was thinking.

"And you know what he said to me?" Sammy asked.

"What?"

"'You know, sweetheart, we could get a reconstruction loan on the house and open it up as an inn. You always said we were lucky to have a home this big and too bad we couldn't share it. We could do it, Sammy. I can manage a lot of the construction, and you're a great organizer. We'd have to get it re-zoned as a business, but it could work.'"

Sammy smiled fondly at the memory and looked over at Tina. "It was like connecting the dots. All I could think of at the time was, 'But what would Momma and Daddy think? Would they want their house used this way?' Dan told me, 'It's your house now, Sammy, you can do whatever you want with it.'"

Sammy gazed at the garden, blinking back a few tears. "We just stepped out in faith, Tina. We became innkeepers less than two years later. Those first years were the hardest, trying to get the loan, living in a home torn apart by reconstruction, followed by licensing, marketing, and advertising the inn. We took classes in hotel management, and our lives became an adventure again, doing the work together."

Sammy stood up, sliding her shoes back on. "Well, my break is over. This is your day off, and I don't want to see you worried over anything. Enjoy the sunshine and that book."

"Let me know if you need any help, Sammy," Tina called,

but Sammy waved her off.

Instead, Sammy walked back in the house thinking of happy years with her husband Dan. Everything clicked until that one awful day.

"It's a lovely springtime, Dan," she whispered.

But all this reminiscing wasn't getting the housekeeping done. Grabbing a bag of mixed hard candies from the cupboard inside the sideboard, she refilled the candy jars, straightened the magazines, and puttered around the bottom floors of the inn. She just couldn't seem to settle today. She was glad to see how peaceful Tina appeared, though. She seemed to have lost that haunted look.

In the month since Tina arrived, Sammy had made several phone calls to local abuse shelters, putting together a list of organizations in Orange County that could offer therapy or counseling sessions for Tina. Each time Sammy brought up a suggestion, Tina brushed it aside. Was it enough that Tina realized she could confide in her aunt if and when she wanted to? Sammy frowned. Although her niece's bruises had faded on the outside, they were still deeply embedded internally along with grief, confusion, and its companion, anger.

But now and then, Tina had days like today, when her smile peeked out like the sun.

Most of the time, Sammy kept silent because she had experienced many of those same feelings when Dan had died. Yet Sammy still felt uneasy. She cautioned her inner voices. *Patience. I need the patience to help her because that man de-*

stroyed every vestige of confidence my niece ever had. She's not telling me something. It feels like she's holding something back. Sammy still didn't know who Ruiz was, although she had a feeling it was all wrapped up in Tina's reticence to talk or leave the house.

Turning to make her way back to the dining area, Sammy found her way blocked by Matt Phillips coming through the arched doorway.

"Mr. Phillips, how nice to see you!" She smiled. At least she wasn't wearing a stained shirt today. "How is your father doing? Stronger than ever by now, I hope. St. Mark's has an excellent reputation for patient care. I hear their cardiology unit is excellent."

"He's doing so well, Mrs. Cooper, that Dad will be released from the hospital tomorrow. I need to check out this afternoon so I can make sure his apartment is ready for him." His brown eyes met hers, and Sammy felt a frisson of delight dance down her spine. "And I thought we were going to dispense with formality and go on a first name basis."

"Alright, Matt then. I'm so happy that he's better. You mentioned that he lived in a retirement community in San Clemente?" Matt nodded, and Sammy continued, "I like it there. The city is so distinctive with all its roads leading downhill to the ocean. Did you know that San Clemente was one of the first planned communities in Orange County? In 1925, Ole Hanson, who founded the city, laid out the city streets and the seaside village. The train tracks run right along the ocean."

"I did know that, although I haven't heard it mentioned in years. I love Southern California, although it doesn't have the wild beauty that the coast of Northern California has. I lived in Monterey until about 16 years ago when my daughter and I moved to the San Fernando Valley. Dad fell in love with Orange County and settled down here. I do try to come south as often as possible to see him, but my job keeps me busy, and the L.A. freeways are another form of torture."

"I've lived here all my life," Sammy responded. "Gable House was built in the late 1940s. Mom loved the ocean, and Dad built her this home a few years after they got married. My two sisters and I were born here. I was their surprise baby. My dad never did get that son he wanted, so my mother had to compromise with my upbringing and let me tag along with him."

Matt opened his mouth to reply, but Sammy held up a hand.

"*Not* that it's a bad thing," she clarified with a laugh. She'd had no choice but to live up to her name, and that meant being a tomboy when she was growing up. "I was always better at sports than my husband, Dan. We went to school together. I don't mind bragging that I was better at bat than him, the better swimmer, and I even beat him in tennis half the time. Lord, he hated me when we were kids!"

"Please forgive me, Sammy," Matt started, his jovial tone growing cautious, "but I was in town the other day filling some of Dad's prescriptions. I mentioned to the store owner that

I was staying here. He said it was a shame that your husband died in a car accident."

Sammy stiffened and stood a little taller in the doorway. "Yes, a drunk driver hit him in a head-on collision in San Diego." She sucked in a breath. She *hated* when people brought up the accident. "Matt, I have to get back to my chores. I hope you've enjoyed your stay here. Let me complete your checkout."

"May I ask you a question?"

She nodded slowly. "Alright..."

"Would you tell me about your niece Tina?" Matt asked. "I couldn't help but notice her bruises. I've several contacts with counselors and can offer my—"

"Tina is healing from some recent tragedy in her life. Thank you for your concern." Sammy turned and started to walk out of the room, but Matt interrupted once more.

"Please give me just a moment more of your time," he begged. "I'm your guest, of course, but something else you should know..."

"I'm listening." But Sammy wasn't sure she liked where this was going.

"Okay, Here goes...I'm a mental health counselor. Actually, my title is crisis counselor. I often work with victims of traumatic stress. But I should have told you earlier. Remember I mentioned I was a friend of your brother-in-law Ben?"

Sammy's mind raced. She'd meant to call Ben, but they'd been so busy these last few weeks, she just forgot.

"Remember I mentioned him earlier when I checked in?" Matt continued. "When I called him to let him know my dad was going to have surgery and that I'd be in the area, he asked me if I could stay at Gable House and possibly keep a professional eye out for your niece."

Sammy's heart pounded in her ears. *Ben* had put Matt up to this? This was their brilliant plan to help Tina? "Well, really! And you both just decided there was no need—" Sammy tried to say, but Matt kept talking.

"And before you say why didn't I tell you before, well, I was here at Ben's request. Not that I don't love bed and breakfast inns, because I do."

Sammy put her hand on her hip and gave a very un-ladylike snort of disbelief.

"Ben stressed that Tina was a very quiet person who had been severely abused over the years and didn't trust anyone," Matt said. "He only asked me to keep a watchful eye out for her while I was here and to let him know what I thought."

Sammy opened her mouth like a fish, wondering if he'd been honest from the start whether she would have thought as kindly about him. At the very least, she would have said something to Ben, and boy was he going to get an earful now.

"I've observed Tina quietly for the last few weeks," Matt said, voice low, "and I told Ben that while I definitely think Tina needs professional counseling, she's not ready to open up to a professional yet, at least not a man. I think she's gaining more emotional support just being with you for the time being."

Sammy rubbed her temples. That was the same conclusion she'd come to. *At least I'm on the right track.*

"I've watched her come out of her shell. She's smiling more and seems to be relaxing a little with some of your guests. Today I called Ben and told him I was uncomfortable with the fact that I haven't been more outspoken with you and that I was going to speak with you. You're very good for her, Sammy, but based on the little Ben has told me about her life, she has enormous issues to face and resolve."

"Matt, stop." Sammy held up a hand, and to her surprise, Matt actually stopped his monologue. "You should've said something to me when you first arrived. Now it makes me feel like you've been staying here under false pretenses, sneaking around, withholding information. I need to speak with Ben about this. It makes me angry that you both thought you could play armchair analyst and you, at least, should know better! Isn't this against your ethics code or something?"

Matt had the good sense to hang his head as Sammy ripped into him. She knew both he and Ben meant well, but this wasn't the way to help someone.

"You're right," Matt finally said, lifting his head to meet Sammy's gaze. "And I sincerely hope I haven't ruined our friendship. The reality is that I was here for the exact reason I gave you. My father was in surgery and is just now well enough to go home. I do love being here, too. I *hate* hotels. The fact that I do what I do for a living makes no difference, but I agree with you. I should have been upfront with you, and

I hope you'll forgive my arrogance, and that of Ben. I want to reassure you that I never approached Tina, and I only spoke with you today because once I leave, I'd like to see you again."

"Oh, you can bet I'll talk to Ben about it," Sammy snapped. "I wondered why he's been scarce around here for the past few weeks, but I'll take that up with him."

"Sammy, I only have three more days before I have to get back to work. Right now, I need to concentrate on getting Dad discharged from the hospital and back home. I'll be coming back south next week. Hopefully, you'll allow me to stop by, but I'll respect your decision if you won't. Speak to Ben. He'll vouch for me. We can certainly speak more when I come back this way if you allow me that opportunity."

Sammy gave Matt an unsmiling gaze. She could see the sincerity in his eyes and opened her mouth, but she realized there was no point in saying something further. She stepped around Matt, stopped at the registration desk, checked him out of the inn, and wished Mr. Phillips well.

Late in the evening, Sammy wandered back to the kitchen and found Tina studying one of the cookbooks next to the kitchen's computer. Quietly, she studied her niece, still annoyed that Ben hadn't seen fit to tell her he discussed Tina's history with Matt. But she had to concede Matt had a point. Tina was better confiding in a woman, and the two of them had made some headway. Maybe if she encouraged Tina to talk to her a little more, it might serve as a start for healing.

"What recipe are you looking for?" Sammy asked. "Maybe I can help you."

Tina didn't startle at her aunt's voice as she would have just a few weeks ago. Sammy considered that it was a step in the right direction.

Sammy came closer and placed her hand on Tina's shoulder. Tina smiled and shoved her hair behind her ears, then pointed to the recipe she was reading so avidly.

"Oh, I'm just looking at some of these recipes. Here's a great one with puff pastry and sausage that might work out for appetizers. We have that wedding anniversary-vow renewal ceremony in the gazebo next month. I thought we might try something new," Tina said. "I'm quite a good cook, Sammy. I think I could be more helpful to you in the kitchen and free up some more of your time with the guests…"

Tina's smile faded, her words trailing off. This might be a moment for a chat.

"You are doing great!" Sammy exclaimed. "I've received several compliments about how kind you are, especially with the older guests. A penny for your thoughts! You are one of the quietest persons I know, but sometimes all you need is someone to talk to. After Dan died and everyone went home to their own lives, it was a lonely time for me. Thankfully, the inn and my guests kept me busy. I'm a good listener if you ever feel like talking."

"Oh, I'm used to being alone." Tina waved a hand, but Sammy didn't miss the way her posture stiffened. "The vow renewal party next month made me think about our anniversary, that's all. It was our tenth anniversary on the night everything happened."

Sammy opened the refrigerator and pulled out freshly squeezed orange juice made earlier that day. She poured two glasses and walked over to the table, encouraging her niece to join her. Tina straddled the bench, leaning one hand on her head in thought.

Slowly, she began speaking.

Chapter 11

Tina

Waking up in a great mood the morning of their anniversary, Jarrod had told Tina they'd check out the new restaurant opening on the other side of town.

"We'll make a night of it, have dinner and go dancing, just you and me like we used to," he'd said. "I even promise to lock my gun in the car, so you don't have to be such a fraidy-cat." Jarrod never went anywhere without his handgun hidden away. It made him feel powerful given the work he did, and he swaggered more when he wore the concealed weapon.

Playful that morning, Tina had basked in his good mood, growing more and more excited at the thought of a night out. She ignored that nagging sense of anxiety, hoping for the best, no fights, no arguments, just a happy evening. With the gun locked away, perhaps she could relax.

Tina looked up at Sammy, who was quietly wiping the condensation from her glass. "Was it so wrong of me to want to get away for one night? Anniversaries are supposed to be happy, aren't they?"

At Sammy's nod of affirmation, she went on.

"I thought we might be going to that new restaurant in town. I took such care to dress up. All I wanted was to enjoy one special night, out of so many nothing evenings."

Carefully, Tina had put her makeup on. Not too much or other men would notice her. But not too little or Jarrod would complain she didn't want to look pretty for him. She always wore her hair long and loose, and that night had been no different.

Sammy reached over and ran her hand down Tina's long brown hair. "When you were younger, your hair would glow with beautiful copper highlights. You would sit on the grass outside with Sara, and I could see the sun light it up from the window. How long has it been since you had it cut?"

Tina twisted a long lock around her finger, thinking about her hair. The last time she cut it, she received a broken wrist for the trouble. "It's been about five years, but I like it long."

Poking around in the closet, Tina had pulled out her old black velvet blazer worn to the last three family gatherings and dressed it down with a silky gray blouse, some black boots, and her best pair of jeans. *Maybe I can wear my pearl necklace and earrings tonight*, she'd thought.

Glancing at the old alarm clock on the nightstand, she judged there was still a bit of time till Jarrod got home. Quickly, Tina pulled the step stool out from under the bed and dragged it over to the closet. Climbing up, she stood on tiptoe to reach way behind the pile of old sweatshirts that Jarrod never wore and pulled out the old yellow box hiding behind a small panel of wood she had loosed a few years back. Not much was safe from the pawn shop anymore, though she was determined to keep her mother's pearls tucked out of his sight.

"I remember my wedding day. Momma placed them around my neck, and she was so proud she had something to give to me that was from her. Momma said, 'Your grandma gave these to me for my sixteenth birthday. I almost sold them once. I probably would have if I'd kept them in my possession, but when you were born, your Aunt Susan agreed to hold them for you.'"

Tina clutched her hands together with sadness, glancing at her aunt. "Momma's pearls were broken that night. I was only able to save a few from the floor."

Both women took a moment to sip their juice, and Sammy spoke up.

"I remember those pearls. Sharon was the oldest and a spoiled beauty. You look so much like her." Sammy smiled, and Tina smiled back. "Grandma was so excited the day she put them around your momma's neck. She wanted to give Sharon a sweet sixteen birthday party, but Sharon laughed and asked her for the pearls instead. Sharon loved jewelry."

Tina told her aunt how she fastened the necklace around her neck the day of their anniversary, gently touching the beads, ensuring they were affixed securely. She'd sat on the linoleum floor in the apartment bathroom, remembering Momma's laughter and silly stories and how much she missed her. Tina ached from the loneliness, praying for that one happy evening.

Tina wrapped her arms around her body. It was hard to speak, hard to force the words out, but she felt a little better, telling Sammy some of her memories of that day. And Sammy was right. She was a good listener.

Tina closed her eyes and remembered her apartment. "The house was spotless. I didn't want Jarrod to have any reason to stay home. After I finished getting dressed, I went back out to the living room. I straightened the old ripple afghan on the easy chair. I brushed away any dust and made sure everything was perfect." Then she'd sat down and waited for her husband to come home.

Finishing her story, she gulped down the rest of her juice. "I'm tired, Auntie. I'll see you in the morning. Thanks for listening."

"Get some rest, Tina." Sammy smiled and stood with her, grabbing the juice glasses. "See you for breakfast."

Climbing the stairs, Tina thought about what she didn't tell Sammy.

Tina had started to place Momma's box back in its little hidey-hole the night of her anniversary. When standing on the step stool, she'd found a small lumpy bag poking out from under one of Jarrod's shirts. Curious, Tina opened the bag, her eyes widening at the contents inside.

"Oh, God, now what is he up to?" She'd stuffed the bag in Momma's box, then shoved it back out of sight behind the panel. Tina had taken special care to seal the board in place.

Better to keep those in a safe location when they weren't home. Now instead of the pearls, there was something else hidden away in the yellow box.

As Tina climbed into her bed at Gable House, she couldn't help but wonder: had hiding that hidden bag from the closet shelf been a premonition?

The house was sleeping, everyone but Tina. She stood in her room, feet planted firmly, shoulder distance apart, ready to practice shooting the Ruger SR22. The safety was on, the magazine empty and on the floor, but she hated handling the gun. She stood straight and gritted her teeth, forcing herself to go through the steps one more time.

Visualizing the video she'd watched on YouTube, Tina inhaled and began. Safety on, pretend to insert the magazine loaded with ten rounds of .22 Long Rifle rimfire cartridge. Gun gripped in one hand with a finger on the trigger guard. Flip the safety off. Pull the slide back with another hand. Now with both hands firmly holding the gun, look down the sight of the gun, target in sight, pull the trigger, click, release the magazine.

She slumped forward, exhausted. Every night for the last month, Tina practiced with an empty gun, always praying she'd never have to use it, but if the time came, she would have the nerve and shoot straight. She put the SR22 back in the holster, placing it and the magazine and shells in her drawer.

Tina crawled in bed, but when she closed her eyes, all she could see was the gun in her hands. *It's no use. What if he finds me?* Her heart started to pound.

Tina stood up once more, wide awake now. She moved cautiously to the little sliver of a window in her room and peeked out the curtains.

It was too dark to see outside, though. *What if he's out there right now?* Tina wondered. *Oh, God, oh God, oh God, what have I done? What should I do?* Sinking back down on the bed once more, she pulled the covers up to her neck, staring at the ceiling until she finally fell into a restless sleep.

A week later, Tina woke up to a sunny morning, realizing it was another day off. Sammy kept encouraging her to leave the house, so she finally agreed. Maybe fresh air would do her some good.

Disheveled and sweaty from the half-mile walk downhill, Tina wandered into the harbor square. She knew she needed the exercise but ugh! Now she was going to have to climb up the hill again. She wouldn't stay long. It was almost four weeks since she arrived in Dana Point, and she knew Sammy was right. If she didn't get away from the inn for just a few hours, she was going to go stir crazy.

She could feel the hard steel of the gun concealed within

her clothing. All of a sudden, she felt silly. Surely Ruiz wouldn't still be looking for her. *But what if he is?* she thought as she made her way to the old plaza center. *I should have stayed home!*

She made her way to the old wall where cement blocks formed sitting areas near the old fountain. Here she could see everyone around her. Relaxing a bit more, Tina pulled her long hair up off her neck into a ponytail and held it in place with one hand. She took a deep breath of ocean air, letting the fragrance linger in her nostrils. Nobody was going to come after her in broad daylight, not when there were plenty of witnesses around.

Relax, she told herself.

Leaning back against the wall, the breeze fanned Tina's face as she gazed at the sailboats tied up along the wooden dock. The water slapped against their hulls and turned into a dirty white froth of foam. Seagulls flew overhead, diving for fish, or coming closer to snatch at the bits and pieces of bread and other food items dropped on the walkway. If Tina squinted hard enough, she could see sea lions bobbing in the water just outside the breakwater.

She laughed at the comical parade of dogs walking their owners. Restaurants and retail stores competed for business while the small kiosks in the middle of the harbor square fluttered pennants of pink and green, blue and purple, all waving merrily.

Tina loved it here. It was her place, her harbor. As a kid, it was the place she always ran to when she needed to get her head on straight. *Maybe some things never change,* Tina thought.

The old fountain looked the same. If anything, the yellow and blue and green ceramic tiles were uglier. As a kid, Tina and her cousin Dave would run around and around the wet fountain edge, trying not to slip into the icy cold trough. Mostly, though, they would lean over and count the quarters and dimes and nickels that tourists threw, wishing they had enough nerve to grab a few of those coins and buy an ice cream cone. They did it once, but Sara, that big tattletale, went snitching to Sammy, so they had to throw the money back in. Sammy even made them throw in their allowance as punishment. Tina tucked her legs under her, getting more comfortable on her cement block as she savored the memory.

The harbor square was a center of activity for locals and tourists alike. You could always tell the locals because they walked about with a sense of purpose and didn't stop to look around, or at least not for very long. On the other hand, tourists meandered in and out of souvenir shops bragging to each other when they believed they found a bargain. Most tourists refused to wear a coat because it's 'never cold and it *never* rains in Southern California.'

But who am I to complain, she thought. *It keeps Sammy's B&B filled and her wages paid.*

"I would French braid your hair if I were you. In fact, I can do it for you if you want," came a woman's voice from Tina's left. "You'd feel a lot cooler. Your hair is thick, but it needs shaping. It's too long and too flat on the crown of your head."

Tina jumped, squeezing her arms against her sides and feeling reassurance from the items tucked away. She should never have been caught daydreaming like that. What if it had been Ruiz?

Nervously, she felt the bulge of the concealed holster. Tina was pretty certain she could shoot it if she had to. At least she was able to hold it steady now, though she hadn't fired it yet. She didn't know if she ever would, but she wasn't going anywhere without that gun.

Feeling slightly reassured, Tina found herself looking at a petite, beautiful woman with wavy black hair pulled back with combs. She was smiling down at Tina and had the sweetest baby on her hip.

"Hi! I'm Angela Franco, and this is my son Nicholas, Nicco for short. It's a gorgeous day today, especially considering it's only the end of March. I bet you're new here." Angela tilted her head and smiled at Tina. "You don't look like a tourist even though you have that 'I don't know what to do with myself' look about you. You know… that look like 'Gee, I don't know where I'm at, but now that I'm here, where's my camera?' Though I could be wrong, am I?"

After Tina shook her head no, Angela went on, "Okay then, that means you just moved here! I figure that's correct because I haven't seen you before, and Nicco and I always come out about this time of day to relax and get some sun. So, what's your name, lady with the long brown hair?"

"Umm, I'm Tina, and yes, I just moved here." She glanced

between Angela and Nicco, then smiled. "Your little boy is so cute!" Tina crossed her eyes and grinned at the toddler. Nicco let out a wail.

Angela started laughing. "Momma's boy, this one. It takes him a little bit to warm up to people, but once he does, watch out. He'll want you to hold him forever."

"I love kids. I don't have any, but my cousins have several," Tina explained. There was no harm in talking to this nice woman, right? She seemed so friendly. "I enjoy them whenever I can. How old is he?"

"Eighteen months, and he weighs a ton let me tell you. May I sit down?" At Tina's slow nod of affirmation, Angela sat and breathed a sigh of relief. "So, Ms. Tina who just moved here, where are you from? And where are you staying? It's okay to tell me it's none of my business, but I sure hope you won't because I enjoy people and like to make new friends. My husband is in the Marines based down in Oceanside, but I don't like to live down there. Dana Point isn't that far away, so I convinced him we had to live here. Since he worships the ground I walk on, I got my way." She smiled at Tina, and her smile was contagious. Tina smiled back and couldn't stop.

"Don't you ever take a breath?" Tina laughed, and Angela shook her head.

"Well, I've got a lot to say!"

Tina laughed again. "Well, let me see. I'm Tina, umm, just Tina, currently helping out on the hill at Gable House. It's my day off, and yes, the day is gorgeous, and no, you may not

French braid my hair, but it's very nice to meet you too."

Tina looked up at Angela and Nicco. For the first time in what seemed like forever, Tina felt happy. Maybe she'd stay and visit for a while longer with this new friend.

That night Angela Franco hugged Nicco to her breast and rocked back and forth, trying to decide what to do. Finally, when her husband and son were asleep, she pulled out the piece of scratch paper with the phone number Ruiz gave her when he provided the crack cocaine she so desperately needed.

Angela didn't realize how much she was going to like Tina when Ruiz told her to keep an eye on Gable House and look for any opportunity to make contact with the woman. She'd been keeping an eye on that house every day, going to the harbor, trying to run into her and make friendly with Tina Oliver.

How did that woman get mixed up with trash like Raymond Ruiz? She seemed shy and just a bit lonely. Angela looked down at the paper again. She could feel her skin itch. Thank God she had quit the habit when she got pregnant with Nicco, but now, here she was again. Her husband would divorce her if he ever found out she was using again, and he'd take the baby, too.

She walked out to the front porch and heated the pipe. She dialed Ruiz to let him know she'd be meeting Tina again on her next day off.

She just had to make friends, he told her, get a good look at the inside of Gable House. Can't be that hard.

You can't refuse a man like Ray. He'd as soon slit your throat if you do. Angela looked out over the dark street and up at the moon. *Oh, Tina, please be careful. Give him what he wants.*

Chapter 12

Donaldson

O wen Donaldson squeezed his bloated belly behind the booth and sat down on a cracked Naugahyde vinyl seat cushion.

"What a dump! I sure do know how to pick them," he snickered as he looked around the old bar with its smoke mirrors and dusty bottles that looked as though they had never been taken down from the shelves. A single waitress stood chatting up the one other occupant at the other end of the room, and the bartender was idly watching an episode of court cases on the old portable tv.

"Crap, where's that bastard Ruiz? You'd think I have nothing better to do." He directed a flat-eyed stare at the waitress until he caught her attention and asked for a Heineken. She slapped his beer down in front of him, twitching her skinny hips as she ambled back to the bar.

Owen was no prize to look at, and that was just the way he liked it. He had bags under his eyes and a humped nose from one too many fights. There was a jagged scar up the side of his neck ending at a point behind his right ear. He didn't need anyone to take a second glance at him or express an interest in his conversation, but if they did, they'd be amazed at his intelligence which was clearly at odds with his appearance. His bank accounts were fat and laundered, hidden away along with the private home he owned in San Francisco.

"Where is Ruiz?" he murmured as he toyed with his beer. To be honest, he rarely drank much in public, preferring to keep his brain clear when he dealt with the scum who made his deliveries. "He should have been here by now."

Owen knew how to keep his industry under the radar and how and when to grease the pigs to keep them quiet. After all, smuggling was his business. Never mind the drug sales that were used to cover up the more prosperous gem smuggling that went on right underneath the noses of the rich and not so famous.

So here he was in this Stockton hole-in-the-wall. Goddamn Ruiz for keeping him waiting. Owen pushed himself up and away from the table, then made his way to the men's room to take a piss. If Ruiz didn't need to know where Oliver's wife rabbited off to, he'd have punished Ruiz long before now for letting Oliver lift the diamonds from Sonia, Ruiz's heroin-using, addict common-law wife.

Owen was pretty sure Ruiz didn't even know the value of the packet she lost, and it was worth far more to Donaldson than the $50,000 in cash Ruiz was whining about.

He checked his watch. The man was 20 minutes late.

Ruiz pretended he didn't care where the now-dead Sonia

had been concerned. She had been a whore but a capable one, enticing men to look the other way while she robbed them blind. Donaldson grinned into the bathroom mirror. She'd been one fine piece of ass, and he should know as he'd fucked her first, then recruited her as a courier for special clients several years ago.

Owen sat back down at the booth. He took a sip of his beer and grimaced. *Ugh! Warm now.*

And what of Jarrod Oliver? *Mistake. Stupid of Oliver to try and outsmart me,* Owen thought. In the long run, he'd proved his weakness, always running off at the mouth, thinking he had the brains to run an operation that had taken Donaldson years to build. At the very least, Oliver should have been smart enough to know that Owen had enough employees who would snitch at the drop of a hat, hoping to gain a higher position in his business. Owen preferred to call it OD's World.

During the past six months, Jarrod Oliver got too bold with the clients, too outspoken, and too dangerous to keep around. Stealing the diamonds confirmed the very reason that idiot had been on a short leash. If Ruiz hadn't killed him that fateful night for his own personal reasons, Owen would have ordered it done.

There weren't many people that could control the ins and outs of the shipyard merchandise. Never mind paying the warehousemen to look the other way or finding new and innovative ways to smuggle gems from other countries and into the over-inflated coffers of certain gem merchants in the San

Francisco and Los Angeles jewelry districts. The drug cartels were getting almost impossible to work with, preferring their own agents.

Oliver had been no more than one step above the typical rats and cockroaches that Owen used to run the merchandise. Donaldson turned his head to the side and scratched his scar. Oliver deserved his death. He should probably thank Ruiz for that.

Owen grunted, finally hearing the throaty pipes of Ruiz's Harley. Frowning, he squirmed on the cracked cushion. He knew what Ruiz thought about him, what they both thought of each other. He knew they'd both kill each other if they could. Owen fingered the small revolver that was always just a touch away. He had to figure Ruiz was on the run now; his photo had been a three-day wonder on the news channels.

Ruiz slipped into the seat opposite Donaldson, looking around in disgust at this dirty establishment. Ruiz stared across at the other man and opened the conversation with, "Owen, you always pick bars that look and smell like trash."

Donaldson lifted an eyebrow. "Save it for someone who doesn't know you as well as I do, Ruiz. Playing with trash is what you're good at. You're late."

Ruiz leaned in and tapped his two fingers together, mimicking a smoking gun. "I found Oliver's wife."

An hour later, Donaldson was alone again, his third beer barely cold. He whipped his head around and stared at the old man sitting at the bar, calling him over to the booth.

"Tell Espinosa to follow Ruiz," Owen said as soon as the man took a seat. "Keep tabs on him so he doesn't try to pull any tricky shit without my knowledge. Espinosa will know when to contact me so I can get to Oliver's widow."

Owen steepled his fingers in front of his face. *Who does Ruiz think he's playing with?* He knew all about Ruiz's background. The man was good with his knife and guns, as well as the martial arts he was trained in. He'd been raised to leader status in Hispanic neighborhood gangs and was in and out of jail for ten years, though never convicted for murder. Ruiz had impressed Owen with both his skills and his psychopathic tendencies. A man without a conscience was a good enforcer.

He considered Sonia's death and grunted. When Ruiz killed the woman, it had been because she'd stepped over the line. Donaldson didn't want his enforcer thinking he could do the same to him.

Ruiz was outliving his usefulness.

Chapter 13

Tina

"The purpose of brochures, advertising, and promotional materials is to communicate a message to your audience," Sammy lectured. "Our menus have to be cheerful and attractive and sound so delicious your mouth starts watering before you even catch a glimpse of the food."

Tina tried to pay attention to her aunt as she droned on and on about the menus, but she was starting to get sleepy. She'd stayed up far too long last night, trying to decide the safest place to hide the stolen money. She finally settled on the third-floor storage room, under the large cushion of an old fainting sofa that had been stored there when the house was renovated. Tina felt more settled with it out of her sight.

She'd just about made up her mind that she was going to sit down with Sammy and maybe Uncle Ben and tell them the whole story. The scare at the harbor was still too real. *Soon,* Tina thought. Then she would call the police. She couldn't keep living her life like this one day at a time. It felt more like a prison than prison itself. She'd been at Gable House a month and wanted to stay.

What should she do? No matter which way she turned it around in her head, it came down to the same answer. She had to stop hiding. Now that her head was on straight, she realized she was in more trouble than she would have been if she had trusted the crooked police in the first place. She turned her attention back to her aunt.

"It needs to be decorative but readable. I've got templates set in place for the menu shape and size, with decorative fonts to use for the typeface on the document," Sammy continued. "Each week I change the menu itself. But this week, you can do it. Just play with it for a while, okay? Here are samples of old ones." Sammy stepped away from the computer so Tina could take her place and patted the menus folder for Tina to review.

"Are you sure you want me to take care of the inn this afternoon while you go shopping?" Tina was more than a little bit nervous about being alone. She was petrified. "Maybe we can just lock up the inn and I'll go with you."

"Tina, I need you here today. I don't know what time my friends are arriving. Miss Ginny and Geri Arnett are on their way down from Napa this afternoon. They'll be staying for a week. They absolutely love anything made with fresh apples, so this weekend's breakfast menu is going to include lots of wonderful treats. I have to go shopping today."

"Ok but..."

"Are you ok, Tina?" Sammy asked, her voice gentle. "If you don't feel ready, I can work the schedule around, and I'll go to the store later."

"Um, no, no. It's ok. I'm just nervous." Tina straightened up in the chair and smiled sweetly at her aunt. "It's just my first time alone, that's all."

"Ginny and Geri are special friends of mine and have been coming to the inn four times a year almost since we opened. I can't wait for you to meet them. They're…" Sammy paused, then grinned. "They're interesting!"

Sammy looked at Tina and gave her a quick hug. "You'll be fine Teensy, have fun getting to know the program. When you feel comfortable, type out the changes in the menu for this weekend on the menu template. Perhaps you can use a red or green border and find some clip art with apples. It's nice and quiet today, so you should be just fine on your own. And I've got old menus backed up, so don't worry about losing any information, okay?"

"Okay, Sammy," Tina agreed.

As Sammy headed out the front door of Gable House, Tina blew her aunt a kiss, already distracted by the computer program and its possibilities. She loved working on the computer. In fact, she really liked everything about the inn. If only she could forget about Ruiz, she'd be so happy. *Ruiz!* Jumping up, she ran to the front door and threw the dead bolt.

But once she settled back down at the desk, Tina was soon intrigued by the graphics tools and filters and the ability to create your own or use artwork such as clip art or photographs. She bit her lip, concentrating on finding just the right graphic to place on the menu.

An hour later, Tina stretched long and luxuriantly, pleased with her first attempt at the menu. Just around the corner, the front doorbell pealed long and loud, the door rattling as if it would lift off its handle.

"Hello, Gable House! Sammy? Who locked the door? Sammy, we're here! We brought you some Napa wine! Sammy, where are you?"

"For Heaven's sake, Ginny, can't you wait?" Tina heard the complaint of the second woman trailing distantly behind the other.

"No, I have to go pee, Geri, you know that."

Tina unlocked the door as quickly as possible.

"Hello there, I'm Ginny Arnett. Why was that door locked during the day? I'm just going to pop into the Lavender room if you don't mind. Don't worry, girl, Sammy always gives us the same room, and I'll leave Geri here as your hostage till I get back."

Bemused, Tina had only a second to take in the round face of Ginny Arnett before blinking rapidly at the mirror image of the other woman walking through the door.

"Honest to Pete, Ginny, you're like a bull in a china shop!" Geri Arnett yelled after her sister. Exasperated, she puffed out her cheeks in blow-fish fashion.

"Hello Miss Arnett, welcome back to Gable House. I'm Tina. Sorry about the door. I used to live near San Francisco where you always lock your doors. Sammy stepped out to the stores, but I have your registration paperwork all ready for your signature."

"Hello there, Tina." Geri sighed. "There's no stopping my sister. Can you be a dear and help me with her suitcases? They're all scattered in the front entrance. She drops them and runs, leaving me to pick up the mess. So typical!" Geri Arnett scowled, then shrugged before striding back out the front door.

Tina hurried out after her, glancing around the parking lot. It was just the Arnett's car and suitcases. She picked up the forlorn luggage and followed Geri back into the inn.

"So glad to be here at last," Geri continued. "It was a nine-hour drive from Napa, which isn't too bad considering all the traffic. Ginny's been squirming and whining since we reached Los Angeles, but would that girl stop driving? No. Just plows on through."

Tina blinked, setting the suitcases down just inside the door. The Misses Arnett had to be at least seventy-five years old and as long-removed from girlhood as mothballs.

"Geri, look at what Sammy left us on the bed!" Ginny called as she came down the stairs. "Just the sweetest apple doll. It's a 'grandma' holding her grandchild. Maybe she remembered Cousin Charlie's granddaughter is due to have another little one next month. Now, *she* would make a good apple doll. Eight months pregnant and big as a house! You'd need another apple for her belly as well."

Tina couldn't help it. She burst out laughing, gazed into

the wickedly sparkling eyes of Miss Ginny Arnett, and fell in love. Miss Geri opened and closed her mouth like a carp once or twice, then started laughing herself.

"It's what I keep her around for," Ginny said, grinning over at her twin sister. "She's such a priss that it's fun to shake her up." Ginny turned her merry black eyes to Tina. "So, I think you must be Sammy's niece. When I called her last week to reconfirm our visit, she mentioned you were finally here to help her. It's about time, I must say. I've heard her talk about you for years, how you used to come and stay when you were younger, just like one of her three kids, she said. She told us about the mischief you and your cousin Dave would get up to."

"We're happy to meet you," Geri said. "Ginny and I like women who can cause a little mischief now and then. Sammy also told us you've fallen on some very hard times. We're very sorry to hear that. Well now, it's no secret Sammy needs help around here, so I'm sure you'll help each other! She works way too hard." Pausing, Geri looked around the room. "Now, what is that dear innkeeper feeding us for breakfast tomorrow? Snacks don't count. It's the full breakfast we want! We need lots of energy to shop on."

Tina looked from one to the other. Identical twins. About 5-feet-3-inches in height, they had beautiful almond-shaped black eyes and slightly bulbous, upturned noses. Their rosy cheeks didn't come from a blusher brush, and their big ears stuck out from two very different hairstyles. Geri wore hers cut very modern in a longish silver bob with a fringe of bang, while Ginny's silvery-white hair was cropped short overall two or three inches, styled in controlled disarray and directed away from her face.

Both women seemed feminine and self-assured, though they had an opposite style of dress. Ginny wore a pair of blue overalls with a deep purple cotton t-shirt tucked underneath. Peeking out from underneath the overalls were bright blue sneakers. Geri wore a pale rose-colored smock gathered at the waist with a pair of black silk pants and loafers. Tina was thoroughly enchanted by their new guests.

"Ahh, I'm finishing the menu right now," Tina said as she sat back down at the desk. "I already know you love apples because Sammy is preparing a real treat for you both. Let me just print out a copy for you."

Snatching the menu copy from the humming printer, Ginny and Geri oohed and ahhed over the upcoming apple cheese blintzes and smiled over the waffles.

"Perfect dishes, of course. Sammy knows I love waffles," mentioned Ginny, "but you have three misspelled words."

"Let me see that." Geri grabbed the paper away from her sister and perused its contents. "Yes, you'll want to correct the spelling, and you should probably add a bit of leading to even out your columns since you've changed the font that Sammy generally uses for her menus. Here, let me show you."

"Miss Geri, how do you know all this?" Tina asked. "It seems so easy now, but it took me forever to get it figured out."

Ginny chortled and rocked back on her heels. "Well, she should know! Geri was an office manager for 40 years. She's a whiz with all kinds of computer software, and she still does volunteer work at the library. I was a high school history teacher."

The door opened and the women turned around at the same time. Sammy smiled at the trio hanging around the computer and spoke up. "Well, ladies, I see you've arrived safe and sound, and you're already giving my niece computer lessons. But the question is, where's my wine?"

"Sammy!" All three good friends embraced while an entertained Tina looked on.

This is going to be an interesting week, Tina mused.

Chapter 14

Sammy

S ammy, I'm leaving now. You'll be okay for a while?" Tina asked. "Shall I pick up anything at the store for you?"

"Hmmm, oh sure, Teensy, I've told you three times to go out and get some fresh air." She peered up at Tina from her chair at the kitchen table and softly smiled. "There was a time when I didn't have to tell you to go outside. You and Dave would be out the door so fast I couldn't catch you if I wanted to. It should be a quiet afternoon, I just have to finish these cheddar cheese puffs for this evening's appetizers, and then I'm going to put my own feet up for an hour or so. Could you try and be home by 4:00, honey? We've got a full house this weekend. In fact, when you get back, let's sit down and discuss the next few weekends' activities and chores."

"Sure, but I don't have to go," Tina said. "I know I told Angela I would meet her, but I can put it off."

"No!" Sammy exclaimed. She was so glad Tina was finally leaving Gable House. Putting off her friend date was the last thing Sammy wanted. Besides, Sammy needed Tina out of the house for the afternoon so she could work on a surprise.

"You need to get out every so often. From what you've told me, Angela seems like a live wire. You go, enjoy yourself! Make sure you have gas in the car because the mall is about ten miles away."

"All right then, see you later."

Tina grabbed her purse and sweater and went out the side door to the small parking area, dragging her steps. Sammy watched through the window as Tina looked around the parking lot before finally getting into the small economy car.

Sammy jumped up fast and called to Geri, who was loitering in the salon.

"Geri, crane your neck around the window and make sure she's gone!" Sammy called. "I thought she'd never leave. I'm going to grab my handyman to help us move things, then I'll go get those bags from my room and meet you upstairs on the third floor. Let's hurry, the new furniture will be here in thirty minutes."

Sammy hurried out of the kitchen and into her own inner sanctum. She loved her little private studio at the back of the kitchen. It was peaceful and feminine and gave her pleasure. Here she hung her small art treasures and kept her favorite books. Her bed was a large four-poster with a canopy in green silk with gold-shot thread. Thick area carpets that your toes could curl into covered the hardwood floor. All around her she could view pictures of Dan and her kids and grandkids.

But today, she and Geri were going to go decorate Tina's room. Sammy had wanted to surprise her niece with a room update almost since she'd arrived.

It took three trips up to the third floor with linens, curtains, and bath items. Thank God for Geri and her love of the antique stores where she found a lovely barrel chair in the softest shade of gray and matched it up with a small ottoman. She'd also purchased two small crystal bedroom lamps at a well-known thrift store in Laguna.

In view of the room's tight space, Sammy had ordered a new mattress for the simple but feminine carved cherrywood headboard, pairing the bed with one small nightstand and dresser that had been all been in the storage room at the other side of the attic. Her part-time maintenance worker, Hector, had cleaned them thoroughly and gave the pieces new life with a good coat of beeswax, and now stood ready to assist.

"Oh, my gosh, the dresser looks so beautiful!" Sammy exclaimed once the new furniture was in. "What a great job you did. Tina is going to love it." Hector's ears turned red with the compliment.

Sammy and Geri stood in the threshold of Tina's room, surveying the space with excitement. They looked at each other with grins and stepped over the threshold.

Sammy emptied the old dresser drawers to make way for the new, feeling sad that Tina had brought so few clothes with her. She opened the bottom drawer and gently pulled out the afghan and saw her sister Sharon's old yellow box. She ran her hand over the top, smiling at the memories. Curious, she started to open it, but it was locked, and probably a good thing.

Every woman deserved a few secrets.

The patient handyman moved not only the old bed set but the scarred dresser into attic storage, just in the nick of time before the mattress was delivered. He brought the barrel chair and ottoman upstairs while Sammy fretted over where to place the new bed. Finally, he rewired the cable for the small TV in its updated placement on the wall, disappearing with a tip of his cap to the two busy ladies.

Sammy and Geri hung a simple window treatment of soft buttery yellow sheers, welcoming the late afternoon sun through the small corner window.

Crisp cotton sheets and pillowcases of snow white with small yellow and purple sprigged flowers covered the new mattress. Next, the two women layered a warm thermal blanket the color of soft heather, then finished with a down comforter and duvet cover in yellow and white stripes.

Sammy stood in the center of the room, turning in a slow circle. "Oh, Geri, this chair fits right under the eaves, and it will be perfect with Tina's afghan my mother crocheted. And look at these lamps!"

Geri gave a well-satisfied nod. "Shopping was so much fun knowing what you wanted me to get. I know this is your gift to Tina, but would you allow me to give her this mirror? See, it will hang perfectly on the side wall over here." Sammy turned to see Geri holding a small but exquisite square mirror framed in silver filigree.

"Oh, my goodness Geri, are you sure? It's so feminine;

she's sure to love it."

Geri's organizational skills took precedence in the tiny bathroom. She unwrapped new nickel-plated bathroom accessories and added fluffy yellow towels and a small hamper. Hand creams and face soaps made their way to the vanity cabinet shelves as well.

Both women mischievously grinned as they dragged the last big plastic bag over to the new bedroom dresser. Sammy snipped the price tags off of the new clothes, and she gently placed soft sweaters of rose and blue and Tina's favorite color—purple—inside. She added two pairs of jeans, new socks and undergarments, and four colored tee shirts in soft brushed cotton. Three new pairs of earrings lay inside a small glass keepsake box.

"I wish I could have bought her new boots," Sammy lamented, "but I just didn't know how to ask for her shoe size. As it is, I had to sneak a peek at her laundry to catch her clothes sizes."

Sammy placed a vase of freshly cut spring daisies and fern on the dresser. Then, with a satisfied nod, she pronounced the room complete. Geri turned to Sammy and gave her a brief, hard hug.

"Thank you for letting me be a part of your surprise," Geri said. "She's going to love it."

Together, they gave the finished bedroom one last look and walked down the staircase arm in arm.

Chapter 15

Tina

Angela Franco waved wildly from the food court at the mall. "Hey! Over here, come on over here! Nicco was hungry, so he's already started."

Tina grinned at the chubby baby with a French fry in each dimpled hand. "Hey, Nicco! Those look good. Can I have a bite?" Tina bent down and took a pretend nibble of a very mushy potato, earning a giggle from the baby.

"See, I told you he would warm up to you!" Angela said. "I know Nicco, we like the lady with the long brown hair who needs a haircut, don't we?"

Nicco squealed with laughter and stuffed his fist and his mush in his mouth. Tina and Angela cracked up. Over the next hour, they munched their way through pizza, salad, and root beer and discovered things in common that all young women enjoyed: men, makeup, men, music, movies, and men.

"...So then I told him he was an idiot. Why would anyone sleep by the bed with a shotgun? I said I'm not going to live like that, and I don't care if you do have family in the mafia, I'm not going to marry them! And then we broke up, which

I think was very sensible of me, don't you?" Angela sighed. "I did miss the sex, though. And after Michael, I met Neal, who was a real jerk, but fantastic in the sack... but wait, it's your turn!"

Tina blushed and warmed up to the topic under consideration. "I'm trying to remember sex back before my husband. I was still pretty young, so I don't have that many experiences to choose from, but I do remember the time I went to an amusement park with my girlfriend, and she picked up this Marine and left me to spend time with his buddy who wore this stupid cowboy hat all night. I don't even remember his name."

"His name isn't important!" Angela gushed. "What *do* you remember?"

Tina smiled. "I *do* remember driving him back to his motel a few blocks away and thinking how adult I was when I took him up on his offer for a drink. So, I'm standing there in his room, feeling stupid because he said he had to go to the restroom, and he comes swaggering out with nothing but a cowboy hat and his... Ahem! It looked like one of those skinny balloons you blow up for animal hats after the air leaks out. I couldn't help it. I started giggling, and he got mad. I almost ran out of that room!"

Angela tilted her head to the side. "No, really, tell me the truth," she said. "Was it deflated before it was blown up?"

"I swear."

Both women started laughing. Tina had forgotten what a

pleasure it was to spend time with other women, easing into a new friendship.

They walked for a while, window shopping in the large two-story mall as they talked about small, inconsequential things.

Eventually, Angela stopped to grab a cleaning wipe from her bag to clean her son's face and hands from the cookie she'd given him earlier. Crouching down to play with the baby, Tina felt little Nicco tug on her long hair, tangling his sticky fingers in the long strands. Laughing, she carefully disengaged his little hand and pulled her hair away from her face.

Catching her own profile in a store mirror display, Tina thought she looked a little messy as well and took a minute to secure her hair in a long, loose braid down her back.

"Okay Tina, I really want to know why you won't cut your hair," Angela said. "Like, is it a religious thing? Because I won't say anything further if it is, but don't you know how pretty you would look with it layered and some highlights?" she asked. "I tell you, when Nicco is a bit older and Brian is stationed in one place long enough for me to work again, I'm going to go back to working as a hairstylist. I know just how you should look. Trust me?"

Tina looked down for a long moment and then tipped her chin up in a gesture of defiance, taking a deep breath. Now that Jarrod was gone, there really was no reason to keep it so long. Besides, it was always getting in her face and in the way when she was cleaning the rooms or baking in the kitchen.

Slowly, Tina ran her hand down her braid and made a decision.

A new start, a new me. Jarrod be damned! she thought impulsively.

"You win, Angela. Let's go get it cut, then I'll think about the highlights."

"Yahoo, Nicco!" Angela exclaimed, leaning down to kiss the baby's cheek. "She's going to do it! There's this salon right here in the mall, and I know just the right stylist. It might cost you a little bit... do you have money? I like to have some cash for a tip at least when I come here. Oh, well, it doesn't matter, I'll talk her into a discount and help you pay for it."

"Oh, it's okay, Angela. I can pay for it," Tina said quickly, "but I'll have to get some money from the ATM. I have a little bit of money saved up since I came to work for my aunt."

"Speaking of your work," Angela said as they strolled to an ATM near the salon, "I really *really* want to get a look inside your gorgeous Gable House. I looked up some magazine articles online, and it seems so gracious and elegant! Please say yes and invite me for your next day off."

Tina paused. She didn't want to offend her new friend. "Well, we really don't do that, per my aunt's policy," she said, "but maybe next week you can come over to see just the bottom floor, and we'll go outside in the back gardens. I'll make you a picnic lunch. Ok?"

Tina was happy. The constant worry in her heart eased a little with both of her snap decisions. It made her feel... *normal.* Quickly, though, she glanced around to the crowds of shoppers. *How could I forget?* she wondered. Ruiz was still out there. Would life ever really get back to normal for her?

"Sure! It's a date," Angela said. "I'll bring the sodas and Nicco!"

Tina pulled her attention back to the other woman and discussed the newly planned picnic. Overall, Tina enjoyed her afternoon off. After the initial shock of seeing her hair fall to the floor, she left herself in the hands of the stylist and Angela, who oversaw the entire procedure. She didn't have enough time or money for highlights but left with a future appointment and a bag full of hair products.

Angela tapped Tina on the shoulder. "Nicco and I are going to step outside. I need to make a phone call."

"Okay," Tina said, smiling. "I'll wait here."

"Yes, I'm going next week, I'll be able to get a good look around at the entrances and the back garden, and I'll let you know where they are," Angela said. "She's really harmless, so I don't get it. What's she done to set you on her trail? And Ray, if you want me to continue being her friend, you better have more than a stingy bag of rocks for me next time."

Pensively, Tina drove home and pulled into the lot, about ten minutes past four. She sat in the car for a minute, realizing that she hadn't given one thought to the money, the diamonds, her gun, or Ruiz the entire afternoon. She'd barely even thought about Jarrod today and only then when the stylist cut her hair. Looking into the rear-view mirror, she almost didn't recognize the woman staring back at her.

Closing her eyes, Tina gulped hard. Tentatively touching the shortened locks brushing her shoulders, all she could think of was the "Reflection" song from an old Disney movie Mulan that she and Momma used to watch on the VCR over and over. She felt different, almost brand new.

Cautiously she drew her gun out of its hidden holster, and taking the cartridge out of the chamber, she dropped it and the Ruger inside her purse. Maybe tonight she could finally confide in her aunt and make a fresh start.

Finally, taking a deep breath, Tina stepped out of the car, feeling like a pretty woman. Better yet, today, Tina felt beautiful.

"Sammy, I'm home!" she sung out as she walked into the kitchen. "Whew, no time to go change now!"

Throwing her purse in the kitchen cubby drawer, she washed her hands and prepped the large serving tray with cream and sugar and gourmet tea bags for the afternoon guests. She readied the large coffee server, then filled the matching pot with water for tea. Appetizers were already laid on two beautiful platters of dark green depression glass.

Sammy shot around the corner and into the kitchen. "Oh, there you are! It's been busy! Mr. and Mrs. Sandoval arrived. I just got them settled in their room, and a Mrs. Ralston called and said she and her husband were on their way and will be here by 5:30."

"Ok!" Tina replied.

"Ginny and Geri will be checking out sometime tomorrow, but we still have one more couple, the Halsteads, arriving for the weekend. They're celebrating their first anniversary, so we'll want to make their room extra special. I ordered a gift basket with champagne from the specialty shop in town, so you need to be on the lookout for that."

"Ok, Sammy," Tina said. She gathered her courage, then continued, "Auntie, can we sit down and talk awhile later? I know we're busy, but…"

"Huh? Oh, sure." Sammy took a deep breath, clearly not really paying attention to what her niece was saying. "Plus your Aunt Susan and Uncle Ben are coming to dinner tomorrow night. I'm so glad you want to visit with them. Ben said they've just been sitting on ice till you were settled. We'll need to prepare breakfast for eight persons tomorrow, and—oh my goodness, your hair looks fantastic!"

Sammy finally stopped her rustling around the kitchen and walked over to Tina. Tina smiled shyly.

"Oh, Teensy, you look so pretty! Your eyes look so much larger without all that hair in your face, and it curls so softly down to your shoulders. I'm so proud of you! That must have been such a hard decision for you to make."

Tina's eyes grew watery, and she brushed at them with the back of her hand, then shrugged. "I had her cut a ponytail for me," she confided. "I'll keep it with my treasures. Maybe someday I'll be able to look at it and think of Jarrod more clearly. He was so adamant that I never cut my hair that it almost feels like a betrayal."

"Well, I think you did just the right thing." Sammy smiled again and squeezed Tina's shoulder. "Let's get this show on the road, then we'll circle around and discuss tomorrow's breakfast and chores, okay?"

It was almost 7:30 by the time Sammy and Tina finished up with tea, appetizers, late registration, and the general business of running a Bed & Breakfast inn. They shared a small quiet dinner of meatloaf and baked potato at the kitchen table. Both thought the day was a complete success, and Tina totally forgot what she was going to talk to her aunt about.

The sky had gone dark with just a scattering of stars over the ocean when Tina finally decided to call it a night.

"Sammy, I'm going to go up and relax now," Tina said. "Thanks for loaning me your car and allowing me the day off to go to the mall. I hadn't realized how much I missed having a girlfriend to gossip with. Angela's like a talking doll. You just pull the string and she talks and talks and talks. Nicco is the cutest baby you've ever seen, all chubby with these rosy cheeks." She yawned and stood up from her seat at the kitchen table, grabbing her purse from the cubby. "I'm tired. I'll see you in the morning."

Sammy looked up from the dishwasher. "Goodnight Tina." Just as Tina made it to the door, Sammy added, "You've really made my life so much easier this last month."

Tina turned and smiled at her aunt. "I love it here, Sammy. I'm happy to help."

"I'd like you to stay on permanently if you're ready to consider it. I know you've been trying to figure out how you fit in, but I don't have any questions about it at all. I'm less lonely with you here, you learn fast, and you don't have to be told twice about what needs to be done."

Tina felt overwhelmed. So many emotions had been running through her heart today, she didn't know what to say.

"I'd like to train you as an assistant manager so I can start going away more often. Think about it, would you? We can talk more when you're ready, but I don't need to wait till the end of summer to know you fit in perfectly."

"Yeah, sure, I'll think about it," Tina managed to choke out. "Goodnight, Auntie."

Tina climbed the stairs thinking about her full day. She stroked her shorter hair, shaking her head from side to side to feel it swing around her neck. Sammy was right; the haircut was perfect.

"Oh, my God!" Tina gasped as she opened her bedroom door. Turning around in a circle, she took in all the details her aunt had painstakingly put together. "Oh, my God!"

She sighed as she sank down on her new bed, dropping her

purse to the floor. She found her grandmother's yellow afghan on a lovely little chair. On top of her pillow was a brand-new cell phone. Everything was so perfect.

"Oh!" Tina jumped up, racing down the stairs to fly into her aunt's wide-open arms.

Chapter 16

Ginny

Ginny Arnett sat on the bench in the gazebo, swinging her bare feet and staring out at the ocean. There was something about being barefoot on a bright sunny day that made her feel young and lazy. She took a long drink of water from the bottle never far from her side.

The morning sun was warm against her back, and she enjoyed listening to the birds and the wind chimes tucked away under trees. The flowers in the garden were in full bloom, their scent lingering in the air. This morning her sister was off somewhere in town, picking up a few odds and ends for their return trip. To be honest, Ginny was enjoying this little bit of time to herself. She wouldn't trade her sister for a million bucks, but that woman never slowed down. "Aren't we supposed to be retired?" she'd tease, though Geri could never take the hint.

"I'll slow down when I die!" Geri would respond, to which Ginny would just stand her ground and reply, "If you don't slow down, you'll die anyway." Honestly, Ginny didn't know how they got along some days, but after a lifetime of taking care of each other, what would she do without Geri?

Ginny had led a full life in the Napa, California area, watching her students grow and take their place in the community, marry, and have children of their own. She was godmother to seven of those babies, sharing photos with pride, watching them thrive. There was nothing she enjoyed more than a roomful of kids. Speaking, listening, watching their eyes light up when she'd finally get it through their thick skulls what she was teaching. She missed it.

Geri was always more formal, more corporate. She'd enjoyed the company of adults and politics and artsy movies. Boring! God forbid Geri should let out a fart instead of holding it in. Ginny twisted her lips in a wicked smile, lifted a butt cheek off the bench, and let it out. Startled at the sound of laughter behind her, she turned.

"Heard you all the way from over here!" Tina giggled. "And I'm staying right here for a few minutes anyway. Sammy sent me to tell you Miss Geri is back and asking for you because it's time for you to head home."

Ginny wiggled her skinny fanny on the bench. "Caught me, did you? What would be the fun of being an old lady if you can't do what feels natural?" She laughed. "I was saluting Geri, the starchy old biddy. Every time we come down to Dana Point, we stay still for a few days, then she drags me around to soak up culture and art museums and classical music. Then another few days I get to relax while she goes running around buying up the stores. She calls it 'antiquing.' It gives me time to myself, but today I'm bored and not looking forward to that ride home. Geri can wait awhile."

Ginny looked over at Tina, motioning for her to sit down. "Please do an old lady a favor and come over and talk to me. Take your shoes off and keep me company."

After a pause, Tina sat down next to Ginny. "I've got thirty minutes off for lunch, so I'd love to join you, that is, of course, unless you're going to continue farting up a storm." Both women laughed. "Sammy said I'd find you here because you love to sit and dream in this spot. It's so peaceful."

"How do you like living in a beach city?" Ginny asked. "Do you enjoy working at Gable House? Sammy seems to love your company."

"You know, Miss Ginny, I've loved this home since I was a little girl, but I don't know if I've earned the right to a permanent place at Gable House yet." Tina fiddled with the hem of her shirt. "I think I've been more of a headache to Sammy than I've been worth this last month."

Ginny looked Tina up and down with her sharp eyes and decided she liked what she saw. "You're honest, that's a good thing. Innkeeping takes time to learn. And anything worth learning takes even longer."

"I guess," Tina replied.

"Sammy told us you were pretty bruised when you arrived..." Ginny started, waiting. When Tina didn't react, Ginny continued, "But she also mentioned that you're settling in and handling all the routine tasks. Plus, you're mastering the computer, gardening, and a good portion of the baking."

Tina shrugged and tucked her hair behind one ear. "Well, since Sammy told you, I don't mind admitting to you that I was knocked around ruthlessly by my husband."

Ginny blinked, surprised Tina would just blurt that out. But she held her tongue.

"I wonder sometimes how much more of his fists I could have handled. Working at Gable House is good for me and keeps my mind off of ... off of—oh, many things.

"Since Dan died, Sammy's been all work and very little play. Tell you the truth, we've been trying to get her to take some vacation time for the last three years, but she never does," Ginny said. "Your cousins never did show an interest in running the inn. Oh, they all put their time in, but it didn't stick. She said you're the only one who used to trail her from room to room with a dust rag. Maybe now that you're here, she'll relax a bit.

"Geri and I have been friends with Sammy and Dan for many years," Ginny rambled. "I thought my heart would break for her when Dan died. Many's the night we'd sit in her big kitchen over a cup of cocoa and gab the night away. So if you're talking about more than just the physical bruises in your heart, Tina, then I already know about some of them. We've talked about you, Dan, her kids, our lives, our loves ... and yes, even though I'm an old spinster..." Ginny paused. "Does that sound awful, the word spinster?" She shrugged. "Even though I'm an old spinster, I've been in love. It just never culminated into the magic of marriage." She leaned back and wiggled her eyebrows at Tina.

Ginny watched as Tina laughed. She sat quietly, resting and wondering if Tina would relax enough to confide in her. She knew that sometimes it felt safer to talk to a stranger who had no judgment call to make.

Tina looked out over the ocean, then back at Ginny.

After a minute, Tina started to speak. "Marriage. There wasn't much magic there, Miss Ginny. A lot of mystery, maybe. Stubborn would more aptly describe me. I found him so romantic and sexy. He watched over me, and at first, I thought he was being attentive. I'd always wanted someone to pay attention to just me. Finally, I figured out he was obsessive. I thought I could fix him. He'd knock me down, and I'd get up, followed by his second act of 'I'm so sorry.' Then it would be peaceful for another few weeks." Tina sighed and closed her eyes. "He would argue with his bosses, people he knew. He just didn't know how to keep his mouth shut. Then he lost his job. People didn't want to hire him because of his bad reputation. When he couldn't find honest work, he started dealing drugs and was out of the apartment for longer periods of time."

Ginny didn't interrupt the flow of Tina's words, knowing she needed to unload her feelings to an unbiased listener.

"I wanted to run. But every time I put my things in a bag and tried to leave, he'd show up. He had the apartment and me watched. I think in the early days of our marriage, if I'd really wanted to leave him, I could have." The younger woman glanced at Ginny. "That doesn't say a lot about my strength of character, does it?"

Tina stopped talking for a minute, rocking her body on that cement bench, back and forth, back and forth. Ginny gently placed her hand on Tina's shoulder for a moment, hoping Tina knew it was okay to go on.

"He always threatened to hurt my mother," Tina blurted. "One time, he called me from her apartment just to let me know he could break in. I don't think Sammy would have told you, but my mother was a recovering alcoholic. I grew up tiptoeing around alcoholics. She wasn't a mean drunk, but Jarrod was. After so many years of drinking, Momma found Alcoholics Anonymous and finally got sober, but she was so unhealthy and thin. I always thought you could snap her arm just by holding on to her too hard. I got pregnant once. I was so happy about the baby, nothing seemed to bother me. I wanted a little girl so bad; I'd dream of how we'd get away and go live someplace far away, without a single spot of hate. Momma was still alive then. She was Sammy's oldest sister, Sharon." Pausing, Tina sniffled. "Anyway, Momma insisted on visiting for a few weeks when I had morning sickness."

Tina continued, "Jarrod was good and acted the perfect husband for the whole first week she was there. Eventually, he got bored with that, so he went out and got rip-roaring drunk. He came home in the middle of the night all loud and demanding sex, calling me a bitch and a 'man castrator.' I tried to hush him up so he wouldn't wake up Momma, but he took that as a no and beat the crap out of me. We woke Momma up anyway. I lost the baby that night. I was more ashamed that Momma had to see my life was a sham. She convinced me to leave him. That lasted a week till he showed up drunk with two of his drug buddies, threatening to hurt my mother." Tina sighed. "So, I went back to him. After that, nothing seemed to matter. I stayed home where nobody could see the bruises. I got fatter and fatter. I thought being fat would make him lose interest, or at least I would bounce when he knocked me over." She drew in a shaky breath, then wiped at her eyes and laughed. "Whew, I'm sorry! Why am I telling you all this?"

"Because I'm a good listener, Tina, and you need to talk." Ginny smiled and squeezed Tina's hand. "Sometimes it helps to talk to a person you don't know very well. Sammy said she gave you some abuse counselor names and phone numbers, but you haven't gone. Just my opinion, of course, but counseling sessions could give you an outlet for your anger and grief, as well as some peace of mind. You're like a great big tea kettle that's been simmering and starts to boil. You know the tea kettle is going to start whistling in a minute, but you can't predict exactly when. I'd say you've kept it on simmer for a very long time."

"Oh, I went to a few counselors early on, but they kept trying to make me talk about Jarrod. I didn't want to spill my guts about our marriage. All I wanted was some advice on how to live with someone who hits you. I grabbed a few pamphlets, and I went home. They called me once or twice. I was afraid he would find out, so I told them not to call me anymore because if the phone rang when Jarrod was home, he always answered it."

Ginny watched the young woman squirming on the bench as she tried to make herself comfortable. After years of travel with Geri, Ginny could sit almost anywhere and make herself comfortable. Together, they just sat quietly, staring out over the ocean. Finally, Ginny swung her leg over the bench to straddle it. After taking a swig of water from the bottle of water, she started to speak.

"I was a real party girl in my twenties, oh so many moons ago. I graduated from college, got my first teaching job, had a great group of friends. We'd go dancing or drinking on weekends, just enjoying life and having a hell of a good time." Ginny smiled. "You know, Geri was always more reserved than me. She had a few close friends, and she preferred coffee to beer." At that, Tina finally laughed a little.

"Anyway, I started teaching U.S. History at the junior high school in Vacaville, and there was a math teacher I couldn't take my eyes off. I know what you're thinking, weenie math teacher, huh?" Tina laughed again. "He had blonde hair and gray eyes that looked right through you. Whenever I got upset over some trivial thing, he had this way of making me laugh till I'd forget what I was mad at." Ginny sighed. "He was everything I thought I wanted in a man."

"What happened?" Tina asked, frowning.

"I was twenty-eight and still a virgin. It's not that we

weren't ready for sex, but back then, birth control wasn't as easily accessible as it is today, so couples were a lot more careful. Steven and I were pretty serious by then. We planned for the perfect first time. Neither of us wanted to get married yet. Geri and I were still living at home, and you know I wasn't going to do it at home."

"It was a beautiful summer night in July of 1956. We found this hotel in San Jose where nobody knew who we were so nobody could point fingers. They still did that back then. We had the most romantic night, something I'll never forget. But Steven couldn't keep his mouth shut, and he told his roommate who told another friend, who wasn't a friend.

"One Saturday night not long after that first time, Steven and I went to dinner in town. We had a few glasses of wine. We weren't totally drunk, just tipsy enough to teeter as we walked. The parking lot was at the back of the restaurant. You had to walk through this long hall and step out into the back alley. Three men were waiting for us. One I recognized from a few parties I'd gone to."

Ginny paused and sucked in a breath. It was easier to talk about now, sure, but it was still hard. "Two of the men jumped Steven, and the one I knew grabbed me and held his hand over my mouth when I tried to scream. They beat Steven up and dragged him down the alley and then they turned their attention to me. They yanked me into a nearby building and into this dark back room that was more like a closet than anything else. They took turns at me, Tina. They took turns raping me, calling me a whore, and saying they knew how much I loved it 'so give it over.' I lost every shred of innocence I ever had. They left me there bleeding and battered, and I thought I would die there. An employee from the restaurant found Steven by the dumpster where those bastards left him unconscious and called the police."

Tina reached over and squeezed Ginny hand but didn't interrupt.

"The police found me a few hours later. I was able to walk if I leaned on someone, so the police took me to the station but not a hospital. I didn't know where Steven was. I called my parents, but they were out that night. Geri came to get me. Back then, the police weren't as sympathetic to rape as they are currently." She frowned. "Not that they're very sympathetic nowadays either, but at least there are more laws in place to protect the victims. Anyway, I told them what happened and gave them a description of the men. Afterward, Geri took me to a hospital where a male doctor and a nurse cleaned me up and muttered about 'bad girls.' Then we went home. Geri sat with me all night and the next night and the next. Our parents were kind but older. They didn't know how to cope with what happened to me. Steven avoided me.

"Then the rumors started. I was the talk of the town, and I couldn't understand why Steven didn't defend me. I went back to teach the following week and tried to pretend that everything was all right, but everybody was whispering behind my back.

"Steven came to my classroom at the end of the day. He tried to apologize for not coming to see me, though he wouldn't look me in the eye. He mumbled that it was his fault because he told his roommate about us, who it turned out had a big mouth. He said it was best if we played it cool for a while and not see each other. He arrogantly told me he didn't know whose baby it would be if I were pregnant. Besides, I was okay, wasn't I? Then he left. And honestly, worse than the rape was finding out his love wasn't real. Betrayal hurts, Tina. I never spoke with him again.

"It was Geri who stood by me when everything fell apart. My sensible sister. My reputation at the school and with our social crowd was ruined. I felt like a worm, trying to cross the sidewalk before getting stepped on.

"Thankfully, I wasn't pregnant. Two months later, Geri and I moved out of our parent's home. We found an apartment in a town near San Francisco about 50 miles away. She took a job as a legal secretary. At first, I was afraid to step outside the door. She came home one day with a referral to a psychologist and bullied me into going. Well, I told you how organized she could be, didn't I? Don't let that prissy exterior of hers fool you. It took me a long time to heal, to remember how to laugh. It was a year before I found enough courage to teach again. Geri took care of me the entire time."

Ginny stopped talking. She reached over and put both arms around Tina, hugging her close. "There now, we both shared our hurts. You know, there isn't anything in this life that can't be overcome and conquered. The worst memories of your life with your husband will always be there somewhere in the back of your mind.

"The hardest part is letting the pain and resentment go. If you don't, your heart will heal, but it will never be fully whole again. Tina, you are a beautiful woman. I know you don't believe it anymore, but you are. Your aunt is worried sick about you, but I told her you'd be okay. I can see the inner strength in you that keeps you moving forward. If it helps you at all, remember my story. I'm just another stubborn old lady, but I'm strong and happy."

Tina laughed at that. "You're not a stubborn old lady, Miss Ginny."

"So says you." Ginny smiled, then reached down and grabbed her sandals. "Now then, will you walk with me back into the house? I've talked far too long. It's time for us to pack up and go!" She smiled at Tina and stood up. "If Geri's back, I'll bet you apples to oranges our bank balance is lower, and I'll have to make room for all the items she's been stashing in our room. She's got this thing for old stuff. I tell her we're already antiques, so why do we need more, but she only gets that steely look in her eye and ignores me."

Tina stood, then pulled Ginny into a hug. "I'll remember your story," she whispered. "I'll remember you."

Chapter 17

Owen

Ruiz and Owen met in the gaslight district of San Diego. Owen was in the mood for a good lunch, and business had been excellent during the past month. In fact, he thought the new enforcer he'd hired was just as good, if not better than, Ruiz. The man was too new to consider crossing him.

Owen needed loyalty. Ruiz had become a liability. The police were still patrolling the streets up north, but it wouldn't be long before they extended their search here in the Southern California communities. Owen had legitimate business down here in Southern California, so the trip wasn't wasted. Ruiz's face was now on the daily police patrol wanted sheets—and damn him, Owen was still missing the diamonds.

The diamonds had come from Africa and Asia—mixed with legitimate diamonds, of course—and had been smuggled into the country through various means. The entire pickup had been bungled. Owen would need to involve himself if this fiasco was going to be unraveled.

He was aware of Ruiz's new hideaway in the city of Chula Vista, located just north of the Mexican border. He forwarded additional funds to Ruiz the last time they met, enough to keep him going for another month. *But the buck stops here,* Owen thought.

He almost didn't recognize Ruiz when he walked into the restaurant. Ruiz was forced to disguise himself now. Every trip outside would surely mean additional caution. Owen laughed to himself. The Ray Ruiz he knew best was always well-groomed, wearing either slacks and a nice shirt or even a suit. Now bearded and wearing his hair long over his ears, Ruiz was dressed in a pair of jeans and a sweatshirt, Nikes, ball cap, and Ray Ban shades. Dapper meets casual was Owen's first thought.

Ruiz made his way to the corner table and asked for a glass of water only. Donaldson lifted an eyebrow, but otherwise said nothing.

"Owen."

"Ray."

"Owen, I've been setting up several possibilities on the diamond pickup. We only need to allow another two weeks and this entire misadventure will be over."

"Misadventure, Ray?" Owen scoffed. "You consider getting my property back on the level of a 'misadventure.' Why hasn't this woman been handled by now? Do you think the fact that your name and face has been plastered all over the papers has anything to do with it? Did you consider the security, the location, the people constantly surrounding her? What have you done to correct the situation?"

"Listen, Owen, I've got it all worked out."

"Oh, you do? Talk to me, Ruiz."

Chapter 18

Tina

Tina squatted down to pull the dandelions growing among the perennials. It was a beautiful Tuesday morning with just a hint of clouds on the horizon. Tina counted the days she'd spent here at Gable House and realized that more than five weeks had passed. Five quiet weeks, with a chance to cook and learn the hotel business with her aunt.

No more bruises and curses from Jarrod, no more placing the blame on her for all their problems. Her nightmares were less frequent, and so far? No Ruiz. Strangely, she wasn't as frightened as she thought she might be by now. She'd gone shopping, went to the harbor, and made a friend, and he still hadn't found her.

Tina dug down deep in the ground and furtively dropped in the box she'd brought, sifting the dirt through her fingers as she filled in the hole. Yanking on nearby weeds, Tina let herself drift in time, lulled by the monotonous work at hand and the distant sound of the ocean.

She was nineteen when she met Jarrod at the bowling alley. She hadn't been bowling but was hanging out with a group of friends at the karaoke bar. Her friend Stacy tried to sing a rendition of "I've Got You Babe" with her current boyfriend of the month. Tina had laughed so hard at their off-key rendition that she snorted Pepsi out of her nose. She'd glanced up to see a big white handkerchief fluttering in her face.

"Who uses handkerchiefs in this day and age?" Tina had asked, and she'd peered over the hankie into a pair of deep blue eyes on the face of a tall, heavily muscled and good-looking man. "Well, thanks, I guess," she said, then dabbed at her face and blew her nose with the hankie. "Since I blew snot and got makeup all over it, I suppose I'll have to wash it."

"You could, but then I'll have to come to claim it from you." The first words Jarrod said to her.

Tina had loved the sound of his voice. A deep baritone with a slight southern drawl that sent chills down her spine. "Cocky" was her overall opinion as she gave him a second glance. He swaggered some in tight blue jeans, a pair of scuffed brown work boots, a green t-shirt, and an old blue dickey jacket that read 'Jay's Auto Parts.'

"In that case," Tina replied, "I guess you'd better take your handkerchief back now." She flung his hankie and his smooth confidence back at him, leaning back and away to watch the singing. He laughed and dropped it neatly in a nearby trash can.

Tina was a looker, put together in one fine package. She wore her hair layered and streaked with ash blond highlights. She was tall and slim, her body curving in all the right places.

She knew how to handle over-confident men.

"So, what's your name?" he tried again.

"Not interested." She flicked him a glance and tried to enjoy a new singer rocking to an old Cindy Lauper tune. He stood there, staring at her a while longer before he walked away and tried his hackneyed conversation on some other woman in the far corner of the entertainment center.

"Geez, I thought that jerk would never leave," Tina commented to Stacy.

"Well, Jarrod can come on a bit too strong, but he's pretty hot on the dance floor. In fact," Stacy said, "I've heard that he gambles his money away on pool games and women. He's adventurous in the bedroom but a little intense. His car is pretty nice. It's that red souped-up Mustang out in the parking lot, the one we passed when we got here."

"Oh, yeah? Interesting. So you know him?" Tina leaned back so that her breasts showed to greater advantage in the scoop cut blue blouse she was wearing. She snuck a glance at the man being discussed. Yep, he noticed.

Stacy took a drink of her Pepsi. "I don't know him, but I've heard about him. He's been coming here for a while. Mostly just dances and leaves either by himself or with some woman. My brother knows him from work at the parts shop. Says he's got a smart-ass attitude and warned me away from him. Said there was a fight once and Jarrod stepped in and slugged it out with some guy who was trying to intimidate one of the sales girls. He almost got fired, but they let him stay because the girl stood up for him. He had to pay for the damages, and he put the guy in the emergency room. Now he just does his work and goes home. Took the sales girl home, too." Stacy shrugged. "That's what Tommy says anyway."

From where she sat, Tina gave Jarrod a veiled look and felt the first pinpricks of interest. She watched him lean against a counter in the other corner of the room and start up a flirtation with an older woman who looked about thirty-five or forty. He leaned forward, his arms folded across his chest as he listened to whatever the woman was saying. Tina noticed his smile, his laugh, and the way the light played on his light brown hair. When he turned around and winked at Tina, she knew he'd felt her interest. She looked away. When the karaoke stopped, and the jukebox started slamming out tunes, she felt that flicker of interest grow stronger as he took to the dance floor.

Tina remembered the way they danced around each other, looking, laughing, flirting. Jarrod had a certain confidence that attracted her. *Thinks he's hot, but I can get him,* is what she'd thought as he whiled away his time with other women. She studied his moves and his arrogance, and she'd considered how good he might be in bed.

Knowing her own attraction to the opposite sex, she danced a bit more and made eye contact with the man who now didn't take his eyes off her. Tina had been flattered and hadn't had enough experience to brush off the sexual tension from a man who grabbed what he wanted by any means. She went home with him that night.

She'd slept with him, loved him, married him, was obsessed by him, hated him, watched him die.

"Tina, you're going to get sunburned without a hat!"

Tina jolted out of her reverie and turned her face up to look at Miguel. He was offering her an old frayed baseball cap. Strands of her hair were blowing across her face and stuck to the tears rolling down her cheeks. She pulled the ball cap down around her ears.

Embarrassed, she looked back at the weeds and noticed the clump of dirt she'd forgotten to smooth out toward the back of the bed and casually reached over to pat it down. She knew Miguel noticed, but he didn't say a word. Instead, he squatted down next to her and looked over her work. The sun seared the back of his neck as he checked the flower beds and a pile of weeds she'd pulled so far.

Finally, realizing Miguel wasn't going to go away, Tina sat down and crossed her legs, pretending to relax. "Whew, it's hot out." The statement was clumsy, a clear overstatement. *Please don't dig,* Tina thought.

He glanced toward Tina but hesitated to speak. Finally, clearing his throat, Miguel said, "Did your aunt ever tell you how I came to her house to garden?"

Tina shook her head.

"No? Well, about seventeen years ago, after I retired from the Marines, I came to live with my sister and her family to be a part of their life. I liked the noise and the craziness of all the *niños.*"

Tina gave an inward sigh and wondered why it was that people wouldn't leave her alone for more than a few minutes. Then she blushed with shame for thinking such an uncharitable thought. She wiped the tears from her face, hoping that he'd think it was just perspiration.

"The children would run free like little puppies and would climb up into my lap for a hug, grab the peppermint sticks out of my shirt pocket, then jump back down. It never failed to make me laugh. It was a good life. I never had a family of my own, so I sure enjoyed those babies. My sister and brother-in-law had four children, their youngest a beautiful little girl. I was usually free to run errands for my sister during the day. I bought this old 1966 Volkswagen bus. It was orange, a little bit like the color of a pumpkin. I hung curtains and took out the seats, and it had this shag carpeting in the back."

"I remember seeing a van like that. There used to be an old hippy couple living in the complex where Momma and I stayed once," Tina said. "You owned one?"

"*Sí,* I used to take the *niños* out for a picnic or to the beach in the summer to give my sister time alone. My nephews would beg me, '*Tio,* let's go to McDonald's, let's go to the beach.'" Miguel smiled. "Yes, I loved my life, and my sister's cooking, and the *cerveza* that was always in the refrigerator. I always figured I'd get married someday, but I wasn't in any hurry."

In spite of herself, Tina grew interested in learning the story of a younger Miguel. She thought he must have been a happy person because she often heard him laugh and take a few minutes to talk with the guests. She snuck a peek at his face. "So ... you never got married?"

"No, but I thought about it a few times. One day, my sister asked me to take Rosita, her seven-year-old, to the toy store and buy her something. Rosie was feeling sad that her brothers were all going to a movie that she wasn't old enough to see. I was drinking, just a few beers, but I wasn't drunk by any means, so off we went to the toy store where Rosie bought a doll and little doll clothes."

Tina thought it would have been nice to have had a little girl. She'd be around seven now, if she hadn't had the miscarriage.

Miguel stopped talking and handed Tina a handkerchief to wipe her tears. "I'm sorry, Tina, I didn't mean to upset you. Want me to leave you alone?"

Tina slowly shook her head. "Please go on. I'm sorry. I don't know why I'm so sad today."

Miguel pressed his lips together, but he nodded. "We were on our way home, and Rosie was begging me to take her *muñeca* out of the box. I was driving one-handed and trying to open the doll box with my free hand. I looked away from the road and ran a red light. A car hit my passenger door. Rosie was killed instantly. The other driver went to the hospital with multiple injuries. Me? Barely a scratch."

Tina's heart clenched.

"I remember the doll clothes scattered all over the floor of the car and Rosie's blood on the plastic box near the doll's face," Miguel whispered.

"Oh, God, Miguel, I can't imagine how devastating that must have been." She reached out and touched his hand, quickly drawing back as if she'd touched fire.

"I went to jail for five years on drunk driving and manslaughter charges. *Mi familia?* They love me and forgave me, but when I came home, I couldn't bear to sit around the house knowing Rosita would never smile again at her *Tio.* I saw the sadness on my sister's face, and I knew I reminded her of what happened, so I moved away to work as a day laborer for a local landscaper. I found the dirt and the flower gardens, and the sound of the ocean helped me to heal."

Tina's eyes were red and puffy, but the tears had stopped. "Are you ok now?" she asked quietly.

"*Sí,*" he answered. "It's been many years since then. *Mi patron* sent me here to plant some flowerbeds one day, and the gardens seemed to speak to me. Sammy liked my work and asked me to be the permanent gardener for Gable House. It seemed the best decision at the time. Now, I'm a partner at the landscape company, and to comfort my own heart, I come here and take care of Sammy's *flores,* where she lets me have control of the plantings. But I cannot ever forget Rosie."

"It's hard to forget such memories," Tina whispered. "I try, though. Sometimes a day almost passes where I seem to forget, and then the memories hit me out of the blue."

"I know how that feels, Tina. I also can't escape the memories of the terrible accident, any more than you will forget what you went through, but I tell you this. Life is neither good nor bad. Most of us won't escape some form of heartache. I am fifty years old, Tina. I know I look older," he said with a wry chuckle, "but heartache tends to age you more." Miguel placed his hand on Tina's shoulder, hoisted himself up in a standing position, and walked away.

Tina remained in the garden, sifting the dirt through her fingers as she thought about Miguel's story. She thought of his sister and her family and how Rosie's death must have crushed them. *They must love Miguel very much to forgive him so completely*, she thought. Could her aunt maybe forgive her? Tonight her aunt and uncle would be coming, and Tina needed to talk to them and Sammy. Maybe she could borrow Miguel's strength to tell the truth about what she did.

She stood and glanced over to the lemon and orange trees. She was drawn to the ripe yellow fruit, its tree branches bending, ready to drop their heavy load. She gathered as many as she could in her hands. A few had fallen from the tree. Tina frowned, deciding to grab one of the wooden baskets Miguel kept on the side of the house and gather more.

She'd just turned the corner of the building when she spotted the cutest little silky terrier yapping at the heels of the well-dressed woman who was ignoring the pup's cries for attention.

"Oh, thank heavens, someone is here who can take this dog off my hands for a while!" a woman said. Tina knew she was a guest but couldn't remember her name. "I know I'm not supposed to bring him, but I couldn't get a dog sitter. My husband insisted that I come with him on this business trip. Now I have to get ready to meet him for a business dinner, and there's nobody to watch Beggar. You work here, I've seen you. You can take him off my hands." The woman shoved the dog's leash into Tina's free hand. "Oh, perfect, so kind of you. Here's his leash!"

Somehow, Tina found herself juggling lemons, oranges, and a sporty little blue dog leash. She looked down at the dog, who was small and sweet, though he had a bit of an overbite. The woman dashed into the house, not even bothering to hold open the door for another woman with her hands full.

Tina rolled her eyes, juggling the fruit until she managed to free a hand. Opening the back door to the kitchen, she muttered, "Well, when life hands you lemons, make lemonade."

For some reason, that made her giggle.

"Now what am I going to do with you, little dog? Beggar?"

Huge black eyes smiled up at the sound of his name, and he gave a quick yip of greeting then started to sniff around.

"Oh, no, Tina, that dog is not coming into my kitchen!" snapped Sammy. "Oh, that Mrs. Sandoval. She knows not to bring him to Gable House, yet every time they visit the inn, she manages to sneak him into their room. I'm going to have to speak with them. I won't be able to accept their reservations if they try this even one more time." Sammy looked down at the little bite-sized dog and shook her head. "Hello, Beggar. Looks like you've got a new babysitter. Remember Tina, your aunt and uncle are coming to dinner."

"Yes, I know," Tina said. She was glad her family would be here for dinner. She actually felt better knowing that this time tomorrow, everything would be out in the open.

Taking the fruit from Tina's hands, Sammy laid down the law. "Out, out, *out* of the kitchen! Go entertain that dog somewhere that I won't see him. We're not supposed to allow pets in the inn. And this is why!"

Tina looked down just in time to catch Beggar raising his leg on the kitchen baseboards. "Oh, ew! Come here, dog." Tina grabbed him up in her arms and felt the urine dribble down her arm as Beggar tried to wriggle free.

"OUT!" Sammy ordered them both outside with no sympathy whatsoever for either of them.

Chapter 19

Sammy

Sammy heard a light tapping on the kitchen door. Looking up, she was surprised to see Miguel.

"Sammy, I was working in the garden today," Miguel said, holding up a yellow box. *The* yellow box. "I came around the corner and saw Tina trying to bury this. She did a pretty good job, but I know my garden."

Sammy's mouth opened to speak, but Miguel was quicker. "Tina is very depressed. I found her crying in that flower bed this morning. The soil was disturbed in the area she was weeding. Perhaps I should have left this where she put it, but I started to worry." Looking down at the box, Miguel sighed. "I have a bad feeling about this box she buried. I don't want to invade her privacy, but I think it's best if you keep this in a safer place."

Sammy felt like a robot as she accepted Sharon's yellow keepsake box, taking it into her hands and thanking Miguel for being such a good friend. The box was given to Tina when her mother passed away. Each of the Gable sisters received a box like this one on their 17th birthday. Her own was green, and Susan's was red. Each box came with a key and contained a hidden compartment.

Sammy last saw it when she redecorated Tina's room. What did Tina hide in there that she felt it needed to be secret? Sammy didn't break the lock. Whatever was in there belonged to Tina. Whatever was in there was surely Tina's choice, for better or worse.

Sammy just hoped Miguel was wrong and that there was nothing dangerous hidden inside, but hiding the box worried her now more than ever.

Tina had been headstrong and stubborn as a child, but not dishonest. In a role-reversal, Tina had been her momma's savior. No matter how drunk Sharon became, Tina would lovingly help her momma stand up, feed her, put her to bed. Tina became the parent and never resented her less than fortunate circumstances. Hers was a caregiver's personality.

Sammy kept Tina in the summer months when school was out. Sharon was afraid of leaving her alone in the apartments or motels where they stayed. Tina followed her around the house, helping her dust, fold clothes, learning to cook. Susan's husband Ben was Tina's surrogate father, and it was normal to find the two of them deep in conversation.

Sammy sagged against kitchen counter. As a teenager, Tina's sweetness became brittle. When a new man took an interest in Sharon, Tina distanced herself from the family, taking part-time jobs in the summer for spending money. With Sharon rarely home, Tina stayed out late, began to party,

became a little wild. Sammy knew that part of Tina's trans-
formation was partly her fault. With three teenagers of her
own to raise, she hadn't paid as much attention to her niece as
she should have. After Tina married Jarrod, Sammy had been
relieved, happy that she needn't worry any longer.

Sammy felt guilty for her part in Tina's neglect and abuse.
With Jarrod's death, she hoped to guide Tina to a better life.
Sammy picked up the yellow box and shook it but couldn't
figure out what it might be. What was in there? Should she
confront Tina?

Sammy decided to lock the box in her bedroom safe until
she could speak with her niece.

Tina held tight to the leash in her hand and wandered the path
of crushed gray rock toward the back of the property. There
was a green and white gazebo in the middle of a large patch
of grass, giving shade and comfort to whoever sat in the swing
chair or benches. It was a huge draw to guests, as was the
panoramic view of the ocean and harbor. She looked down at
Beggar, who was running between her legs and had managed
to wrap his leash around her.

"Bring him over here so I can pet him a little."

Looking up, Tina followed the sound of the voice to find
Mr. Thomas, a retired businessman from Iowa, already sitting
in the gazebo. Sammy told her that he and his wife regularly

came out to California in the early spring to thaw out.

Tina tugged on the leash to clear a path around her legs, managing to drop it. Free at last, Beggar went scampering away in the direction of a bird.

"I will as soon as I can figure out how to get him to stop!" she called out as she ran after the dog. "Okay you little Beggar, what did I do to deserve this?" she muttered, grabbing at the leash and missing. Sensing a game, Beggar raced around her, and Tina laughed as he spun circles, dancing out of her path each time she came close.

"Come get a piece of this cookie," Mr. Thomas said. "He'll come to you right quick enough if you tempt him with this." He was holding a sugar cookie from the kitchen in his hand.

"Thanks, Mr. Thomas."

Smelling the treat, Beggar ran on shaggy little legs just as fast as he could toward them both. Laughing out loud, Tina grabbed at the little monster and managed to latch onto the delicate pieces of silvery hair flowing from Beggar's body. He yipped his annoyance at the pinch and the yank of the leash.

"Got him. Thank you, sir. He's an ornery little fella, isn't he?"

Mr. Thomas beckoned Tina closer. "Bring him here to me so I can play too."

An imposing man even in the wheelchair he was sitting in, it was easy to see that Charles Thomas approached life with a great sense of humor and interest in the world around him. Sammy told her that Mr. Thomas, who had Multiple Sclerosis, was the former CEO of a large manufacturing firm.

Tina deposited the squirmy little Beggar into Mr. Thomas' lap. Peeking flirtatiously up at the man, Beggar scrambled up to his shirt and licked his cheeks in a slurpy little doggie kiss. With a booming laugh, Charles struggled to contain the little guy, chattering with him just like an old friend, and Beggar acquiesced into the perfect lap dog.

"So, you're the little man's babysitter today? The Sandovals and I have crossed paths here before," he mentioned with a grin. "He's a funny fella, this Beggar dog. I enjoy him. We have three Shih Tzus at home that keep me highly entertained. Our daughter is taking care of them while my wife and I soak up the sun."

"I'm still trying to figure out how it happened that I'm his master today, but it's nice to meet up with you," Tina said, tucking her loose hair behind her ear. "You clearly know a lot more about animals than I do."

"You don't have to be an expert. All you need is lots of love and patience and a firm voice. A little bit like the patience my wife has with me, bless her, she's a trooper." Charles chuckled. "I sent her out to the malls this afternoon. She loves to shop for our great-grandchildren, but the winters in Iowa keep us more indoors than out."

"The malls out here are wonderful," Tina said, sitting down in the chair opposite him. "And they have all types of one-of-a-kind gifts at the harbor."

Charles stroked Beggar and glanced over at Tina. "You're

Sammy's niece, aren't you? I've met her daughter Sara and Sara's husband before, but you weren't around, and I've been coming here for about eight years now."

"Yes, I'm Tina. I used to visit all the time when I was a kid, but I married and moved away. Now circumstances bring me back. I'm thankful. Gable House is a great place to work and live."

He peered up at her from beneath shaggy eyebrows. "Circumstances are one of those words that people use to smooth over a whole bunch of something they don't want to speak about. I have to figure without being a buttinsky that you're making do with the circumstances."

Tina shrugged. She didn't want to talk about the past with anyone, let alone Mr. Thomas, but then she thought of Miguel's story. "I think that's what we're all trying to do," she finally said. "Make do, I mean."

"Well, here is a fine place to do it. I've got a grandson running my business into the ground. Want to meet him? He's only been divorced twice, and that's pretty much the going rate before settling down with your third and final spouse!" Mr. Thomas chuckled.

Startled, Tina started to respond but then caught the wicked gleam in his eye. "Uh, well, gee. Does he like dogs? Cause you know, I'm thinking of going into the dog-sitting business. I'm doing *so* well here. It's the perfect opportunity to talk with men. See? I met you, didn't I?"

His booming laughter rang in the air and reached the ears

of his wife, who was walking toward the gazebo. Mrs. Thomas sat down gracefully on the gazebo swing chair.

"Here you are, dear! It looks like you've caught a girl and a dog in my absence. You seem to have got the better deal. I walked all over the mall and didn't find anything I wanted to purchase today." She eased her shoes off and sighed with relief. "My feet hurt!"

The soothing, easy sound of Alice Thomas' voice made Tina feel comfortable. She was a slightly younger version of her husband, short and chubby, with smiling eyes the color of sapphires. *Alice looks exactly right for Mr. Thomas,* Tina thought, and she smiled shyly at the older woman.

"This is Tina, Sammy's niece, dear. Beggar is here to visit."

"It's a pleasure to meet you. So Mrs. Sandoval left you with Beggar, did she?" Alice grinned cheerfully at them both, watching her husband play with the dog in his lap. She pushed back, gliding the swing back and forth with one foot easily tapping the cement floor. Turning to Charles, she reached up a hand to brush back the thinning strands of hair out of his eyes. "Ready to go in? Sammy promises a nice tea and those sugar cookies you love."

"A lot, you know! I already had two sugar cookies and some iced tea. I've got one more you can have if you kiss me." Holding up the last sugar cookie, Thomas grinned at his wife.

Tina glanced shyly away from the couple, still in love, still making their world a happier place even after all these years.

"Looks like Beggar fell asleep," Charles stated. "See, Tina?

A bit of love and patience and he's putty in your hands. Just like my grandson if you want an introduction." He handed the dog back to Tina.

"Oh, you stinker, Charles!" Alice laughed and turned to Tina. "Did he give you that twice-divorced, running my business into the ground story? That poor grandson of ours is very devoted to his husband, a wonderful man who goes by the name of Robert!" Alice bounced out of the swing, slipped her flats back on, and took hold of the wheelchair expertly.

"But he likes dogs!" Charles called out over his shoulder as his wife wheeled him into the house.

Light-heartedly laughing to herself and thinking maybe the dog needed to answer the call of nature again, Tina wandered out the side gate and around the front of the house along the pathway toward the parking lot. She almost tripped over the little pup, who had managed to get his leash wrapped around her legs again.

"Geez, Beggar, what in the world am I going to do with you?"

Tina tapped her foot, patiently waiting for Beggar to do his business. "That-a-boy, let's get you back to the yard. Hopefully, your momma will be home soon."

She never even looked up till Beggar yanked on the leash and started barking, shrieking his warning. Tina sucked in a breath, looking around for any sign of trouble. The dog wouldn't be freaking out for no reason.

There, movement in the brush not twenty yards from the

property. *Ruiz!* She grabbed the dog and ran back to the yard, slamming and bolting the gate behind her. White as a sheet and out of breath, she hugged the dog close and froze against the side of the house waiting for all hell to break loose.

"Ohmygod, ohmygod, ohmygod, what am I going to do now?" Shivering with fear, she put the squirming dog on the ground and followed him to the back gardens.

Chapter 20

Ruiz

L ooking at the back of Tina's head as she ran back in the
gate with the dog, Ruiz was pissed off.

Damn, that bitch has the devil's luck.

Ruiz was on the run now that he was wanted for murder,
but he needed that money and Donaldson's gems to get far
enough away and stay gone. Donaldson had his own way of
getting rid of you, and Ruiz couldn't afford to bring any more
attention to himself without striking gold first. He raced down
the hill, weaving across the cars to get to the parking lot and
his motorcycle.

He was riding a different motorcycle now, taken from the
garage of an old biker whose son he'd worked with up north.
The old guy would never miss it considering he'd died last year
and his old lady was in a nursing home.

Ruiz's friend didn't care. The house was empty and the cocaine that Ruiz had supplied him to keep his mouth shut was
sufficient. He liked using the home in Chula Vista as his new
digs. It was situated in Otay, just a few miles from the border
in Tijuana, and there were plenty of illegals as well as county

employees who were willing to turn their heads and look the other way.

Slow and steady, Ruiz made his way back to the freeway headed south, keeping his driving smooth and his speed under control. *Now is not the time to bring attention to myself.* Exiting the freeway, he soon pulled into a quiet, low income neighborhood. There was a grid of about twenty streets under the protection and leadership of the city gangs.

Ruiz considered his new hideaway home as he parked the old motorcycle in the garage, pulling off the helmet and placing it on the seat as was his habit. He was careful to close the garage door behind him. *Not a bad house, not a lot of flash, but it's better this way. No attention.*

The wanted man checked and released the extra locks he'd placed for his own security, making his way through the door leading into the kitchen. After pulling off his jacket and draping it across the kitchen chair, Ruiz stepped into the small bathroom. He leaned against the clean sink, staring into the mirror and stroking his beard.

I don't look half bad, he thought. He'd used a gray rinse as part of his disguise, and it was now overpowering the darker color in his hair. He was getting used to the bearded look and the more casual jeans and sweatshirts he wore most of the time. He shrugged, *As a disguise, it's as good as any.* He almost didn't recognize himself when he looked in the mirror.

Ruiz picked up the phone. "Angela, how is your little family?" he asked. "Your husband, your son? Is everyone well?

I understand your husband is on a brief deployment. My associate tells me you've been slipping outside more often for a smoke. Need a new pipe?"

"What associate?" Angela asked.

"Why surely you know I'm keeping track of you. Tell me, what have you learned about your new friend?"

When Ruiz was sure that Angela really understood he was not someone to cross, he hung up the phone with a cruel smirk. It wouldn't be much longer before he could finally wrap up this operation.

Soon he could put his own plans in place. A little reconnaissance over the border and knowledge of the drug cartels was to his advantage. Once he retrieved the money and diamonds from Oliver's widow, he'd be in good shape to further infiltrate the city gang with its deep connections into drug trafficking, the methamphetamine trade, and the Mexican cartels and mafia.

Donaldson be damned, Ruiz thought. The sooner Ruiz broke away from him the better. His reputation as an enforcer would soon bring him more work.

Ruiz sat down at the kitchen table and reviewed the list of Gable House vendors and security systems.

Chapter 21

Tina

Tina picked up Beggar still hooked to the leash, ran to the front door, and locked it. She sped up all three flights up to her room, where she sat trembling in her chair, stroking the dog. Beggar could only stay still so long before he jumped up, pawing at her face, his rough little tongue licking her hot cheeks.

Looking into those big brown eyes full of trust, Tina felt a new resolve. It was time to do the right thing. It was time for her to tell her truth, to trust her family to take care of her. Uncle Ben and Aunt Susan would be here in a little bit. They were going to be so disappointed, but it would be worse to tell Aunt Sammy.

She nodded in resolve, petted little Beggar one more time, then put him down on the floor. Tina opened her top drawer and removed the holster and gun from her purse. Cautiously, she loaded the magazine. Then, after checking to make sure the safety was on the Ruger, she clipped the magazine into the chamber. Casting her eye one more time on the gun to be positive that the safety was still in place, Tina firmly tucked it back in its holster and then into her purse once more. She wasn't going anywhere without that gun.

Her purse on her arm, she walked to the storage room, Beggar following behind her without hesitation. Carefully, Tina squeezed her bulk in between all the furniture and pulled the money out from beneath the cushion of the sofa.

"Beggar, where'd you go you little monster dog?"

The pint-size canine was growling and tugging at a half-rotted dead mouse under an old chifforobe.

"That's disgusting Beggar. Let it go. Beggar, you let it go NOW!"

The dog gave one quick bark and backed away. Tina picked up the package and walked out of the storage room with the money and gun safely tucked in her purse. Beggar wasn't far behind.

"Sammy," Tina asked, approaching her aunt, "may I use the master key and put Beggar into Mrs. Sandoval's room? I took him to do his business and actually, he's not a bad little dog. I think he'll be all right. I'm willing to bet that he's alone a lot." She struggled to keep her voice steady.

"Alright Tina, then come on back downstairs," Sammy said, handing the keys to Tina. "Susan and Ben are on the way. Dinner's almost ready."

Tina got the key to the second-floor room. "I think you must be my good luck charm," she whispered to the dog. "You saved me from the bad man." Beggar barked an affirmative, and she squeezed him tight, opening the door to his room.

"Now then, Beggar man, you be good. I promise I will be too. No more running away for either of us."

Slowly walking downstairs, Tina entered the kitchen, placing her purse on a shelf in the cupboard nearest the table. She snuck up behind her aunt and wrapped her in a big hug.

"Sammy, I'm so sorry for all the trouble I've been. I love you."

Sammy turned into the hug, and Tina felt her safe arms wrapped around her, almost erasing Tina's fright and guilt. But Tina knew by Sammy's silence that she was waiting for answers, just the way she used to wait for Tina's confession when she did something wrong as a child.

But Sammy simply nodded. "I love you too, my Teensy girl. Finish setting the table for me. Oh, my gosh, they're here already!"

Susan and Ben Owens were as different as night and day. She was a tall, elegant redhead who even now in her sixties caused people to turn their heads and take notice. Not the most tactful member of the family, Susan nevertheless traded on her reputation for getting things done.

Ben was a compact man with kind blue eyes and a quiet strength that wasn't obvious to many until you got to know him. He was the steady beat in Susan's heart, and they worked hard to accept each other's differences.

Aunt Susan stood at the door of Gable House with a stack of the latest mystery novels and a box of Sees Chocolates under her arm. If she had one other weakness in addition to Ben, it was her love of sweets. Tina's momma and Sammy used to call her "Gooey" as a kid because her hands and face were always sticky. As her aunt rang the doorbell imperiously, Tina ran to open it.

"Sammy! We're here," Susan called out as she stepped over the entry. "Why was this door locked so early in the evening?"

Tina stood to one side, waiting for the storm to sweep through.

"Teensy girl! Oh, it's Tina now, isn't it? Look what you've done to your hair, and you have sunshine in your cheeks! I'm so happy to see you looking healthy again. You are well, aren't you? Are you sleeping better now? We've been so concerned about you," Susan gushed. "Although why you stayed with that low-life unfaithful husband of yours, I'll never know. We could have had him jailed! I don't know how many times. Here, I brought some new books for the library."

Susan dropped the whole stack in her arms. Tina blanched and bit her tongue to prevent the retort that was on the tip of her tongue. As usual, Susan spoke her mind to her family with no consideration of hurting anyone's feelings. She just winded up for the pitch and threw her thoughts out there for anyone to catch and absorb.

"Hi, Aunt Susan," Tina said, shifting the books in her arms. "It's good to see you too. Where's Uncle Ben?"

Susan's voice floated over her shoulder as she waltzed into the kitchen. "He's parking the car. He insisted on driving that old Corvette this evening. He babies that car more than me.

He's probably going to put talcum powder on its hood."

Tina dropped the stack of books on the library table.

"Don't worry little girl. I'm right here," Ben called. "Where's my hug?"

She walked into Ben's arms, hugging her favorite uncle tight. "Uncle Ben, it's so good to see you!"

He leaned back and gave her a sharp appraisal. "You look, uh, different, honey. What's this? What did you do to yourself? My goodness, you cut off all your hair!"

Tina pulled away smiling, "You like it? It feels so much lighter."

Tina was so nervous. The thoughts in her head kept flying away, and she was afraid of disappointing the most important people in her life with her story. She couldn't have told you a thing about what she ate for dinner. Aunt Susan was chattering to Sammy, and Uncle Ben was finishing his dessert. It was time.

She opened her mouth to speak, but all that would come out of her mouth was, "Um..." She cleared her throat.

Ben looked up and immediately dropped his spoon on the table. He grabbed Tina's hand and said quietly, "Best you try again. We'll all listen. It will go right in the end." He looked over at Sammy and his wife and announced, "Ladies, we need to listen to Tina. I think she has something important to tell us." Sammy and Ben's eyes met, then he turned to Tina. "Go ahead now."

Tina didn't know how her uncle knew her so well, but

he did. And that brought her some comfort. She turned to Sammy. "Sammy, it's getting dark, and I know the guests have keys to the house. Can we please lock the front door again, all the doors? Please?"

Tina swallowed hard as she watched Sammy immediately get up to check each point of entry. Tina knew, if only her aunt allowed her to stay, the doors were going to have to be kept that way for the foreseeable future.

As Sammy locked the front door, Tina hurried over to where she'd stashed her purse. When her aunt got back to the kitchen, Tina was waiting, holding the bag of money in her hands.

"Tina—" Sammy started, her eyebrows knitted together.

"I found this money in the car, after Jarrod was killed," Tina said quickly. "Please, sit, and I'll explain."

Sammy dropped back in her chair, and Tina sat too. She wasn't sure her legs would be strong enough to hold her up.

"At first, I thought it was Jarrod's because he always had money in his pockets, though he rarely gave any to me. But then I remembered that the man who killed him told him he wanted his money. I counted it, $50,000. I used a little to get here. Just before he left the bar, Ruiz told me he wanted it and he always got what belonged to him."

Tina cringed at how ugly her story sounded. She couldn't bear to look at the faces of her family surrounding her, waiting for her to explain. She looked at the floor instead and missed the shock on Sammy's face when she mentioned Ruiz's name.

"He was waiting for me near the carport the morning I came home from the police station and the morgue. I didn't know about the money then, but I found a bag of diamonds in the closet the day that Jarrod was killed. I hid them where they wouldn't be found."

Everyone was silent, waiting.

She looked only at Uncle Ben. "Ruiz had a gun and a knife, and I was so afraid he was going to kill me too. Why would he keep me alive when he killed Jarrod so easily? I was just one more person to get rid of if I turned over the diamonds. So I lied and told him I didn't know about anything. Jarrod used to tell me all the time that his boss, Owen Donaldson, paid the police money so they'd look the other way about the drug sales. I couldn't trust the police up there. I didn't say anything. There were two men who got out of a car when Ruiz was talking to me. Ruiz ran and I ran away to save my life. I came here."

It took two hours and more than a few starts to get Tina's complete story out in the open. She began by telling them of the murder, the threats, and finally running with the money and diamond packet. She ended by admitting the diamonds were hidden in Sammy's back yard flower garden.

She didn't cry. Pale but steady, Tina told her truth, ending by letting them know she spotted Ruiz in the parking lot that afternoon. She apologized to Sammy for bringing danger to the house, said she was ready to speak with the police now. They made an appointment with a detective for the next day, hoping Ruiz wouldn't try an attack before then. Ben and Susan stayed the night in one of the empty guest rooms.

Tina sat in her bedroom chair all night, shivering, crying and afraid, but somehow, she felt lighter, more ready when she realized she would have to talk to detectives tomorrow.

Please Auntie, please don't send me away, please don't send me away.

Chapter 22

Tina

Tina sat in the wing chair in front of the fireplace, shivering. How could the rest of her body be so cold when her lips were burning from chewing them so much? Raising her head, she faced the two detectives, a woman, and her male partner.

"Ray Ruiz threatened me twice," Tina said. "The night he stabbed my husband and the day after when I drove Jarrod's car home."

The policewoman tapped her pen on the pad of paper. "Okay, Mrs. Oliver, when it comes to trial, the judge and the jurors are going to need to hear what happened both times you saw him, but let's concentrate on the second time you saw him. Can you talk it through with me now?"

Tina whispered, "I can't. I just can't. You don't know what type of people Jarrod knew. Ruiz said he'd kill me, and I believe him. You didn't see his face and…" She glanced over at her aunts and uncle sitting on the sofa. She felt their quiet sympathy.

Ms. Ginny said the pain of violence never went away, Tina

thought, *but if you stood up to it, strength came after.* Tina wrapped her arms tightly around herself and rocked back and forth. Finally, she took a fluttery breath and faced forward again, carefully picking her words.

"My husband is dead because of me. If we hadn't gone out that night, I think he'd still be alive. But there is a bigger part of me that knows it isn't my fault." She glanced up at Sammy, who was shaking her head 'no' but otherwise remained silent.

"Jarrod was a bully, a thief, and a cheat. He threatened my momma, my family, and said he would kill me if I left. He knocked me around so hard, I started to pray that he would die. I guess God answered my prayers."

Tina closed her eyes, trying to tell God she was sorry, but the thoughts were all jumbled in her mind. She sat in her chair silently weeping until her uncle knelt down beside her, putting his strong arms around her.

"Not your fault, baby, not your fault. Jarrod's violence was a part of him. God didn't let him die because of your prayers. Jarrod died because he couldn't, or wouldn't, stop the violence. That's all that was left of what might have been a good man once. It isn't your fault he stopped being one."

"I'm so sorry, Uncle Ben," Tina whispered. "I'm sorry, Sammy, I love you so much, and I never thought of what might happen. I just needed to run home, and I wasn't thinking straight."

Ben leaned forward. "Tina, the police already know who Jarrod's murderer is. It's been in the papers and on the news stations. It's only a matter of time before they find and arrest him."

Susan grabbed a Kleenex box from the side table and silently handed it to Ben. He pulled a few tissues and wiped Tina's tears from her blotchy face, then kissed her forehead.

"If you don't agree to discuss everything you know with the detectives," Ben continued, "then you do yourself an injustice. You'll lose yourself in your terror. If you don't allow yourself to believe that you deserve to live and be happy again, then he wins. Don't let this man, Ruiz, and Jarrod's violence continue to keep you in hell. It's ok to be afraid, Tina, but remember how much we love you. We'll always be right here by your side."

Tina leaned her head against Ben, then looked at Sammy, who was holding hands with Aunt Susan. "I'm so, *so* sorry," she whispered to her aunts.

Licking her lips, Tina straightened in the chair. Ben patted her on the shoulder and went to sit down next to his wife once more.

Tina balled her hands into fists and took a deep breath. She looked up at the female detective. "I didn't think of the danger when I first ran home. I do now. His name is Raymond Ruiz. He worked with my husband. My husband handled drug pickups and money deliveries for this man named Owen Donaldson. Ruiz was the enforcer for Donaldson and did his dirty work, because... you know, that was his job, to punish or kill people who didn't follow the rules. The day after Jarrod died, Ruiz found me when I went to the apartment. He was dirty and sweating. He, uh, he smelled sour, and he had B.O., you know, he stunk bad."

The female detective nodded, jotting something in her notebook.

"I'm sure he couldn't have gone home that night because of the police search," Tina continued. "I don't know for sure, but… well anyway, Ruiz was waiting for me, crouched behind another car when I parked Jarrod's car when I came back from the mortuary. He admitted that he wasn't sorry for killing Jarrod. He told me he did me a favor because Jarrod was a lying, cheating bastard who put his hands on things that didn't belong to him and that I should remember that. He said to turn over the money and diamonds. He told me I should know it wasn't worth what he'd have to do to me if I didn't give it to him."

Tina shuddered, slumping down in her seat as she kept speaking.

"Ruiz said his wife told him that Owen Donaldson sent her to get a package from a client," Tina tried to explain to the detective. "Ruiz and his wife, Sonia, and Jarrod all worked for Donaldson, but they each had different responsibilities. She provided entertainment for the clients and was often sent to pick up items that weren't part of the drug deliveries. Ruiz told me he was at home with her two kids while she… did that."

"This is good," the female detective said. "Please, keep going, Mrs. Oliver."

Tina swallowed. "Ruiz said that when Sonia came back home, she looked worse than usual, she'd been beaten and used up like the whore and heroin addict she was." Tina looked up at the police officers. "Those were his words, not mine."

The officer nodded, so Tina continued. "Ruiz told me that he made Sonia tell him who it was. She met and stayed with the client awhile, then accepted the diamonds from the client. She admitted to Ruiz that she and Jarrod got together after the pick up, which they sometimes did to exchange the money and merchandise so that she wouldn't have to drive to Donaldson's office."

Tina's face was red with embarrassment, but she continued with her story. "Ruiz said that Jarrod was fucking Sonia ... he'd had ... had ... rough sex ... with her. He bloodied her lip and left bruises all over her face, her neck, arms, and her thighs."

Tina couldn't stop blushing in front of her family. "I think that's probably true because Jarrod liked to hurt me, too. My husband enjoyed telling me I didn't know how to be treated gently like a lady.

"Ruiz told me Jarrod stole all the money owed to them both. Jarrod raped and beat Sonia and took off with the items. Ruiz said he searched my apartment after the police left but didn't find anything, then asked where my husband put the items. I said I didn't have them."

Tina swallowed hard. "I got scared. Ruiz grabbed my neck and my hair. He said the police were already looking for him and that he wasn't going to go to prison for murdering a bastard who deserved it anyway, so I better not open my mouth to the police. He told me if I said anything to the police, I'd be dead anyway because their boss, Donaldson, had ears in the police department. So I'd better find the money and the shipment or end up dead like Jarrod. He started to pull me with him, to go into the house and look for it."

Tina looked up at the policewoman and then looked back down at the floor. She felt trapped.

"I lied," Tina whispered. "I told him I didn't have his money but that I would look. I knew if he got me in the house, he would kill me.

"I got very lucky then because two men drove up and parked their car nearby while he was talking to me. They were staring at us. Ruiz took off real fast, and one of the men chased him. The other one told me he was an undercover police officer, but he scared me almost as much as Ruiz and wanted to go with me to my apartment. I didn't see any ID on him or the car to mark it as police. I started to yell and scream that I wanted a policewoman as a witness. But the man didn't call anybody. After a minute, he took off in the car, so I don't think he was a policeman, or if he was, he was one of the crooked ones that Donaldson paid.

"I ran to the apartment. I threw some clothes and other stuff in a bag, drove Jarrod's car downtown, got on a bus, and rode around for a day or two. Finally I ended up in Los Angeles. I went to the train station and got a ticket to San Clemente. Then I came here."

Tina finally looked up. Her family was staring at her, but it was without judgment. They looked scared.

"I'm sorry Sammy," Tina said. "I didn't really consider how much I was putting you or Gable House in danger. I didn't know where else I should go to be safe." To the detectives, she admitted, "If Ruiz hadn't found me yesterday, we wouldn't be talking now."

"Oh, sweetie." Sammy's voice shook, her face crumpling. Tina hated watching her aunt's heart break. "It's okay. It's all going to be okay. You've endured so much."

Picking up speed now, Tina just wanted to complete her story, lay down and sleep for a week. "I found the money the day after Jarrod died. I picked the car up from the bar, and was driving it to the mortuary, but kept feeling this lump under my leg as I was driving. I pulled the car over into a gas station to look. Jarrod had stuffed a bunch of rags and the money underneath the metal springs and against the lining of the car seat. It was Jarrod's car, and I rarely drove, so I can't tell you how long it was there. I didn't know which police to trust and which were crooked. If I said anything about the money, they would arrest me thinking I was a part of Donaldson's ring. Ruiz would have killed me whether I gave it to him or not. So I kept it. I'd never seen so much money in my life. Jarrod was dead. All I could think of at the time was that it was more money than I'd need to take care of myself."

Tina looked over at Sammy's hands, twisting in her lap, a sure sign she was upset. More than ever, she felt the guilt of putting her aunt in danger. Tina tried to convey her confusion and reasons for her actions. "My first plan was to fly to the east coast," she admitted to Sammy. "The money would let me start over, but I knew that would make me a fugitive and bring you more heartache because you wouldn't know if I was alive or some kind of a crook. But more than ever, I just wanted to come home to you."

She turned to the police. "I don't know how much money Jarrod made from selling drugs or what he did with the money, because I never saw it. I don't know of any accounts or any other deals he might have made with Donaldson."

"When you're beaten, and your family threatened continuously, you stop thinking of anything but survival. You just lay there and take it until you die," Tina continued, her voice cracking. "You always wonder when you're going to die. When I couldn't work any longer and he got more involved with the drug dealing, Jarrod paid for whatever we had. I was given money for groceries and sometimes for clothes. I think he must have made a lot of money over the years since he started working for Owen Donaldson, but I have no idea what he did with it, and that's the truth."

Hysterically, her voice rising, Tina tried to explain. "I thought about the money all afternoon the day after Jarrod died. I guess I felt that I needed it more than the police. I wanted to use some for Jarrod's cremation, but they said an autopsy was necessary first. I didn't want to go home, but my mother's box and afghan were home. It was pretty much all

I had left. The rest of the money was still in the car when Ruiz threatened me in the carport. It's around $50,000. I shoved it in a backpack and took it with me and used a little bit for a train ticket. I have the rest and will give it to you now."

The policewoman nodded. "Mrs. Oliver, thank you for letting us know your location so we didn't have to keep searching for you. I'm sure your aunts and uncle had something to do with that. We know you're tired and afraid and don't want to sit here talking to us. But we can't let you just send us away."

She stopped and asked the other officer for a file. "We have a copy of records from the police in Emeryville. Ruiz murdered two people that week. After he killed your husband, witnesses said he got away through the crowds. His wife spoke with the police, and, after, they drove her and the children to a shelter. The police in that area had undercover agents in Donaldson's employ as well. That may very well be who was in the car when Ruiz spoke to you the day following your husband's murder, though I can't say for sure."

"What about Ruiz?" Ben asked. "Have they found him?"

The detective shook her head. "Police have continued to search for Ruiz in Northern California, but thanks to your coming forward, we now know to look for him here."

She paused for a moment, trying to find the right words to impart to Tina the danger she was in. "His wife wouldn't stay at the shelter the police took her to, and she left. Ruiz found her at her sister's home. Ruiz walked up to his sister-in-law's front door and shot his wife in the head while she was handing the baby to her sister."

"Oh, my God," Sammy whispered.

"The sister-in-law told the police that Ruiz never said a word," the detective continued. "He just killed her. This time, he didn't even have a crowd to cover up his getaway. He walked to the street curb, driving away in his wife's car. Police found the car abandoned about four miles away. The sister and other witnesses and neighbors have said he has an old Harley motorcycle, so be aware."

Tina nodded. A motorcycle. She could watch for a motorcycle.

"Police searched your apartment again for anything illegal. They found cocaine and heroin. You've been searched and tested for drugs at the police station after your husband's murder. Your tests came out clean, but you're still under investigation. We don't have any reason to arrest you now, but I get the feeling you haven't told us everything you know."

The male officer leaned forward in his seat. "Mrs. Oliver, if you've been lying or know anything else, you'd better speak up now. For the record, he broke into your apartment a few weeks ago and must have been looking for something else. He left his old clothes on your bedroom floor. It looks like he may have taken some of your husband's things. Creepy when you think about it."

Tina bit her lip and looked down at the floor. "I told the other police over and over again. Jarrod went out and sometimes didn't come home till very late or not at all. It was his job, or maybe it was women because I could smell perfume and liquor on his body. Yes, he was involved in a bunch of illegal things. He would show up with strangers, including Ruiz and their boss, Donaldson. But I had nothing to do with it."

Tina put her hands up, trying to hide her face with her hair, but realized her hair wasn't long enough anymore. In complete misery she admitted, "He beat me and loved on me and beat me some more. Sometimes I pushed back, but since that only made it worse, I mostly did what he asked. I was often afraid, but I wasn't blind. He went outside of the house to do his 'work.' I was aware that he kept drugs in a drawer in the bathroom, although I never touched that drawer. I stayed at home and kept my home spotless. Do you know what it's like to have nothing, to feel like a non-person? Don't think you can sit there and lecture me, because I bet you have never been on the floor, hurt so bad you didn't want to get up again."

How can these officers not understand? Tina wondered. She'd already told them about the crooked cops and the threats. Jarrod would've killed her if she'd even tried to report him.

"I was taking care of a guest's dog yesterday and took him out the side gate to do his business," she said, steadying her voice. "I'm sure I saw Ruiz hiding under some bushes yesterday out beyond the parking lot. There was someone there, anyway. That's why you're here now. I want you to protect my aunt and her business. If you need to arrest me, ok, only keep her safe, please, keep her safe."

"Mrs. Oliver, we'll need to go to the police station and

turn in the money."

"Wait!" Tina exclaimed. "Take the diamonds too. I buried them in the garden in Momma's yellow box."

"Tina," Sammy said slowly, "I have your box. Miguel was terrified for you. He cares for you, you know. He saw you bury it and thought you'd placed a gun or something else in there that you might use to hurt yourself. He felt you might wish to commit suicide, so he brought the box to me. It's in the safe."

Sammy excused herself and brought the yellow box from the safe. Tina took the key from around her neck and opened it. Everyone leaned forward as she lifted the packet out of the hidden compartment and displayed several diamonds of varied sizes and quality.

Tina looked at the detectives. "I don't think my husband had anything to do with the diamond smuggling, honest. I believe he was there at the right time when Sonia picked them up and took them because he wanted to hold something over Donaldson's head."

The detectives looked between Tina, Sammy, Susan, and Ben.

"We'll need you to come to the station to make your statement again," the female detective said. "And we'll be sending patrols through this neighborhood multiple times a day until we catch Ruiz."

Sammy breathed a sigh of relief. Police patrols, that was good, even if it was scary. "Is there anything else we can do to keep Tina safe?" she asked.

"I recommend hiring an armed security guard for the inn," the male detective said. He flipped open his notebook and wrote something on a piece of paper, then slid it to Sammy. "Give them a call."

"One more thing," the female detective said as she stood. "No more guests until this is over. It's safer for everyone that way."

"I'll cancel my guest's reservations for the next month," Sammy said.

"Sammy, no!" Tina cried.

"It's okay, Teensy," Sammy said, her voice soft. "It'll be a financial hit, but I can afford it. Don't worry."

"I'm so sorry," Tina said, her voice breaking.

Sammy pulled her niece into her arms and hugged her tight. "It's okay, Teensy," she whispered. "We'll keep you safe. It's all going to be okay."

Chapter 23

Matt

The Southern California weather was invigorating this time of year. Matt had the windows rolled down, the radio blasting, and thoughts of Sammy on his mind. From Los Angeles to the 5 Freeway South to the 605 interchanges, he couldn't make up his mind. From the 605 to the 405 just past Seal Beach, he thought he lost his mind.

As Matt drove through Orange County, his mind was set. He was going to ask Sammy out on a date and let the chips fall where they may.

Of course, he still hadn't told her everything about his job, but he was going to risk it. Hopefully, she wouldn't turn him down. Sammy Cooper was plenty worth the risk. He thought about their goodbyes when he left last month and felt hopeful.

Don't get too cocky, Romeo, Matt thought. *Just play it slow. Just play it slow.*

Tired of the monotony of freeway driving, Matt turned off the 405, exiting south onto the 133 highway toward the Laguna Beach area. He drove slowly through the busy main roads of town, eyeing the locals and tourists alike as they wandered the busy streets, noses pressed against the store glass or gathering in groups to have a cup of coffee at the local bistro. Southern California was so much more casual and relaxed than Northern California ever had been or could be. Couples of every gender walked hand in hand, and it was the norm to see a rainbow banner hung from a flag pole on homes and businesses alike. Art galleries and antique stores bid for people's attention with colorful window dressings. Dog walkers, some coordinating five leashes, vied for space on the sidewalks.

Matt thought of Monterey and its coastal beauty, but for some reason, he just couldn't summon the same enthusiasm for his hometown that he normally held. Matt sighed. His heart wasn't in it anymore.

Maybe it's just age, he reflected, his mind wandering to Sammy's green eyes and smiles.

And what about Tina's trauma? Ben had told Matt what he could of Tina's upbringing, but it still left a wide gap in any good aspect of Tina's life after marriage.

Glancing up at the street light in front of him, he realized he'd passed Laguna Beach and was heading straight toward Dana Point. His first image of Sammy sitting on the kitchen floor flashed through his mind, and he grinned. She was so earthy, with a big gusting laugh and those green eyes of hers that saw everything. She was somehow both businesslike and personable, and he couldn't wait to get to know her better. She was cozy.

That's it, he thought, *she's cozy and fun and damned impressive.*

He thought of stopping by Gable House but decided the

better of it. His father was waiting to eat lunch till he arrived, and it was nearly 1:00 P.M. now.

I'm going to have to adjust my schedule to Dad's. Pay more attention to his needs if I'm going to be down here more. Matt zoomed his sedan past the intersection leading to Gable House and with brief regret, he headed toward San Clemente.

Matt unlocked the front door and stepped into his dad's small apartment.

"Hey, Dad, I'm here!" he yelled into the empty front hallway. "What are you up to?"

"In the kitchen!"

Matt poked his head around the wall of the tiny kitchen just in time to see Jim Phillips take the last bit of apple and 3-point the apple in the wastebasket.

"I was munching on an apple because my stomach is about down to my shoe flaps by now. Was the traffic bad?" Jim straightened up with a grin and wiped his juicy hands on his old blue jeans.

"Mmhmm, caught up with a bunch of road construction through Los Angeles, but made up some time when I took the 405 freeway," Matt explained. "What are we eating?"

"Nothing son, I made nothing. I've got some of those Lean Cuisines if you insist, but I decided that I'd rather go to a good Mexican restaurant. Enchiladas sound so good, although

I know you'll try to talk me out of it. You can always eat most of it. I just want to try a few bites anyway," Jim grumbled. "I'm so tired of healthy food. Damn doctors are always trying to take away the pleasures of life. What's left? I don't smoke and now I'm not supposed to eat anything with flavor. What the hell is the sense of getting old? Might just as well stick me in the old pine box now. Crap!"

"Whoa! Where is this all coming from?" Matt questioned. "When we spoke this morning, you were in a great mood, took a walk, and even flirted with that Sally person from apartment 5B. Dad, what's up?"

"Aw, got some statements in the mail from the hospital and the doctors, and did you know they charge a fortune for anesthesiologists, and another bill for the doctor who assisted with the surgery, and more crapola that I didn't even know about. I can't figure out all these insurance papers." Jim heaved a big sigh. "Why bother talking about it? Let's go eat, son. If you let me have some enchiladas with cheese, my mouth will be busy chewing, and you can't hear me complain like an old woman nagging her man to death!"

Matt crossed his arms across his chest and chuckled. "You're pissed, huh? But what do you expect the doctors to say to a patient who has diabetes and a heart condition? How am I supposed to say yes to giving you food filled with cholesterol?" Jim glared at Matt. "I tell you what, Dad. No enchiladas, but we'll go to that soup and salad place around the corner that you like."

"Yeah, sure," Jim grumbled, waving a dismissive hand. "Better than a dang apple."

Matt rolled his eyes. A change of topic was necessary if he was ever going to get his dad back in a good mood.

"Say, Dad, do you remember I was telling you about the Bed & Breakfast I stayed at while you were in the hospital?"

"Yeah, why?"

"It was a beautiful home, lots of light and airy and welcoming," Matt said. "Sammy Cooper owns it, she goes by Sammy, and I can't get my mind off her."

"What kind of a name for a girl is Sammy? She's a girl, you say?"

"Well, yeah, if you can call a woman in her fifties—at least I think she's in her fifties—a girl. She's funny and helpful and has pretty green eyes. Sometimes she's chatty, but mostly she's quiet and personable. Good cook, too." Matt grinned over at his dad because he knew his father loved a good home-cooked meal.

Aiming a sharp glance at his sixty-two-year-old son, Jim asked, "Sounds to me like you are plenty interested in this woman. She's not married, is she?"

Matt shook his head. "A widow. Her husband was in a car accident. I can't quite get a handle on whether she likes me or not, though. I can't decide if she's just friendly because she enjoys talking to me, or if she's nice because that's important in her line of work. I figure it's both of those things. I can't figure her out yet, but I really want to ask her out to dinner."

Jim leaned against the kitchen counter. "What's she look like?"

Matt thought about Sammy's smile. Once, when she caught him looking at her, she'd realized she had flour all over her blouse. She'd blushed so hard, but Matt grinned. He didn't care about the flour. And it was so cute when she took off like a shot into the kitchen.

"She's got red hair, Dad." Matt grinned, knowing full well his dad had a weakness for redheads. "What I do know is that she keeps crossing my mind at the oddest times."

"Well boy, sounds like you have as good a chance as any other man." Jim Phillips cackled and hooted at his son. "You're not too ugly. So what are you waiting for, Christmas? Hell, you're not getting any younger, ask her out!" Jim scratched his head, smoothing down the sparse bits of hair still left on his scalp and shot his son a keen glance. "Red hair, huh?"

Matt laughed. "Come on, let's go get some lunch."

In the car, Jim buckled his seat belt before looking over at Matt. "I'll tell you right now, there's plenty of women around here who wouldn't mind making me the enchiladas that you don't want me to eat. A man has to stay on his toes if he wants to stay single where I live."

"Is that so?" Matt asked.

"There are more women than men living in these apartment complexes for seniors. There's this one lady who sits down at the end of the hall outside on my floor, and whenever I pass by, it's, *'hello Jimbo, how is ya doing today darlin? Going to take the community bus to the casino?* I'd be willing to bet she drove her old man crazy with that voice of hers."

Matt cracked up at the drawled falsetto in his father's voice. "You really want those enchiladas?"

"Yep," Jim answered.

His dad's favorite Mexican restaurant was just a few minutes away. After they ordered and their food arrived, Matt decided to bring up Sammy's niece. His dad usually had good perspective.

"Dad, I'm not sure what to do," Matt started. "Do you remember my friend Ben?"

"Sure do," Jim said, cutting into his enchilada. "Why? What's wrong?"

"Well, the reason I stayed at Gable House to begin with was that Ben asked me to give him my personal opinion of his niece's well-being. Ben is Sammy's brother-in-law. Ben told me their niece had been abused and that her drug dealer husband was recently murdered."

Jim's eyebrows shot up, but he said nothing as he started on his lunch.

"I checked on the file at the police station," Matt said. Because of his position on LA PD's staff as a crisis counselor, he'd been able to pull some strings. "But I can't really touch the case because it's under investigation. I told Ben that without clearance to the case, I couldn't approach her or give him any professional opinion, other than it would be in his niece's best interests to engage in trauma and abuse counseling. In any case, I don't think a man would be able to reach her, at least not at this point."

"Alright…" Jim nodded slowly.

"I told Sammy what I do for a living before I checked out, and I know she thought I was intruding, but if she agrees to go to dinner with me—and I sure hope she does—I'm going to make a fresh start with her."

"It sounds like you went in with the best intentions," Jim said after a moment. "And it sounds like you really like her. You said she's a good cook, right?"

Matt nodded.

"Well, you better make things right with her," Jim said, "so I have something to eat besides those Lean Cuisines."

Matt stood at the entrance to Gable House, taking inventory of his physical and mental assets and grew despondent. Sixty-two years old, not too old, but hitting retirement years. Dark brown hair shot with silver now. His body was still strong, though definitely showing a little paunch. He had a bit of a limp but was still game for nice long walks. He had good teeth, brown eyes, and money tucked away in the bank.

Why is what she thinks so important to me? he wondered. Matt hardly knew Sammy, but he was so drawn to her.

"So, are you going to stand there for another five minutes, or are you going to go in?"

Matt jumped and turned to see the main object of his thoughts, smiling at him from the walkway behind him.

Sammy's hands were full with a basket of flowers, her hair was mussed, and again, she wasn't wearing any makeup. Matt thought she looked beautiful.

"I was just coming by to see you," Matt began in an uncertain voice, "to let you know how much I enjoyed my stay." *Well, that sounded lame*, he thought. *I already said that in the guest log they keep in the bedrooms.*

"Thank you, Matt. We enjoyed having you as our guest. Are you here to visit your father? Would you like to reserve a room for this weekend? Because I'm so sorry, but we're not accepting any additional guests right now." Sammy rubbed her face with a dirty hand and sneezed. "Oh, I just don't believe it!" she laughed out loud. "How do you always manage to find me at my worst?"

"I do? Because I don't think so. Here, let me take these flowers from you." Matt grabbed the basket, and they both stood there, blocking the entrance, staring at each other.

"Oh, thanks," Sammy finally said, "but I was just going to go to the back gardens to cut a few more flowers for the sideboard in the dining room."

"How about I tag along to carry your tools?"

Matt followed Sammy through the side gate leading to the back yard. If anyone had been reading his mind right then, he'd have to confess he wasn't looking at the lush floral pathways, the citrus trees, or the panoramic view of the ocean.

Instead, he was enjoying the curve of Sammy's backside in a pair of cotton slacks and the way her curls lay all tangled around her neck.

"Here we are." Sammy paused beside a bed of Gerber daisies with a delicate fern growing against the wall of the house. "Miguel usually keeps a basket back here for me to grab whatever I need, usually a quick bouquet during the week. Isn't the garden lovely?"

"Actually, I think it's you who makes it lovely," he said quietly.

Sammy's mouth fell open, and she turned around slowly, her wide, astonished eyes on Matt's face.

"Listen to me please, Sammy," Matt said, a little embarrassed but ready to make his case. "I've been thinking about my visit, and even though it was hectic with my dad and all, what I remember most is how welcome you made me feel and what a pleasure it is to speak with you. I came here today to ask if you would like to go to dinner with me. I've taken four days off to visit Dad. I know you'll be busy through the weekend, but I thought Sunday evening would be perfect since most of your guests leave by then."

The little voice in the back of Matt's head chanted, *Say yes, say yes, say yes.*

"Oh, gosh! Well, we don't currently have any guests. Um, Sunday?" Sammy pursed her lips, then nodded. "Yes, I'd like that very much, Matt. I haven't been to a dinner someone else has cooked in ages. Yes, I'll go to dinner with you."

Matt couldn't believe his ears. He wanted to punch his fist in the air and do a victory dance. Only now they were both so embarrassed that neither knew what else to say. Quickly, they planned for him to pick her up at 6:00 P.M. to go to dinner at the Chart House.

As he walked back to his car, Matt couldn't help wondering if she really wanted to go out with him, or had it just been so long since she'd been to a restaurant that she'd go out with Quasimodo?

Either way, I don't care, he thought. *She said yes!* He laughed and threw his keys in the air, feeling like an ass when he didn't catch them.

Chapter 24

Tina

Tina and Sammy tried to maintain a semblance of normal routine in the house, even though it was a Saturday and not a Wednesday baking day. Sammy stood at the kitchen counter whisking butter, cream cheese, sugar, and eggs to make a batch of cherry cheesecake muffins.

"You know," Sammy said, "we can probably just freeze some of these bakery items. Then we can thaw them out and see how fresh they taste."

Tina, who was stirring a bubbling strawberry compote, thought perhaps her aunt was angry with her. *Well, she would be justified.*

"I wish I could make everything go away, Sammy, and that the inn was full of customers."

Everything is changing because of me, Tina lamented as she stirred the preserves. *Sammy's losing customers and it's so unfair. Maybe I should just leave anyway. Everything would be better, and then Sammy could open up the inn again.* Tina felt like a fly that just kept buzzing around everyone's heads. *Maybe somebody should swat it and put it out of its misery. I'd feel better, not so guilty.* She glanced over at Sammy to find her listlessly spooning unfinished batter into the baking cups.

Tina did a double take and almost burned her hand on the pot while staring at her aunt. Talk about preoccupied.

"Sammy, Auntie Sammy! You still have to add flour and cherries to that batter."

"Oh, for Pete's sake!" Sammy gave the muffin pan a disgusted look and kicked the cupboard, prompting a look of amazement from her niece.

"Give over, Sammy, what's going on with you this morning?" This didn't actually seem to be about the guests at all. "I don't believe it, you're blushing!"

"I am not! You just pay attention to that strawberry syrup you're working on." Sammy blushed even brighter. "I'm just a bit preoccupied, that's all. I have a date on Sunday, oh my God, that's tomorrow night!"

Tina's jaw dropped open.

"Shut your mouth before you catch a fly in it!" Sammy snapped. "Matt asked me out to dinner, and I said yes."

Tina started laughing. "Oh, man, I was just thinking I should be a fly so someone can swat it."

"I still can't believe it, Tina. I haven't been out on a date with another man since before your Uncle Dan and I got married. Look at me! I don't have anything to wear, and it's been so long since I've worn a pair of heels that I'll probably fall and break my neck. Oh, my gosh! I have a date!"

Tina looked at Sammy's shining eyes and listened to the

excitement in her voice, which turned to horror all of a sudden.

"Tina, the syrup is starting to steam! Turn that pot off quick!"

Tina looked down and quickly pulled the pot off the stove. She couldn't believe it! Sammy was actually frightened. Her aunt was never nervous about anything. When Tina was thirteen, she'd watched Sammy push her way right into the middle of a fight between Dave and Tim and some neighborhood kids scuffling over skateboard ramps. She had grabbed a hank of hair from one kid and the arm of another and yanked both of them off their feet. She not only stopped the fight but embarrassed all the boys by being stronger than they were.

Tina looked at the panic in her aunt's face and thought fast, coming up with, "Wow! A date with Mr. 'Tall and Handsome' Phillips. I tell you what, Ms. Sammy Sweetie-Peach. It's your turn for a day off. Let's call Aunt Susan and ask her and Uncle Ben to come over this afternoon instead of tonight. Uncle Ben can babysit me. I'll take care of the house, and you get to go shopping. Aunt Susan's always going out to business dinners and parties. She's like the closest thing to a model in this family."

"I'm not going to a business dinner, Tina, I don't want to wear a suit. I'd look like a penguin with these hips." Sammy sighed. "Besides, you know how tall your Aunt Susan is. She'll try to force me into buying something that would look good on her, and I'll end up like some frump in a dress one size too small and a hem clear down to my ankles. I'm going to call and tell him I can't go. Me! On a date!" Sammy's voice actually squeaked, and Tina giggled.

"Susan's not that bad. She knows all the right stores. She'll find just the right thing for you to wear! You don't even know how beautiful you are. You just don't want to admit that you're scared. I'm going to call her right now."

Tina was already thinking of what to do for her aunt, so thankful she could help Sammy instead of the other way around. For the first time, Sammy said nothing and let her niece take charge.

Susan stepped into Gable House with a makeup box and a twinkle in her eye. "Sammy! The cavalry is here," Susan called out as Tina let her aunt and uncle in the house.

Tina stepped forward and hugged her aunt close. "Thank you. She's been acting crazy all morning."

"Where is she, in her room?" Susan asked. "She's probably trying on shoes from twenty years ago."

"She's in her room alternately putting moisturizer on her face and poking in her closet."

"Oh, poor thing, she hasn't got the slightest idea about clothes! I'll go help her." Susan slipped around Tina and headed for Sammy's rooms, perhaps a little too eagerly.

"Don't worry, little girl," Ben said. "Suzy is just what Sammy needs right now. She'll bully her for a few minutes then coax her out of her nerves. In the meantime, where's my hug?"

Tina turned to Ben's arms and hugged her favorite uncle. "She must really like this man. I've never seen Sammy so weirded out. It's like she's a whole different person."

"Well, I sure hope Matt figures out what a prize she is. Suzy said the last time she fell apart like this was when Dan died, so he must hold a powerful attraction for her."

"Wait, you said Matt. Do you know him?"

Tina stared at her uncle. *Matt never said he knew Uncle Ben,* she thought. *Well, he seemed nice, but how hard is it to say, 'Hey, I know your Uncle Ben.'*

Ben put his hand on her arm. "Matt did tell Sammy he knew me before he checked out of the inn."

Tina was still a little confused, but she shook off the discomfort. "Well, if you're sure. He started to speak to me a few times, but to be honest, I'm not all that high on men right now. I want to run in the other direction and keep running. As for Sammy, she did seem to brighten up anytime he was around and even said he had a nice ass, but you couldn't prove it by me! I didn't look." Uncle Ben chuckled, and she grinned. "Well, all right, I did look, but only after she mentioned it. I should have been nosier when he was here."

"I know Matt well, and I like him," Ben said. "He's a good friend of mine. He'll treat Sammy well."

Tina cocked her head and looked quizzically at her uncle. "Ok, I'll take your word for it. Wait till I tell you what Sammy almost did to the muffins this morning"

Susan was secretly enjoying her little sister's discomfort. She found Sammy sitting on the bed in her bra and panties with half the contents of her closet scattered around her, looking like Eeyore searching for his tail. Sammy jumped up and flung herself on Susan's mercy.

"Oh, Gooey, help me! It's not fair to lose our femininity as we get older. It makes me feel invisible."

"Invisible!" Susan scoffed. "I don't think so. Gable women have never been invisible. By the time I'm through with you, sister, the man will need sunglasses he'll be so dazzled."

Twenty minutes later, Susan swept out of the room with a newly composed Sammy in tow. "Ben, we're going to the mall. Tina, keep the doors locked and don't you dare go out driving around in that Stingray of your uncle's. The police still haven't caught that horrible man, and there's a security guard in the parking lot. We'll see you both later. *Much* later."

Sammy gave them both a helpless smile, following Susan out the door.

Tina and Uncle Ben tried to maintain serious expressions but then burst out laughing as a helpless Sammy was led out of the house like a lamb to the slaughter.

"Uncle Ben, are you hungry?" Tina found her uncle stretched out on the back porch swing with the latest edition of Motor

Sports in hand. "Sammy called. She said she and Susan still had shoe shopping to do so they are just going to grab something on the run. Since we're on our own, let's throw some spaghetti and salad together. I know that's one of your favorites!"

"Oh, I think I could manage to eat a mouthful," Ben replied as he stuck his finger in the magazine to hold his place. "I've been keeping an eye on that security guard all afternoon. He spends 15 minutes in the front of the house, opens the back gate—and sometimes he forgets to close it behind him—then marches around the garden for 30 minutes." Ben shook his head. "I think he needs to spend more time in the front property than back here smelling the flowers. I'm going to go talk to him, then I'll join you."

A few minutes later, Ben joined Tina in the kitchen. She'd already laid out all of the ingredients they'd need. In the fragrant kitchen, they soon found their rhythm of cooking together. Fresh garlic and onion were sautéing in olive oil, followed by meatballs made more delicious with the addition of a little ground Italian sausage. But the pièce de résistance was the addition of Sammy's homemade marinara sauce.

"Yum, if I close my eyes, I can pretend I'm in Italy!" Tina said after tasting the sauce. "I always wanted to go to Venice."

"You should have traveled to many places by now. And you will, Tina. I wish you had come home to visit," Ben gently chided. "We would have loved to see you more often. When we did, it was difficult to pry Jarrod from your side. He was like a guard dog. We missed you, sweetheart, and I can't help thinking you missed us too."

Tina drew the bread knife from the butcher block, slicing the freshly made olive bread in half. Her time with Jarrod hadn't always been bad. At first, there were so many happy moments. *Love seemed the most important thing in the world,* she thought. *The first years were full of hope. We talked about a house and a family. He wanted me by his side all the time.*

She filled the tiny ceramic bowl with olive oil and vinegar for dipping and still said nothing. She tore a hunk of bread from the half-loaf, shoved the rest at her uncle, and dipped her piece. Tina thought about it some more and finally tried to give voice to an honest response that he could accept.

"The first few years, Jarrod was making enough money to support us. We had some good times together. We'd often go away for the weekend. Life was simple when we were on our own with no one around that he had to impress. But I soon learned that Jarrod needed a lot of attention and didn't care to share me with anyone"

She sliced and spread the other half-loaf of bread with a little garlic butter, placed the slices on a cookie sheet, and slid it in the oven before continuing.

"It made me feel special at first. As the years went by and he couldn't keep steady work, he started getting violent and more possessive. He frightened me, Uncle Ben." Tina sucked in a deep breath, then another. "After he broke my wrist and began to stalk me at my office, I lost my job. It became easier just to stay home. He went out a lot looking for work, he said.

My friends didn't come around because he found fault and made fun of all of them. I didn't encourage them. You've got to understand that I didn't want any of you hurt. Most of the time, I lived a quiet life. It was easier that way."

Ben sat at the table watching Tina prepare the bread. Tina peeked at him from under her eyelashes. She knew he was saddened by the way he propped his elbows on the table, waiting for her to explain. She felt dismayed and a little ill that she'd never confided in him.

"Did you know that your cousins went to your apartment to check on you?" Ben finally asked. "Jarrod opened the door a crack and said you were sick and didn't feel up to visiting with anyone. Then he slammed the door shut. I suspect there was little, if any, truth to that. When Sharon told us he beat you, we all piled in the car to get you. I've never understood why you wouldn't leave that day. I wanted to punch that door down."

Ben's face hardened, and Tina saw him blink back angry tears.

"What made you want to stay with a man like that?" Ben's voice cracked. "We could have had a restraining order served against him for your safety."

Tina searched his face and her heart, wondering how much to tell him.

"The third time he hit me, I went to a domestic abuse center," she admitted. "They encouraged me to go to Legal Aid and file papers, but I never followed through on it. Jarrod said a piece of paper wasn't going to keep him from 'what belonged' to him. He said he'd plow through my whole family and leave pieces of all of you on the floor, and if I didn't want that to happen, I better make sure I knew where my place was and not leave." Tina closed her eyes, then leaned down to check on the bread in the oven. It wasn't ready yet. "Jarrod turned into the worst sort of a bully. I became afraid of him, plus he had horrible friends he'd bring to the apartment. If I didn't make sure there was beer or food for them to eat, he would call me names in front of them."

Tina glanced at her uncle, and he nodded, seeming to encourage her to speak further. *If I tell him too much, will it only make him feel worse?* Tina sighed. *I love you Uncle Ben, but you don't need to know everything. Maybe someday, but not today.*

Tina continued, and now she spoke softly and tried not to let her voice shake. "He had this way of standing right over me, daring me to talk back. He'd punish me for standing up for myself. Frankly, I got tired of hurting. I didn't dare get the restraining order. I knew he'd go after Momma, or Sammy, or one of you. It would have killed me to see any of you hurt. A long time ago, I heard this phrase used, 'I made my bed, I had to lie in it.' For some reason, that phrase always stuck with me. Well, I guess I made my bed, and I became afraid to get out of it."

Tina shrugged, then tucked her hair behind her ear. "One time, he kicked me in the ribs so hard that I went to the hospital. They called the police, but I backed down when it came to pressing charges. If he went to jail, it would have been that much worse when he got out. You have no idea of the people he was associated with."

She held her uncle's stare till they both looked away with tears in their eyes.

"He can't hurt me anymore, Uncle Ben, and every time I say that I feel less conflicted. Since I've been with Sammy, I wake up most mornings relieved to be alive and grateful he's gone. I should feel guilty, but I don't."

Ben said quietly but firmly, "You should have trusted us to take care of you. We would have made sure you were safe, you know."

Tina knew her uncle meant well. Really, she did. But it wasn't that easy, especially with Jarrod's connections to some really bad people. "How, Uncle Ben? By putting your families and your businesses on the line? He'd have found some way to ruin you financially, plus he would have reminded me it was my fault because he warned me. You had the boys to put through college, and little Franny was still so young. I thought I was doing the right thing at the time. After I lost the baby, and Momma got liver failure, he left her alone with me most of the time so that I could take care of her. He would stay away for a few days and then come home drunk or high. Uncle Ben, you just can't know how it felt."

Ben didn't say anything as he stood and started filling up a pot with water.

"Jarrod could be so calm and gentle sometimes," Tina continued, "and the next minute, he'd be screaming in my face that I only cared about my mom and it was a good thing she was going to die. That way I could remember who was number one. He was like Dr. Jekyll and Mr. Hyde. I needed to take care of Momma, and when he was there, I had to take care of them both. Sometimes I was so tired that every free minute I had, I would close my eyes and nap." Tina shrugged and turned back to the oven to take the bread out.

Ben put the water on to boil for the spaghetti. Frustrated, he started to say something, cleared his throat, then shut his mouth. "Tina, you are a beautiful woman just like your mother." Ben wiped his hands on a dish towel and drummed his fingers on the counter, trying to make Tina understand how he felt. "Your father was just another lazy asshole. Thankfully he took off when you were too young to know it. Frankly, we always thought your mom did the right thing by raising you by herself, but most of the time she allowed you to do the caregiving. I know I'm hurting you by saying that, and I shouldn't. Sharon loved you so much, Tina. At least you had the summers, and you grew up knowing the meaning of the word family and that we would be there for you. There was a time in your life when you confided in me and then you stopped as you got older." Ben looked Tina in the eye. "I can only apologize to you for not taking care of you better, and we were just dead wrong by leaving you with that man. He wasn't a man in any sense of the word. Tina, that person you married was a waste of your time."

Tina felt defeated by the whole conversation. She took the bread out of the oven and tried to change the subject. "Who is

Matt Phillips, Uncle Ben? Why did you send him here?"

"Matt is a crisis counselor. A good one. I should know because he helped me. I went to him for counseling. I spiraled down into a real depression when my son Michael overdosed."

Tina turned from the stove, shocked. "Michael?"

Ben dropped back down heavily on the kitchen bench. "Michael was my son from a girl I got pregnant when I was single. I didn't raise him because his mother wanted no part of me in her life. I paid court-ordered child support, which she spent on parties and pot. Michael was a kid who fell through the cracks. He never went into foster care, and he had a drug problem when he was in his teens. He wouldn't acknowledge me as his father because she told him the father was someone else."

"Oh, Uncle Ben, I never knew you had another son," Tina said gently. How could nobody have told her? "You are such a good father. If he'd known you like I do, Michael would have been so proud. He would have been so lucky."

"After Michael died, I became depressed," Ben continued. "Susan couldn't help me through it. One morning, a policeman woke me from a drunken stupor laying outside the cemetery in Los Angeles where Michael was buried. The police officer didn't arrest me, but he did sober me up with coffee. He gave me some business cards of people to contact for help. One of those cards belonged to Matt."

He looked up to see silent tears falling down Tina's cheeks. Ben swallowed hard a few times.

"Matt may be able to guide you to the right counselor if you let him, Tina. We're good friends. I asked him to check on you, but not to interfere. You don't have to talk to him if you prefer someone else. However, you should have a guide to help you recognize your true self, to get mentally straight again. Everyone needs help at one time or another, and it's no shame to ask for it."

Tina turned it over in her mind. Sammy had given her some brochures, but Tina hadn't been ready for it. Now, though? Now everything seemed to be pulling her down a different path, hopefully the right path. Maybe it was time.

"Lastly, Susan and I would like to pay for you to finish college. We have the money. I know you're an adult and at thirty you will make your own decisions, but all you have to do is say yes."

Tina stared at her uncle. College?

"Suzy and I will make it happen, Tina. Please think about it. Sammy says you've earned a home here. She thinks you might be willing to work full time and go to school part-time. But if you decide against school, she'll take you on as Assistant Innkeeper." Ben chuckled wryly. "She needs to slow down and relax occasionally. Nobody deserves it more."

Tina nodded, fiddling with the cooling bread. "Yeah, Sammy does deserve a break."

"You think about it, okay? That's all you need to do right now. Matt will fill Sammy in on his background tomorrow. He's a straight arrow, so he'll tell her about our friendship. He can be trusted." Ben straightened up and, noticing the boiling pot of water, added the spaghetti.

Tina sat on the kitchen bench, turning over everything her uncle said. *School. I never thought I could go back to school.* She never thought she'd get the chance. *That would be so wonderful. I would love that so much.*

In the ensuing silence, Tina watched Ben competently finish making their dinner, straining the spaghetti, adding the meat sauce, tossing the dressing on the salad. She filled their plates while he poured a deep red wine. He handed her the wine glass.

She raised her eyes to his, toasting him with her glass. Her eyes were full of resolve as though she were coming to some decisions.

"Uncle Ben, I want you to know how much I love you. Maybe I'll go back to school. But I need to clear things up with the police first. I know some things about Jarrod and other things that I should have admitted when they came to the house. You're right, you know. My head isn't screwed on straight yet."

"Tina—" he started, but she shook her head.

"You're also absolutely right that I need to see someone who can help me get myself together," Tina said, giving her uncle a small smile. "I'm feeling more like myself every day, but I think counseling would help. When all that is done, I promise to come to you, and we'll talk about my future."

"I'll accept that answer, for now, Grace Christina Oliver."

Ben grinned. "There's some Baskin Robbins ice cream in the freezer. I saw it when we were looking for the sauce." His eyes twinkled.

Chapter 25

Sammy

S unday night came too soon. Was she ready?

Sammy sat in front of her mirror, assessing. Her eyes were outlined with a soft taupe shadow and a bit of gold highlight, and she'd swiped lengthening mascara on her eyelashes. She batted them now and laughed at her own silliness. *I can camouflage the wrinkles,* she thought, *but there is definitely some wear and tear on this body.*

She sighed. If Dan were here, there wouldn't be butterflies flying around in the pit of her stomach. Dan had been so comfortable. Maybe he hadn't been the most exciting man on this side of the moon, but, well, he was just Dan. Her teddy bear.

She thought about Matt and compared the two men physically. Not even close. Matt had brown eyes with flecks of topaz and hair more silver than brown. His nose was straight, and his mouth was firm. It looked kissable. She'd like to try, anyway. He had nice long legs and dressed casually elegant. She liked talking to him, and so far, they hadn't run out of subjects to talk about. With Dan, you never had to worry about awkward silences. Dan was always rumpled, like you wanted to take his shirt off and iron it again after twenty minutes.

Listen to me rambling, she thought. Sammy stood up and turned sideways to the mirror as she studied her new outfit. Her bronze silk capelet floated over the attached silk camisole. A satin tie at the waist of her black silk pants added sophistication. Ankle vents showed off a flirty pair of evening sandals. *I've got to give credit to Susan. She sure knows how to dress a girl. I feel like Cinderella,* she mused, *but sexier.*

"Sammy, Matt's here." Tina leaned in the door and provided a quiet wolf-whistle.

Sammy cast worried eyes at her niece, gulping. "Do I look ok?"

"Well, now, I don't know. Let me look at you. I think you might have stuffed your bra too much, so don't let him feel you up." Tina tilted her head to the right. "Yes, definitely too much tissue. Your left boob is *way* larger than the other one."

Yelping, Tina dodged the hairbrush flying through the air and threw her hands up in mock surrender. "Okay, okay, you can't help it if your boobs are lopsided. Seriously, you look fantastic, Auntie. Go get him!"

Sammy found Matt standing at the bay window, watching the sail boats escaping the wharf for an evening ride. The sky was a shot with magenta and purple ribbons as the sun seemed to dip gracefully into the ocean. Matt turned toward the sound of Sammy's heels clicking on the hardwood floor and drew in a quick breath.

"Wow!" he said out loud.

Sammy felt like the belle of the ball tonight. Her eyes were luminous, and though her auburn curls threatened to escape from the combs she used to hold her hair back, it only added to her beauty.

"You look absolutely breathtaking," Matt told her.

Sammy blushed, then turned to Tina to give her a hug. She whispered "Keep those doors locked. Two armed guards are posted out front, and the security system is on. The police are on patrol. Don't go near the windows, and please, don't open those doors." She was so proud of Tina for speaking her truth, but when would the police catch that dreadful man, Ruiz? Was it right to leave Tina alone?

"I'll be fine, Sammy," Tina replied, waving her aunt off. "Go have fun!"

Sammy pressed her lips together, but Matt's hand on the small of her back finally got her feet moving. While he was escorting her to the car, Matt almost tripped over a stepping stone. She laughed shyly. He grinned. All was right with the world.

They chattered about everything and anything, enjoying the fine evening and each other as they drove along Pacific Coast Highway toward the restaurant. About a mile away from Gable House, the car lurched and jerked to the right with a mind of its own.

"Uh oh," Sammy said as an apologetic Matt climbed out of the driver's seat to take a look.

"It's a flat. I'm going to have to change it myself, or we'll have to wait for the Automobile Club to come by, and that might take even longer. Damn! What lousy timing."

"Go ahead and change it, Matt. This way, I can say, 'My hero!'" That earned her a chuckle.

Sammy watched as he pulled over into a small parking lot, took off his suit jacket, gathered his tools out of the trunk, and proceeded with the job at hand, squatting down to unloosen the nuts and jack up the car.

Ten minutes later, the embarrassed man climbed back into the car, panting. "Uh, Sammy? I seem to be feeling just a bit more breeze than is warranted right about now."

Sammy frowned. "Huh?"

"Aw geez," Matt muttered. "There's only one way to say it. My pants ripped!"

Sammy couldn't help it. The laugh started right down in the pit of her stomach and grew into a great bubble of mirth till she couldn't hold it in anymore. She laughed till she cried, the tension of the day draining right out of her. Embarrassed, but obviously delighted that she wasn't upset, Matt laughed with her.

"Well, now what shall we do?" Sammy asked when she could catch a breath.

"I think the Chart House is going to have to wait, but I know a gentleman living in San Clemente who would love to meet a redhead. Would you mind if we go to my dad's so I can change?"

"I'd love to meet your father," she replied.

The sunset was long gone, replaced by the deep blue velvet night sky as they walked up to the pathway and through the front entrance to Jim Phillips's apartment.

"Hey Dad!" Matt pounded on the door, simultaneously opening it with his spare key. "You up?"

"In the bathroom, son. What are you doing back so early? That lady you're so taken with stand you up?"

"No, she didn't stand me up, and you better keep quiet and get out here because I've got the lady with me!"

Matt and Sammy smiled at each other. Sammy took a moment to look around. A small sofa and easy chair took up space against one wall of the tiny apartment, while the other held a large bookcase full of fiction, all jumbled together as well-loved books should be. She glanced at an end table taking up space next to the easy chair and noticed an old Alex Cross novel by James Patterson dog-eared and smeared with leftover chili from the bowl sitting on top of the book. Delightedly, she listened to James Phillips mutter to his son as he exited the bathroom.

"I shouldn't have had that chili for lunch, boy. Better leave the bathroom door closed for now."

"For Christ's sake, Dad! Let me introduce you to Sammy Cooper, owner of Gable House and my date this special evening. Well, at least it was special till I got a flat tire and my pants ripped. Speaking of which, I'd better go change and leave you to entertain our guest. Sammy, this is my father, Jim Phillips. Try not to be so graphic, Dad." Matt turned wicked brown eyes on Sammy and added, "Looks like we're even in the red-faced department."

"Hello, Sammy!" Jim said. "So you're the woman my son is all excited about. Well, let me get a look at you. I'm damned if you don't light up the room. And you cook too?" He bowed at the waist. "Please have a seat, madame, and talk to this old man."

Sammy remembered how frightened she was earlier at the thought of dating Matt, who she was fast learning was truly considerate of others. It looked like she was going to enjoy getting to know his rascally father as well.

"I'm happy to meet you, Mr. Phillips," Sammy replied. "I'm so pleased you're doing well after your surgery. I was checking out your bookcase. I love to read, and it looks like we share a liking for the same authors." She nodded toward the Patterson novel.

"Call me Jim. Yeah, I've always loved a who-done-it. I've got Patterson, Connelly, Parker, Baldacci, and a whole host of others in that bookcase. I also enjoy sci-fi. Keeps my mind occupied when I'm not chasing the women around the complex." He took a breath and continued, "I've seen your place advertised in local magazines. I drove by once, although I've never been inside. I understand from Matt that it's not only beautiful but homey as well. That's a good thing. Do you have an elevator or just stairs to your second and third floor?"

"Well, we thought about installing an elevator a long time ago," Sammy said, "but the money wasn't coming in as much when we first started, and my late husband couldn't see the expense of it at the time. But you know, if it could be worked into the stairwell area so it doesn't look too out of place, I wouldn't mind having an elevator. Why do you ask?"

"I've got some friends who specialize in that type of business. I was just curious. You never know when you can drum up a new customer."

Sammy nodded in approval. "I certainly understand the use of networking, Jim. I'd be happy to speak with your friends, but I can't guarantee them any business right now. Maybe in the winter when it's slower."

"She's a good businesswoman, son," Jim called as Matt walked out of the bedroom. "And I love this mass of red curls she's got going on. Pretty. Maybe when you stop working arm-in-arm with the police force, she'll keep you closer to home. Wouldn't mind taking her out myself if I were younger."

Sammy froze and turned on Matt. Police Force? What police force?

"Hands off, Dad," Matt joked. "I saw her first. Now, we're too late for our reservation at the Chart House, but perhaps we can find a nice restaurant around here."

"Well, you two go on and have a nice dinner. Matt, maybe you could bring me back some banana cream pie for dessert. That Denny's down the street has some nice pie—why don't you go to dinner there?"

She shot a glance at Matt with a question in her eyes. He nodded yes, just as though he already knew her question. *Same as Dan would have*, she thought.

"Jim, won't you please come with us? We can go to Denny's, have dinner, and you can enjoy that banana cream pie you're craving."

"A smart woman, son." Jim grinned. "Yes indeed, I'd sure enjoy that pie. Thanks! Let me just go grab a jacket."

Two hours later, after a lively dinner with his dad as a chaperone, Matt sat in the car with the keys in his hand, not bothering to turn over the ignition. He turned in the seat to face Sammy, who sat with her hands in her lap, quietly waiting.

"I know you have explanations coming to you," Matt said. "I've waited too long to talk to you about this, and now you're angry with me because you think I've been spying on your family. Well, you have a right to be, but first, will you just listen to what I have to say?"

She still wasn't sure what to think. She liked Matt, but first, he'd withheld that he knew Ben. *And now I find out he's on the police force?* But Sammy nodded. "Alright. I'll listen."

"Years ago, I was a psychologist in Northern California," Matt said, sucking in a deep breath. "I'd probably still be in private practice except for one thing. In 1988, my wife went to the drug store at about 8:30 at night because I was coughing. I had a bad cold, and she wanted to buy me some cough syrup. She was attacked in the parking lot and hit in the head with some type of weapon while she was trying to unlock the car door."

"Oh, Matt, I'm so sorry!" Sammy's heart clenched as she thought about how she felt when they told her about Dan's accident.

"Whoever it was that attacked her hit her so severely it left her on life support with extensive brain damage. They stole her car and took her wallet. She never came out of the coma. I placed her in a long-term facility. Three painful years later, I finally made the decision to terminate her life.

"Our daughter Jenny was only fourteen at the time. Neither of us wanted to live with reminders all around us of what had been. The only bearable thing that came from losing my wife was the opportunity to become involved in crisis counseling. Jenny and I moved to Los Angeles. I started assisting the police department with counseling for victims of violent crime. I work with the mental and emotional needs of victims, but I'm not a medical doctor and I'm not a policeman." Matt took a deep breath and fell silent.

"Ben should have told me, Matt, or maybe you should have," Sammy murmured. Matt obviously did good work—necessary work—but she couldn't get over the fact that he'd never told her this. "Even though you told me you were a counselor, you didn't mention your work with the police, and

I can't help but wonder if you're withholding anything we should be aware of. I know Ben meant well, but to be honest, I don't know how I feel."

"I can imagine that's how it seems to you, Sammy, and I'm sorry. But remember, I was primarily staying at the inn to be close to my father and only agreed to give Ben my opinion because of our friendship. I told Ben my opinion was Tina's need for trauma and abuse counseling but that I didn't feel she would agree to that from a man. That's when I told you I was a crisis counselor."

What was she supposed to say to that? Matt wasn't wrong about what Tina needed, but Sammy didn't like that he'd withheld info. *Ben either, for that matter*, she thought. Sammy glanced out the window.

"What I didn't tell you was that a majority of my practice comes through my work with the Los Angeles police," Matt continued. "I read the police report on this Ray Ruiz, and I'm very concerned about both you and Tina. He is a very dangerous man."

"Matt, I don't know if we should see each other right now," Sammy said. She hated that idea, but she had bigger problems. "Tina is very vulnerable, and now that she's in danger—I probably shouldn't even be away from her this evening."

"Sammy, please, please don't shut us down," Matt pleaded. Sammy looked over at him. "During my time at Gable House, I found myself fascinated by you, by how lovely and endearing you are. I watched your gentleness with Tina and watched your interaction and comfort around your guests. I want to see you again, Sammy. I want to spend more time with you, get to know you. I never meant to deceive you in any way, but please, give us an opportunity to get to know each other better."

Sammy blew out a breath, then nodded. "This is new territory for me too. I haven't dated anyone since Dan passed away. It makes me feel awkward and tongue-tied. I can't really stay angry since you're being honest now, but I'm also not sure I can fully trust you. I have to trust the people I care about, and that only comes with time." Matt nodded. "We're very worried about Tina," Sammy continued. "I don't know if I'm doing the right thing for her or not. I closed the inn. It's dangerous to keep it open until they capture her husband's murderer."

"I totally agree," Matt said quickly. "It's dangerous, and we'll go back to the inn now before it gets any later. Sammy, talk to Ben, please. He's known me for years. He'll vouch for my trustworthiness and the work I do, but my feelings for you are personal and very real. I will help you and Tina in any way that I can."

Running her hand over her face, Sammy sighed. "The police have questioned her twice, and I know they want more information about her contacts with persons Jarrod was associated with. Tina's getting stronger every day, but if I try to force information she isn't ready to divulge, she'll run. I feel it." Sammy was so proud that Tina had finally come forward, had finally explained who Ruiz was, but her gut told her there was something Tina hadn't explained yet. "We just want her to be healthy and happy again. You should have known her when she was a kid. So adventurous and daring. She bit off more than she could chew. Jarrod was her poison apple, and I don't know if she can wake up again."

Matt started the engine and drove back to Gable House. The silence left both of them reflecting on the evening's success or lack of. She sat silently with her hands folded in her lap, waiting as he got out of the car and opened the passenger door.

Sammy didn't know whether to be happy or sad. She liked this man so much, her every instinct telling her to trust him. Even so, the date hadn't gone exactly as they'd planned. Maybe it was better to move forward with all their cards on the table.

Sammy looked up as Matt held his hand out to assist her out of the car. She felt the butterflies again. Quietly now, they walked up to the path of her front door. He turned her to face him. His hand stroked the softness of her cheek, letting his lips follow. The green of her eyes darkened with desire. He gathered her in his arms, and she felt the comfort of his caress. He kissed her eyes, her chin and finally, her lips. After taking a deep breath, he took a step back.

"I'll call you next week. Please give us a chance, Sammy. I know we're right for each other. I will earn your trust."

Chapter 26

Sammy

S ammy answered the ring of the doorbell, opening the door to Tina's friend. Angela was a beautiful woman with long wavy hair and big brown eyes which were busy gazing all around the front of the property and at the security guard walking around the perimeter of the parking lot. Angela startled and turned to face Sammy.

"Hello. You must be Tina's friend, Angela. I see by Tina's description that you also have your little cherub Nicco with you." Sammy smiled at Nicco, who was in his stroller surrounded by toys, a six-pack of Pepsi for Mom, and his baby bottle of milk. "I'm Sammy Cooper."

"Hello back," Angela replied. "Thanks for having us over today."

"Please come in, welcome to Gable House. Tina's out in the garden setting up a picnic lunch she made for the three of you. I hope Nicco can eat cookies because she made him some special Cheerio cookies without too much sugar. I'm Sammy Cooper."

"I love your inn," Angela gushed. "I've only ever seen it

from below. It looks like it's standing guard over the sailboats and the harbor, and I've wanted to come here forever! Well, not forever, but since I moved here. Speaking of guards, why is there an armed guard walking around your parking lot?" Angela stopped talking and slapped her hand over her mouth. "Excuse me! Sometimes I just say whatever comes into my head without realizing. Sorry about that."

Sammy just smiled and invited Angela in.

Angela stepped through the front door, gazing around the entryway. "What a beautiful staircase! Are all your sleeping rooms upstairs?"

"Almost all of them, but no, we have a room for the disabled on the first floor as well as the dining room, grand salon, and library for our guests," Sammy explained.

"Oh, how cool! May I take a quick peek in the salon? Does it, like, have a piano in there for people to play? I always wanted to learn to play the piano." Angela didn't wait for Sammy to show her the salon but eagerly looked into the large room to the left of the registration office.

Sammy quickly followed behind, not knowing why she was feeling cautious. *Better to be safe,* she thought.

"This room is gorgeous, Sammy. May I call you that? Tina is full of 'Sammy says,' and 'Sammy does,' so I think of you as Sammy. Oh, look, the library opens off of the salon and goes to the outside! And the dining area is to the right of that. What a great house! But how do you get outside?"

Sammy opened her mouth to reply, but Nicco let out a

lusty cry of protest at being left alone for even one minute.

"Oh, my goodness, I left Nicco in his stroller in the other room. I'll just go get him." Angela scampered back the way she came, her eyes darting in every corner. "Thank you so much for showing me around, Sammy. I'd love to see the upstairs, may I?" She started to go off in that direction, but Sammy placed a hand on her arm.

"It's fine to call me Sammy, as Tina usually does. The bedrooms aren't available for you to look at today, sorry Angela. Maybe another time. Our guests require privacy. Let's bring you and Nicco outside to the garden, shall we?" Sammy guided Angela out through the dining room exit and left her and Nicco with Tina.

Then, Sammy went back inside to the kitchen and sat down at the table with a cup of coffee, slowly stirring the sugar spoon around and around the cup as she contemplated this new friend of Tina's. *Her eyes were everywhere. I'm not sure what there is about that girl that seems a little off, but she seemed nice enough. Nosy?* Sammy sighed. *A lot of people want to see the inside of the house. Tina said she talks a lot and asks a lot of questions, so maybe that's all it is.*

Sammy sat for a while, considering whether to have the police check her out. *No, Tina needs a friend, and I'm just too cautious.* She walked out to the back garden to check on the girls, only to find Angela wasn't paying as much attention to Tina as she was to her surroundings.

Sammy's gut dropped, and she headed back inside before

either Tina or Angela saw her. She dialed the police from her office in the bedroom. *Better to go with your gut,* she thought, *even if we have security.* She'd have the detectives check into Angela's background to be sure.

Later that evening, after she put the baby to bed, Angela sat down and drew up a sketch of the entryways and exits to Gable House. She thought of the beautiful afternoon and how gracious Tina's aunt was to her. She thought about how Tina had purchased a little stuffed bear and a toy truck for Nicco, along with a wonderful lunch of roast beef sandwiches, fresh fruit, and a cucumber salad, as well as the sweetest little Cheerio cookies for Nicco. Tina even sent a care package of cookies and sandwiches home with her.

Angela felt terrible. How could she be tricking her friend, who as far as she could tell, didn't act like she was a thief like Ray said. But she must be, or why would it be so important to Ray that he get into the inn?

I bet it's Ray, that's the thief. Angela thought back to how they met in the old gang territory in Northern California. He was sexy and handsome and always had a little something for her to sniff. *Sex with Ray had always been an adventure. I suppose if I hadn't met Brian, I'd still be living up there, using, and Nicco would have never come along.* Angela sighed and ran a hand through her hair. *But here I am, back to my old habit again. Why did I answer the door when Ray showed up? He could always talk me into anything, and it was just going to be one time.*

Her head was pounding. She was starting to feel shaky. She cradled her head in her hands. Why, *why* had she opened the door for Ruiz?

Brian was on another of his training missions somewhere in the California desert. Sitting in the corner with her fists balled and teeth clenched, Angela was lonely and itchy, in need of another fix.

She could hear the roar of Ray's Harley down the street. Angela got up and went to the door, eager for the extra candy he was bringing her. She knew the routine—candy for sex. It was a good thing Brian was out of town.

Later that night, the high was crashing in her veins. Feeling ugly and dirty, Angela sat up and adjusted her clothing. She allowed herself to think about the euphoria that crack provided, the rush of the hit, the orgasm of the accompanying sex, and the exhilaration of flying.

It was all a lie. She was coming down, and she wanted nothing more than to step out of her body and get clean again.

How could I have turned my back on my husband, my home? she thought. *How could I have put my sweet son in danger?* Angela turned the television on, listlessly changing the channels till she caught a glimpse of Ray's photo on an all-news station. She sat up straight, realizing that she was being played.

Ray Ruiz was a criminal. Angela knew that. But this? A massive man-hunt for him? She sighed.

Brian's going to take the baby away from me when he figures out I'm using again. Now she knew why there was a guard walking around the parking lot at Gable House, and she finally put two and two together. She was making herself an accessory to what, stolen goods? A murder?

Angela threw a blanket on the baby and tucked him into the car seat of her compact car. How could she have been so stupid? She needed to protect Tina, and she needed to protect her baby from Ruiz.

She drove down to the police station, parked, and rushed inside.

"Um, can I speak with someone about a man I just saw on the television?" she asked the officer at the front desk. "I think he's wanted for murder."

Chapter 27

Tina

Tina carefully guided the overloaded grocery cart down the center aisle of the discount warehouse. *Hurry, hurry, hurry,* she chanted in her head. *We need to be home.* She pushed the cart toward the end of the aisle and looked to the left, to the right—no Ruiz.

Tina glanced back down at the list of groceries. *Where in the world are the coffee beans stored? Sammy will know.* Twisting around, she opened her mouth to capture Sammy's attention, feeling safer when she saw that Sammy was right in back of her with the additional cart already full and the security guard just behind her. *Why am I so jittery?*

She touched her side, feeling safer with the loaded Ruger. *It's been almost a week, and he hasn't shown up again. Sammy shouldn't have to keep the inn closed for so long. Ah, here's the coffee.* Reaching up, Tina grabbed a three-pound can of beans and turned to ask Sammy if she wanted another can.

"Ah, here you are. I've been looking for you. You got too confident, my dear." Ruiz's voice was low and calm, like it was an everyday occurrence to join her at a grocery store. He placed one hand on the cart and raised his voice. "Here, *cariña*, let me help you with that."

Tina froze. She tried to move her arm, to go for her gun, but her muscles were locked. She cast a wild gaze to her left and right, trying to find the guard who had been walking behind her and her aunt. Tina drew in a deep breath to scream.

"No, I wouldn't do that if I were you, lady," Ruiz growled. Tina caught a glimpse of metal flash in his hand. "I only want to talk to you. I don't think you want me to hurt your *tía*, do you? I told you I'd be back. Don't bother shouting for the guard, either. Didn't you notice he was new? People never do notice things like that, do they?" Ruiz chuckled. "He's one of my employees, and he's right back there controlling your aunt's every move."

Sammy, please, just stay quiet, Tina pleaded. *I'm sorry, Auntie.* This wasn't supposed to happen. How did Ruiz find her at the grocery store of all places? If he was stalking her, how hadn't the police caught him yet?

Tina took a deep breath, trying to slow down her heart rate, hoping she had enough nerve to draw her gun. She willed herself to stand straight. *Am I going to die now?* He finally had her, and she deserved whatever happened, but not her aunt. *Please, God. Please, God.*

And as Tina sent up another silent prayer, she realized she wasn't afraid as much as she was angry. Who was Ruiz to keep terrorizing her like this? He was a criminal, a murderer.

Looking Ruiz straight in the eye, she was glad she was able

to tell the truth. "I don't have any money, okay? I tore my house apart looking for it, and so did the police. Look, Ruiz, if I had money, I would've turned it over to the police by now. I don't have anything that belongs to you. I could barely afford to bury my husband. He hocked almost anything of value that we had. He wasn't working half the time and…"

"Shut up, bitch! Don't bullshit me. Do you think I care about that? Don't waste my time with your pitiful stories about Oliver's burial." Ruiz said Jarrod's name like it was a curse, something evil. "You know what? I think I'll slice you up faster than I gutted your husband."

Ruiz's face turned red. Any semblance of decency turned ugly at the vitriol coming out of his mouth. Tina's fright was lessening, and her hand moved a little closer to her hip.

"Guess who wants to speak with you even more than me, little dead lady? You see, it's not just the money but that missing packet of diamonds. Have you perhaps overlooked the little packet of diamonds that your husband neglected to return? Do you remember Donaldson, perhaps? Short, fat, ugly man." Ruiz scoffed. "Your husband's employer? He loves a pretty woman. He'll have no problem raping you before he kills you. Donaldson is after you now, Mrs. Oliver."

Ruiz gripped her arm so tight she couldn't move. *Use your brains, Grace Christina Oliver, use your brains.* She felt the cold steel of his knife on her skin, and it felt surreal, almost like she was in a bubble.

"Those diamonds are his. Oliver stole them from my poor,

dead, now extremely dead, wife. What did the police say? That I killed my wife, my beautiful, lying, cheating esposa? My niños are better off without her." Ruiz's voice was cold, calculating. "You know your husband fucked her and took the diamonds, right? Instead of turning them over to Donaldson, he planned on a long vacation, with you perhaps?"

Tina turned her head slightly and looked into the deadly stare of his eyes. Her skin was hot first, then an icy chill ran down her back. "Ruiz, please release my aunt. She has nothing to do with this, and I keep telling you…"

"Did the police tell you they'd find me soon?" Ruiz continued. "Lady, I know more holes to hide in than you could even imagine. You're going to get the money now. I want that $50,000 and the rocks your husband stole."

"I don't—" Tina started to protest, but Ruiz pressed the flat of the blade against the base of her neck.

"Now you just keep your pretty mouth shut and start walking toward the store exit, nice and slow. I'll be right next to you. No, don't turn around. I can assure you I can kill your aunt as easily as I can kill you. We're going to go back to your *tía's* house, and you're going to get both packages. Try anything, your aunt will be dead faster than you. *¿Comprendes?*"

"I understand you just fine, Ruiz," Tina muttered. "You want to kill me just like you killed my husband. Then what's to stop you killing my aunt, you bastard?"

Ruiz jabbed her in the side with the point of his knife. She swallowed a scream.

"You seem to have fallen into a lucky rabbit hole," Ruiz snapped. "Looks like you live well enough, for now. Get me my money or the grand home with its fences and security isn't going to be standing too much longer than your aunt."

Tina wrenched her body away from Ruiz's touch, trying to turn around to make sure her aunt was still ok. Ruiz was still talking as she placed her hand on her hip.

"And if you think I'm a bastard, you have *no* idea what Owen Donaldson will do to your pretty face or your luscious body. You're better off turning all that money and the diamonds to me. I'll deal with him myself and keep the diamonds too."

Ruiz leaned in closer and touched the point of the knife to her breast. "Now then, lady, are you going to try to tell me again you don't have the diamonds? If you don't have what I want, believe me, I won't care if I leave you alive or lying on the floor. Ignore Donaldson or me and you and your aunt are both going to be dead. Now just face forward and walk. Keep your mouth shut. I won't be far away, Señora."

Tina stood straighter. She was so tired, so tired of the threats, the hatred, and the fear. She was overwhelmed, so disgusted with her passive acceptance of the life she lived for so long. She lifted her hand to her breast and felt the sticking point of the knife. Slowly, she started to move forward with the heavy cart and took a step.

No, she didn't have to take this anymore. Surging with anger and incredible disgust, Tina lashed out, "Go ahead! Kill me, and you'll never see your money!"

Tina felt the knife slide its razor edge briefly down the side of her blouse, and pain seared through her body. Her knees buckled, but she could still think. Taking a deep breath, she screamed high and loud.

Ruiz stood still, only long enough to growl. "Bravo, Tina, Jarrod would be proud. Three days. You have three days. See you real soon."

Attendants came running. Ruiz fled, dodging shoppers, bulldozing his way out the doors. Tina pulled out her gun from its hiding place and whirled around, aiming it directly at the fake security guard who had her aunt in his grasp.

"Let go of her or I will shoot you." Tina had her finger on the trigger. Then, she yelled over her shoulder, "Please, call the police!" She ignored the wet and sticky substance under her t-shirt and stood straight, stepping closer to her aunt.

The guard tightened his grip on Sammy. "You may shoot me, but if I let her go now, he'll kill me later for sure."

"Well you should have thought about that earlier," Tina snapped. "He's gone now. Step away from my aunt." She took another step closer, her gun trained on him.

The guard looked at her resolute face and let go, backing into the bodies of two store security guards, who cuffed him.

Tina lowered the Ruger, flipped the safety back on, and released the magazine. Her knees were starting to shake, and the blood was staining her shirt. Sammy ran forward to hold her up and took the gun out of Tina's shaking hands, putting it in her own purse.

The crowd cleared a path, allowing Tina and Sammy to make their way to the front of the store. They were intercepted by the police and the EMTs before they were halfway there. Tina touched her fingers to the sticky wetness of her blood, almost making it to the bench before her knees gave out. She collapsed, crossed one arm, and then the other over her heart, and rocked back and forth.

Tina let the anger and rage flash red, feeling the tremors rocking her body. Heart pounding and nausea rushing over her, she wanted to throw up yet all she could produce were dry heaves.

No more, no more, no more. Please! I can't take any more, she pleaded in her head.

Chapter 28

Tina

Thirty minutes later, Tina was almost back at Gable House with Sammy. The police had escorted them home, and EMTs had checked Sammy and bound Tina's wounds. One of the officers was even driving Sammy's SUV for them.

But all Tina could think about was how her worst fears had come true. Ruiz was *here*, and he'd almost hurt Sammy. She blinked back her tears as the officer parked.

One step forward, Tina thought, repeating Sammy's mantra. *One step forward. Don't be afraid.*

Tina stood with the policewoman, watching Sammy quietly sit on the sofa in the salon. She was still holding her purse with Tina's gun inside. Ben paced the room, stopping as though to say something, but there were no words uttered, and he took up his pacing again. Sammy had called Ben, Ben called Matt, and all four adults were now being guarded in the salon by the police while detectives searched the house.

Tina looked at Sammy's hand, securely held in Matt's. She let Uncle Dan's memory recede in her mind. *Sammy deserves this new happiness.* She could hear Sammy's words to Matt as the police escorted Tina to the kitchen alone.

"Matt, I don't know quite what to say right now. I'm overwhelmed by all of this ugliness. I'm angry and so confused," Sammy said. "What are we going to do now? Do we leave here till he's found and taken into custody? Do we stay? How can we escape from this man who the police can't even capture?"

"It's okay, Sammy..." Matt murmured, then his voice dropped too low for Tina to hear.

Tina turned to the policewoman, who was waiting with her in the kitchen. "May I please speak to my aunt?"

"No, ma'am," the policewoman said. "I need you to stay here until the detective arrives."

"Then I would like to speak to the detective *now*. She's aware of everything happening so far, and there is no reason for separating me from my family."

The policewoman nodded, then spoke into her radio. A few minutes later, the detective walked into the kitchen.

"Mrs. Oliver, it would be helpful if you can tell us where you got that gun," the detective said. "Your aunt won't relinquish it to us until we talk to you."

"I'd like to speak to my family," Tina said. "In fact, we should all speak together. I have no more secrets from my family nor you and the other detective. You interviewed me, have the money, the diamonds, and the story of what happened. The only thing I can do now is describe some of the people that Jarrod worked with. I'll explain the gun, too. Just please let them sit in on this interview." Tina's voice was quiet and calm, but most of all, resolved.

Tina sat at the big kitchen table, outwardly calm, but inside she was trembling. She'd put Sammy in terrible danger all because of her pride and her stupid greed. Who knew where Ruiz was hiding now? And how did he find her in the first place?

When everyone was in the kitchen, Sammy spoke first. "This is my brother-in-law Ben, and Matt Phillips, a friend of ours. Matt is a crisis counselor requested by my brother-in-law and also by me to assess the mental state of my niece. He works with the Los Angeles police departments but is aware of everything Tina has gone through."

Tina looked up at Uncle Ben, who was sitting across the room with his arms folded across his chest. He nodded with a slight smile at Tina. Sammy's tears were running down her face but Matt held her hand. Tina liked that Sammy had a new protector. She liked that her family was here, supporting her.

So, she began to speak her truth. "The gun I used today is actually mine and registered in my name," Tina explained. "Jarrod made me purchase a gun for him because he had a police record. I went to the gun store and actually purchased two guns. I'll give you the name and address of the gun store so you can check the records. What's important is that Jarrod carried a Ruger Mark IV converted for left-handed shooting. I'm right-handed."

"This isn't Jarrod's gun?" The detective frowned. "Where's the gun he used?"

"I hid Jarrod's gun in my hiding place in the apartment after his death. I'll tell you exactly where it is so the Emeryville police officers can pick it up. I never used it, and I only touched it twice. The first time I held his gun was when I bought it, and the second time was when I placed it in my hiding place in the apartment after he died. I touched the holster he carried it in but that's all. Any prints on it will be his, not mine."

But the handgun in my aunt's purse is mine. I bought the second gun for my protection. I have a concealed carry license for my gun. My husband was so drunk when I brought them home, he didn't even notice there were two. I hid mine away."

"Why did you hide the second gun—*your* gun—Mrs. Oliver?" the detective asked, scribbling on her notepad.

"He hit me so hard that sometimes I could barely move for days. I was alone a lot. After a while, I didn't even care if I ever left the house. But I wanted protection from him if necessary or anyone who might come looking for him. I was afraid of him the last five years of our marriage. I loved him, but mostly, I hated him for how he made me feel inside. Like I was nothing. I hated myself most times." Tina swallowed, forcing herself to hold the detective's gaze. "I won't deny I thought about shooting him. I won't deny I thought about killing myself. But I didn't."

"Can you give us a reason for your fear, other than his physical abuse?"

"I know you want to know how much I really know about my husband's business with drug runners. I was afraid you'd think I took part in it. I didn't. I was *never* with him and never wanted to go with him when he went out by himself, but I do know Jarrod was a carrier for drug dealers for the last seven years," Tina said. "I can only give you information on what I know and what I saw."

"Mrs. Oliver, we've learned a lot about your husband, Raymond Ruiz, and Owen Donaldson over the last two months. We know about the drug running and are still gathering information, thanks to the diamonds you turned over to us, about the smuggling. Can you fill us in about how business was conducted and why you felt the gun was necessary?"

"I never questioned how Jarrod paid the rent, although I knew he was dealing drugs. Then he started working for Donaldson and would be gone days, nights. I didn't care where he went as long as he was gone. He always took his gun with him and there were always people watching me if I stepped out of the house. The people he worked with made my skin crawl, ugly people from the inside out." She took a deep breath, exhausted from talking and remembering, but continued. "I found a bunch of money once. It was hidden in this old camping bag at the back of our closet. I wanted to leave him, I really wanted to, but my mother's disease was terminal, and she needed me to be with her during the day. I threatened Jarrod that I was going to turn him in if he didn't give me money for a night attendant. We fought, and someone called the police that night. You can look up the police records, but I didn't press charges. That's when I knew it was important for someone besides me to watch over Momma. I remember thinking it was worth it because she was safe even though I wasn't."

Tina tilted her head to the side and folded her arms over her chest. "I knew it was drug money in the camping bag. I knew it and took it because Momma needed it. It doesn't matter anymore. She died anyway."

I'm so tired, so tired. Tina placed her head on the table for a few minutes, and she was grateful the detective didn't press her for more information. Finally, Tina looked up at Sammy and Uncle Ben. She wanted them to understand why she still kept the gun.

"But I'm away from that life now. I just want to learn to be normal, and I can't even have that. Today is the first day I've ever threatened to shoot anyone. I've been practicing at night for the past month, learning how to shoot it properly. With Ruiz, I know it won't do me any good to just take it out of the holster. I have to be willing to use it." Tina turned to the detective, whose face was calm. "And you want to take it away? No. I haven't shot anyone yet, and I need it. I haven't been arrested. Do you really think you're going to protect me from him? He found us in a store. He hired a fake guard and dressed him in the security company's uniform. You can't even find him! I'm keeping my gun. If and when I actually have to use it to shoot him or Donaldson, you can take it from me then and put me in jail. It's legally mine, and I have no police record for anything but being abused."

"Ma'am—" the detective started, but Tina cut her off.

"I can tell you where Donaldson's office is, but Jarrod said he was rarely there. He preferred to do business around the city in dive bars," Tina continued, her heart racing. "I can provide the names of some of the bars in San Francisco and Emeryville. Jarrod said Donaldson also went to San Diego to work with the cartel down there, but I don't know those bars."

"Teensy." Sammy turned to face Tina. "You had your gun in this house, and I'm not blaming you for keeping it with you, but you knew where Jarrod's gun was all along. That gun may have led to finding this Ruiz character before now. Is there anything else we need to know? We could have been killed today, and I don't think I've ever been so frightened. I don't know what the next steps are. I don't know whether the police can arrest you for anything that's happened in the past, but we're family and we love you so much. When the police capture these men, you are going to have to face whatever penalty the law hands out."

Tina choked on a lump in her throat. She knew there was a possibility she could be charged—she'd hidden evidence and never turned her husband in—but she didn't care. She just didn't want to disappoint Sammy or Uncle Ben.

"But I do know this, Tina," Sammy continued, reaching across the table to touch Tina's hand. "If you've had the courage to face off with that son-of-a-bitch husband of yours for ten years, then you can handle whatever comes at you next. And we'll be right beside you all the way, okay?"

Tina had no words. She tried to stand, to go hug Sammy, but the police stopped her. She swallowed, trying to find the right words to say, but her throat was dry, her tears were stopped up, and her body felt so heavy.

After a moment, Tina turned to the detective. "I swear there is no further information. I'll give you directions to find the hiding space in my apartment. That's where Jarrod's gun is. I'll give you descriptions and directions to Donaldson's office. I was only there once, but maybe it'll help. There are other places where he collected from clients. I don't know the addresses, but I can give you some names and cross streets I remember Jarrod mentioning."

The detective nodded. "That'll be helpful, thank you. What about the grocery store today? Can you tell me more about that?"

Tina's voice grew stronger, and she filled them in about her encounter with Ruiz in the store that morning. "Ruiz says that Donaldson is after me too. They both want the diamonds. So what happens to me now, detective? Do I have to go with you to the station? Just tell me you'll keep my aunt safe."

"Mrs. Oliver," said the detective, "I don't think taking you to the station is going to help this situation, but that's really up to the district attorney. We'd prefer to work with you to catch him. Since you've turned over everything but your handgun, perhaps we can work something out to lessen any violations the DA may charge you with." The detective flipped through her notebook, then raised an eyebrow. "Also, there's a woman with a crack cocaine habit who contacted us a few days ago. When Ruiz told her to befriend you, she put two and two together, and it made three. You're lucky she likes you, Mrs. Oliver. We have every reason to believe she'll contact us when she hears from him again. We've got detectives keeping watch in her area."

"Angela? Angela Franco? With baby Nicco?" Tina asked, frantic.

The detective nodded. "Yes, that's the name I have here."

"She's the only friend I have here. She's been so sweet and generous, I thought she was for real." Tina shook her head and looked over at Sammy, Ben, and Matt. "She knows where we live. She came here for lunch. I wonder how he knew where to find me." Tina shrunk back in her chair and looked at Sammy. "He really is coming to kill us."

Angela stood at the kitchen sink in her small apartment, drinking a tepid glass of milk and gnawing on one of the baby's teething cookies.

"These aren't half bad," she murmured. "Don't have much flavor, but hey! They could be worse."

She squatted down on the cold vinyl floor, picking up toys and straightening chairs, humming tunelessly to herself. Angela enjoyed this part of the afternoon. Nicco was napping, and she could kick back for a few hours.

Straightening, she heard the sound of a car parking outside. "Aw man! I knew it, I just knew when I let him give me that stuff that I'd never see the end of him. Shit! I should have known better. Brian is going to kill me if he finds out what I did." Angela ran a hand through her hair. "I'm so goddam stupid for starting up again."

She pulled out the butcher knife from the drawer and slid it to the side where it was within easy reach. She hoped Ray wouldn't notice.

Angela watched in silence as Ray stepped out of the car and swaggered into the little apartment.

"*Que paso*, how the hell are you today?" Ruiz drawled as he made himself comfortable at the dining room table.

"Oh, please, Ray, the way you choose to act like a barrio hood when it suits you drives me up a freaking wall. And don't be trying your scare tactic shit with me. I know you better." Angela leaned casually against the kitchen counter, wondering how fast she could grab the knife. "How your wife puts up with you I'll never know—oh yeah! I forgot, you killed her!" Her insides were shaking like jelly, but she was damned if she was going to show it to him.

No fear and maybe I'll get out of this alive, she thought.

"Sneaking cunt. Christ, I warned her," Ruiz muttered. "So, I guess by now you've seen my sexy face all over the news, huh?"

"Yeah, I've seen the news." Angela sneered at him. "Fuck you, Ray! You could have told me why you wanted me to watch over Tina Oliver. You killed her husband! Hell, if I were her, I'd have run a lot further than Orange County to get away from you, and if I didn't owe you big time for my *personal recreation* habit, I wouldn't have helped you keep an eye on her either." Angela relaxed into her role of the tough bitch and leaned in closer. "What did she ever do to you?"

Ruiz leaned back against the kitchen counter and plucked the butcher knife from its resting place with his long arm, clearly enjoying the look of fear on Angela's face. "She's got my payoff, and I need it and the diamonds to get away from here. After I kill Donaldson, of course. Oliver stole the money and the packet of diamonds we were supposed to turn over to the boss. I thought he'd have given it to him already, but Donaldson never got it either. He sent me after Tina's husband."

Angela kept her eyes on the knife and barely glanced up at Ruiz.

"Oliver deserved to die, you know," Ruiz continued. "I have to figure his wife has the merchandise stashed somewhere close by, because there wasn't time to go anywhere else that night. I'm going to get it back, too. Donaldson trusts me, so I figure my little plan I cooked up will work and I can kill them both. Now you know why I asked you to start a friendship with her. Happy?"

"Friends with her? You ask a lot, Ray. I've never been so friendly with a little piece of shit-for-brains white bread before," Angela muttered, trying to put as much disgust into her voice as she could. "She's scared to death of her own shadow. Yeah, I made friendly with her. But I ain't seen any of your money floating around. I could barely get her to spend the money for a basic haircut."

Ruiz rolled his eyes, but he didn't say anything.

"Ray, you've never been anything but trouble for me since we were kids. Always pushing me around, you and your gang of snitches feeling me up every time you came near me, snorting a line...you're just goddam trouble. What do you want and what's in it for me?"

"Hell, Angela, you were always asking for it! I never give you any more than you want, and you want plenty. In fact, come here, pussy, and let's have a little fun, eh?" He pushed back from the table and unzipped his fly. "Come on, kitty cat." He reached over and picked up the butcher knife, pulling a plastic bag full of white powder out of his pants pocket. "Got some catnip for ya."

Ruiz reached over and lazily pulled Angela's panties back up over her hips, giving her a pinch and a last friendly fondle. She felt her eyes glazing over as she sniffed and licked the cocaine from his fingers.

"Now sit your ass down here," Ruiz said, "and I'll tell you what I need you to do."

Chapter 29

Sammy

Sammy sliced the strawberries into the bowl, automatically tallying how many she needed for tomorrow's breakfast dessert. Instead of new guests arriving as singles and couples, she had police officers and detectives camped out in her home, patrolling outside. She shuddered to think of how upset Miguel was to find feet tramping among his beautiful flowers and pathways.

Three days is what that murderer had given Tina to turn over the money. He'd left a message on the reservation line of the inn. Now, it was almost past that and nothing had happened. They were running out of time.

Maybe the man was bluffing.

But no, it wasn't poker. Killers didn't bluff.

Tina had given sworn testimony about her life with Jarrod and her confrontations with Ruiz and Donaldson. They needed her cooperation to catch this man—no, not a man. He was a snake. Two men, two snakes who had slithered into her niece's life, not to mention Sammy's own well-ordered life. Two murderers who threatened their very existence. Who was this Owen Donaldson who the police detectives wanted even more than Ruiz? Neither were in custody yet.

Sammy glanced down at the glass bowl full of sliced strawberries and gave herself a mental shake. She looked over at Matt, sitting so quietly at the kitchen table reading the newspaper. She sighed and felt her heart turn over. As unsafe as it was here, she couldn't get him to leave. Just why he thought he had to be her protector, the Lord only knew. Hadn't she been doing just fine the last four years?

I was fine, Dan, just fine, Sammy thought. *I don't know how he snuck up on me. Matt just looks so right sitting in that chair... he's patching up the hole in my life that you left.*

Pushing away her thoughts, she looked over at the man who was gradually taking over her heart. "Here, make yourself useful," she snapped at Matt, handing him the sugar. "Glaze those strawberries for me, would you?"

"Sure, but only if you do me a favor in return. Walk with me. You haven't been out of the house in two days. We need to have some semblance of normalcy."

Sammy looked at Matt like he grew two heads. "We can't leave now. What if that snake appears and we're not here to protect her?"

Matt's only response was to get up from the table and grab her hand. He brought it to his lips. "*Her* is out in the garden helping Miguel and has plenty of protection all around *Her*. Everyone here is going to need protection from you if I don't get you out of the house for an hour. You've been barking at people worse than a dog at a squirrel all day."

"What are you talking about? I'm not upset with anyone." She thought about it, then pressed her lips together. "Okay, maybe I'm just a little bit cranky. But I feel like somebody stuck me in a straitjacket. It feels so restricting, and I can't move!" Sammy sighed. "A walk would be nice. Maybe down to the park at the end of the street. Are you sure it will be alright? No, Matt, I don't think we should go anywhere."

He winked at her and in his best James Cagney imitation, he mumbled, "Look here schwweeetheart, I'm packing, see? You'll be safe with me, see?" He folded back his vest and sure enough, there was a pistol in a holster snug under his arm. "I'm licensed to carry this, Sammy, I think we can chance a walk for an hour or so. Besides, we'll have an undercover cop follow us all the way."

Sammy sighed and threw her hands up in surrender. "You glaze my strawberries while I go powder my nose."

Fifteen minutes later, with a plainclothes officer trailing after them, the couple ambled down the sidewalk toward the multi-tiered park overlooking Dana Point Harbor. Sammy could feel the tension drain from her body as they enjoyed the sights and sounds of the perfect afternoon. Children ran about annoying their mothers, dogs were walked, and persons enjoyed a beautiful spring afternoon. Butterflies danced in the sweet air, landing on bushes of lavender and daisies.

She could see Matt kept a watchful eye out, and her feet felt like dancing with pleasure at the opportunity to hold her man's hand.

"Wait," Matt told her, looking back at the officer trying to be as unobtrusive as possible. He tugged Sammy up the steps to the center of the park gazebo with its grand bronze compass built into the cement floor.

Not the best time or place to do this, she thought, *just what we need, a witness to our kisses.*

"North, south, east, west, here with you is what I love best," Matt whispered as he drew her into his arms for a kiss.

She giggled and closed her eyes, snuggling into his shoulder.

Matt took a half-step back and just gazed at her. He cupped the softness of her rounded cheek in the palm of his hand. "I'm in love with you, Sammy. And I know it takes time to build a relationship like you had with Dan, but please allow us that chance. I feel so strongly that you're my home, my heart, and my future."

Sammy raised startled green eyes to beautiful brown ones, allowing herself to dream. She felt loved, protected—definitely protected. She could feel that gun through his jacket when he held her. She knew she was happy for the first time in years. Even with all this police trouble, she felt secure.

Slowly, they drew away, each lost in their own thoughts. They stood in the gazebo and watched the boats sail in and out of the harbor, enjoying the sunset and the fragrance of the roses planted all around.

Sammy took his hand and they started to walk. Silently,

they walked outside the gazebo, and she stopped at the first of nine Eucalyptus trees pointing high in the sky. She kissed Matt briefly, then walked on to stand under the next. She traced her palm along the line of his cheekbone and tugged at his hand to follow her to the third tree.

"Here is where Dan proposed to me so many years ago," Sammy said. "He was my first love, my high school sweetheart. We built a wonderful life together and raised three children. We were loyal, devoted, and happy, Matt." She turned to face him and smiled. "But I have room in my heart for a new life and a new happiness."

"Put your faith in me, Samantha Gable Cooper," Matt said in a low, firm voice. "Let me protect you. Let me laugh and cry with you. I'll always be here for you if you let me."

"You make me feel so beautiful, Matt. You're funny and loving and the perfect companion. I feel like a new woman when I'm with you." As she said it, Sammy felt the weight of the years leave her shoulders. She sighed and look up at the tree where she and Dan had promised to care for each other so many years ago. The tree limbs seemed to stir in agreement with her heart. "I do love you, Matt, more and more each day. Let's go home now."

Matt smiled and touched her soft lips with his. Arms around each other, they walked in harmony back to Gable House.

They were almost home when Matt turned to her with a question. "Sammy, I wonder how he's managed to stay on top of what's been going on, the security, people coming and going. Has the street been canvassed for any missing persons or people out of town? Have the harbor employees been reviewed or the boats checked for any recent rentals?"

Sammy frowned. "I honestly don't know. I assumed the police have been checking the neighborhood and surrounding areas. We should ask when we get back."

Chapter 30

Tina

Tina wandered the back yard with the garden hose, trying to keep busy. She was sneaking peeks at Miguel tending to his flowers. She enjoyed the way his shaggy hair fell across his eyes and how he pushed it away with impatience, only to see it happen again.

She giggled to herself at the suspenders he wore to keep his baggy gardening pants from falling. He'd told her he wore them because he liked to stretch and move easily when he was planting. Then, he'd laughed and told her it allowed him to eat a nice big lunch without unbuttoning the top button of his Levi's.

Miguel told Sammy he was here because he had work to do in the gardens and he could get more work done without guests tramping over the yards. Tina knew he was just worried about her, just like every other family member.

Why did she feel such comfort in his presence? *He's sweet, that's all,* she told herself. *He makes me feel safe.* He was older by twenty years, and Tina shrugged off the stray thought that she could be attracted to a man his age. Still, the thought had come to her.

Tina glanced at him once more before she turned back to the gardening shed to put the hose away. She pushed the shed door closed, slowly walking back into the house, wishing for something to break soon so they could get back to routine. Tina never noticed Miguel stop working for just the minute it took to make sure she got into the house safely.

The phone rang inside the house. "Gable House. May I help you? A reservation next week? We'll be closed for the next two weeks, ma'am, but if you'd like to reserve a room thereafter, I'd be happy to place a reservation." Penciling in the caller's information, Tina thanked her future guest and hung up.

"That's the second call this morning to make a future reservation," Sammy said. "See? Things are picking up. I think it's the beautiful weather."

Tina was working on the next morning's menus, mostly because she needed to practice her computer skills. She'd learned the police ate anything placed before them. All of this restriction was beginning to get on everyone's nerves. She realized there wasn't much she could do about it. Tina mumbled under her breath about tripping over all these police members.

Sammy didn't act like she was angry with her, and if anyone should be angry, it was her Aunt Sammy. Tina glanced over to the reception desk to ask her a computer question. Sammy had roses in her cheeks and a smile from ear to ear.

"Matt is the cause of that smile I'll bet," Tina blurted out without thinking.

"Hmm, could be you're right for once, Tina." Sammy grinned. "What do you think about this idea? Once this mess is over and our lives get back to normal, how would you like to take over the B&B for four days so Matt and I can get away for a long weekend?"

Tina's heart started to beat fast. Sammy wasn't mad at her? She trusted her? "Huh?" she stuttered. "You're kidding, right? Really? You really think I can do it?"

Sammy smiled and walked over to the computer desk. She put her hand on Tina's shoulder. "I'm serious. It's been a long time since I've gone away, and Matt and I would like to go visit Napa and enjoy Ginny and Geri's neck of the woods. He also wants to show me where he was born and raised. I think you could handle the inn for a few days. You've been doing great ever since you got here. When this monkey business is all over with, I think I deserve just a small vacation."

Tina's face burned. "Yeah right, I've been doing such a great job as your assistant. Putting you in harm's way and turning away customers is *just* what you need." Tina glanced over in the salon and frowned at the person sitting there. "But if those cops don't keep their feet off the furniture, I do know what you'll need to buy."

Tina silently nudged her aunt and nodded toward the living room. Sammy turned and glared at the cop slouching on the sofa with his big feet propped up on the glass coffee table. Tina laughed. She'd felt that glare before. As if he could feel the weight of Sammy's stare, the policeman glanced over and turned red. Quickly, he sat up straight and put his feet down. Sammy smiled at him as though he were a big overgrown teenager.

She turned back to Tina. "Good catch! And that's how you take care of fool men whose mommas should have taught them better manners." Sammy sighed. "We better hope we catch these guys soon. If we don't, I'm going to run out of food again!"

Tina didn't say anything. Maybe they could get groceries delivered—but would that put the delivery person in danger? Could the police go to the store for them? *What a mess,* Tina thought.

"Tina, I hope you stay on," Sammy said gently. "You could be a great manager. I always knew that. You just need a bit more experience, take a few management classes, and learn to smile more."

Tina propped her chin up with her hand and stared out the window at the front gardens. "You know, I think I could do it, and you do deserve..."

The phone rang yet again. Sammy answered with a cheery, "Gable House, may I help you? Yes, Tina is here. Who may I say is calling?" Sammy lifted eyes wide to Tina and Detective Paul Amato, who was now standing in the kitchen doorway. "Oh, hi, Angela, hold on a moment and let me get her for you."

Tina felt like she was swimming in a sea of mud and the air was being squeezed out of her lungs. The detective nodded at her to take the call just as they'd rehearsed.

She gulped some air and picked up the receiver with the speaker on. "Angela, hi!" she said, trying to sound anything but scared. "It's a gorgeous day, what's up?"

"Hey, you! That haircut of yours still holding up? It sure looked pretty. Um, the reason I'm calling is 'cause remember I told you that Brian was away for two weeks for training? Well, it finally ended, and they sent him home yesterday. We'd sure like a chance to go out to a matinee and an early dinner. I was thinking that you really like Nicco, and he likes you, so you'd be the perfect person to ask. I hope you might be able to come over and babysit this afternoon. We wouldn't be gone too long or anything, whatcha think?"

Tina's heart pounded in her chest. She looked over at Detective Amato, who motioned her to keep talking, to give Angela an answer. In a calm voice, more calm than her racing heart, Tina responded, "Well, it's not my day off, but it should be okay since there aren't too many guests. I don't even know where you live, though, so you'd have to give me directions."

A few minutes later, Tina hung up the phone, and started shaking. "He's there, I know he's there. I feel sick." She pushed past Sammy and the detective, running straight to the bathroom in Sammy's room to throw up her breakfast.

Sammy rushed in after her and held Tina's hair back from her face until there was nothing left but a bitter bile.

"Oh, God, it's happening," Tina mumbled. "He's going to kill me."

Angela hung up the phone and wrapped her skinny arms around her body. She could feel the dance of the drug already coursing through her veins. Ruiz hadn't left her alone for two days. Every time she tried to leave or make a phone call, he was there, blocking her way. She thought of Nicco and Brian with deep sorrow as she felt the sharp knick of the knife against her skin.

"Please don't hurt my son," Angela whispered, closing her eyes.

Ruiz drew the point of the knife down across her neck.

Chapter 31

Donaldson

The mid-day sun was bright. Owen Donaldson flattened his body against the wall of Gable House's vegetable garden, barely out of sight. He could see the library's sliding glass door that led into the dining area, but there was still plenty of time. He chuckled.

The cops went right to the scene of the crime. Ruiz laid the ground work by having that woman—what was her name?—make friends with the Oliver widow, he thought. *Their plan to get the cops away from the house is working out just fine.*

Sure, it took longer to retrieve the diamonds this way, but it also drew most of the cops from the house. It had been extremely difficult to get to Tina Oliver, having locked herself up most of the time in this hotel. The security here was quite extensive. The police patrols during the past three weeks were worse, and finally the police protection inside the house required yet additional money spent.

Goddamn Ruiz! If he hadn't blundered Oliver's death in the first place, we wouldn't be in this predicament, Owen thought. *Then, he just had to follow those women to the store.* Typical

Ruiz, always thinking his plans were superior, infallible. *He didn't account for that woman getting courage at the last minute. That fake security guard from the Otay gang down in Chula Vista squawked his lungs out once he was caught. What a waste.*

Owen heard a crunch on the ground from the direction of the back patio and moved into the shadow of the large garden shed. With silencer attached to his Beretta, he was ready to send whoever was coming on their way to meet Jesus. He watched the rookie detective flip his shades over his eyes to soften the noon-time sun. Gazing around the vegetable garden, the detective's shoulders relaxed for a moment. Then, he started moving again.

Donaldson held his breath as he watched the detective step closer to his position near the shed. Owen put his finger next to the trigger of his weapon with its silencer. *Aw, too bad,* Owen thought as the detective slowed. The rookie stared at the tomato smashed on the ground where Owen had stepped.

Fuck, Owen thought. How could he have been that careless?

Owen didn't miss the quizzical look on the detective's face. He was putting the pieces together. *Two and two make three. Damn it, I hate that!*

Taking aim, Donaldson shot and killed the detective. Quietly, he stepped over the dead man to open the sliding door. One cop down and only one cop left since the other two were en route to Ruiz's location.

Just as Donaldson reached for the door, he paused. Was

that a sound by the shed? He turned, looking over his shoulder. *Just the dead cop. Stop being paranoid,* he scolded himself. Nobody was there, not even that useless idiot, Ruiz. *One cop left. That's it,* he reaffirmed as he snuck through the library door.

The old smuggler could be very, very quiet when he needed to be. Hearing voices, Owen crept by the registration desk, standing in the corner of the room and listening to the sound of feminine voices murmuring over the flow of water from the kitchen faucet. He'd learned the layout of the house from Ruiz.

At least Ruiz was good for something.

Donaldson shoved open the kitchen door, gun at the ready. Detective Amato was sitting at the pine kitchen table. Owen shot and killed the detective before he could even get his hand to his gun.

"Ladies, am I in time for tea?" Owen sneered.

Two pairs of shocked eyes turned away from the man now slumped and bleeding all over the table to the man lounging in the doorway with an automatic pointed their way. Owen smirked.

"What, you weren't expecting me? Perhaps you think Ruiz is now under arrest?" Donaldson motioned them away from the kitchen sink toward the table. "Guess again. Your other cop babysitter is lying out back as dead as the squash in your garden. He won't help you either."

Owen looked between the two women. He didn't know

much about Sammy Cooper, but he smiled at Tina Oliver.

"Nice to see you again, Tina. I understand you have a gift that you've been holding for me?"

Tina's heart leaped out of her breast. *One step at a time, one step at a time.* Her mind was racing to match her heart, but bravely, she stepped in front of Sammy, straight and tall and sheltering her with all five foot nine inches of height.

"Are you looking for the diamonds my husband had in his possession, Owen, or perhaps just the money that Ruiz can't wait to get his hands on?" Tina asked. To her surprise, her voice was steady.

"Good. So very brave you've become. Quite the protective little puppy," Owen mused, his eyes scanning her up and down before landing on her face. "You're speaking my language now. I thought you might. The *diamonds*, Tina, I want the diamonds. I don't think Ruiz knows their true value, and I prefer it stay that way," he said. "But why don't you give me the money anyway since I plan on ridding myself of that nuisance Ruiz if the cops don't. I might as well kill two birds with one stone." He chuckled. "In case you didn't know, I really don't like to share."

Steady, Tina, steady, she thought. *He's going to kill me anyway, but maybe Sammy can get away if I stall him.*

"What makes you think I haven't given everything to the

police, Owen? Don't you think I would have told them everything?" Tina snapped. She didn't know where this inner fire was coming from, but Tina knew she was sick of playing this game. "Why should I give you everything? I think I deserve that money for all the years I put up with you and those low-lifes you had working for you, my husband included."

"Be careful there, Tina," Owen growled. "It doesn't do to grow too brave at the end of the story, does it? I wouldn't want to have to kill you too soon."

"But you won't, will you?"

Tina held Owen's gaze. He didn't flinch.

"How else would you know where I hid them?" Tina continued. Sammy tensed behind her, but she kept going. "Maybe my husband was right. He always thought he was better than you. Maybe he hid the diamonds away where you'll never find them. Maybe I never found them. That's a lot of maybes, isn't it? Maybe I know where they are, and maybe I don't, but you aren't going to get them unless you let my aunt go. If you hurt her, Owen, I'll tell you nothing. You're scum, and you've already murdered at least twice today, so yeah, I realize you can do it again. But my aunt hasn't done anything wrong and doesn't deserve to play your game of death."

Tina held her breath, watching Donaldson study her as he would a specimen in a petri dish.

"Well, well, Tina, who knew the little dog your husband kicked around has teeth? Did you know that was how he referred to you? His little puppy who would do everything he told her to." He considered her for a moment, roving over Tina's body with his piggy eyes. Donaldson pursed his lips and gestured with the gun. "It almost makes you interesting enough to screw, but no. It's a bit late for that now. You better hope you're as sneaky as your husband was. I either leave this house with the diamonds, or I leave you dead and ready to join your hubby in whatever cemetery you planted him in. Quite frankly, I'm tired of waiting for what's mine, so I really don't care who gets hurt in the process, guilty or not guilty."

Tina and Sammy jumped back when the explosion of another bullet from Donaldson's gun shattered a stack of serving dishes just a few inches away from where they were standing.

"Aw hell, lady innkeeper," Owen drawled with the gravel voice of an old-time gunslinger, "my gun went off. I hate when that happens. Why look, Tina! Your arm is bleeding. Did you cut yourself?"

Tina didn't move an inch, feeling the blood drip down her arm. "Sammy, stay where you are. Are you okay?"

"Don't aggravate him further, Tina," Sammy whispered from where she stood. "He'll kill you."

"Damn you, Donaldson!" Tina screamed. "If you hurt her, you might as well kiss your ass goodbye because I don't care if you kill me, you *get nothing.*" She wiped at the blood dribbling down her arm. If she could keep him talking, maybe he'd agree to let Sammy go. Or maybe the cops would finally show up. "That's right, I was a little puppy who took too long to figure out where the bones were hidden. But now I know. Let her go."

Owen just laughed and shot the beautiful etched-glass fruit bowl on the other side of the counter. "Well, Tina, how much longer are you going to keep me waiting?" he asked. "I've still got a few more bullets and another gun in my pocket."

"Unlike you, Owen, I'm not carrying anything in my pocket," Tina gritted out with a voice steadier than the pounding of her heart. "I've put the diamonds away for a time when I need to get away from here. Let my aunt go, and I'll get them for you."

Tina knew her aunt would be startled at the bald-faced lie, but even more, by the strength of the hate in her voice. Tina tried to stop the fear running like licks of fire down her back while they played Donaldson's game of 'how long will Tina stay alive.'

"Shall we just go get them?" Tina continued. "I have them upstairs. You can go with me if you want, just leave my aunt alone."

The cell phone was ringing in the dead cop's pocket, and the guest phone was ringing off the hook. Neither sound was truly registering in Tina's brain. *Just get him to leave Sammy alone,* she reminded herself.

Laughing, Donaldson smirked at Tina. "Looks like the cops found out that Ruiz isn't there with your little friend after all, my dear. We needed a game plan to get most of the cops off our track before we could approach you." He gestured to the dead detective at the table. "It's too bad about this one and the dead cop outside, but that's on you, Tina Oliver. You just don't play the game right. Did you put a lot of thought into coming here where there were people surrounding you much of the time?"

"Shut up, Donaldson. Let my aunt go." Tina was running out of words. The fear was back in her head and paralyzing her brain. *Focus, Tina*, she pleaded with herself.

"I must say, you drove Ruiz crazy. Even when you were alone, there were police patrols. Clever on your part. I'll give you this: you've had Ruiz running in circles for the past few months. He almost had you twice, but luck was on your side. Then in the grocery store, you showed you had some guts and saved yourself yet again. Did the police take your toy gun away?" Donaldson waved his gun. "Doesn't matter. I'm tired of waiting for Ruiz to get his act together, so I'm sure the three of us can manage to climb up those stairs."

God, please help me, Tina thought. *Please let me say the right thing to get Sammy out of this house.*

"Somehow, I always knew you were smarter than Oliver figured," Donaldson said. "He always laughed about how gull-ible and stupid you were. Not fit for anything but ass-kicking was what he told me. Guess you wanted some of your own back, huh? Shows some smarts, sure, but you shouldn't have tried to outsmart me and keep the diamonds. Perhaps you and I should hit the bed sheets when I've managed to shake off Ruiz, eh? Now start heading for the stairs."

"Oh, I don't think so, Owen. You're nothing but a weasel in a pig suit, always keeping my husband loaded and drunk for your own use," Tina snapped. "I'm tired of being afraid of you. I'm tired of all of it. So I figure you'll have to kill me before you leave this house. But you'll never get those diamonds if you don't let my aunt go." Tina grabbed Sammy's hand and squeezed it hard. "You could tear apart this whole house and never find them. Set my aunt free first, then we'll get your goddamn diamonds and get this game of yours over with."

"Yes, why don't you just do that, Donaldson?"

One shot between the eyes dropped Donaldson on the floor as Ray Ruiz strutted into the room from Sammy's bedroom just off the kitchen. Tina stared, shocked, as Ruiz kicked the other man's gun in the corner. He stared down at Donaldson's carcass.

"What's that you said? You don't want to share? Good, because neither do I." Ruiz turned and looked back at the woman. "By the way, there's cops swarming all over your neighborhood again." Ruiz directed his statement to Sammy as she clung fiercely to Tina. "Think I didn't know you had the diamonds, Tina? I told you I wanted what was mine, and I intend to get it. You can be my hostage since that bitch Angela is no longer available. One less whore to worry over."

"And you, old lady," he directed his words to Sammy,

"today is your lucky day. Move away from your *sobrina*. You get to live. You need to go outside and tell the cops out there that I'll think nothing of killing Mrs. Oliver here for pleasure just as I did so many others, so they better vacate the premises if they want Tina alive. Hmmm, maybe we should make this a realistic threat, yes?"

Calmly, Ruiz aimed a Glock and shot Sammy in the right shoulder. The women screamed.

"Go now," Ruiz ordered, "before I decide you're not worth it and finish you off."

"You bastard!" Tina leaped at Ruiz and slapped him hard across the face. "Kill me, you bastard! You want the diamonds so bad, just kill me! Go find the diamonds yourself. I don't care."

Ruiz hit Tina across the face with the gun. "Feel familiar?" He held the gun to Tina's temple and looked coldly at Sammy. "Go."

"I'm sorry Auntie," Tina babbled, "I'm sorry I brought my troubles here, and mostly I'm sorry I've hurt you," Tina said. "Go please, I love you."

Ruiz rolled his eyes, but the little widow's words seemed to do the trick. He watched Sammy move forward to the door, her face pale.

"Let's go, Tina," Ruiz snapped, grabbing Tina by the arm.

Matt had been staying in the Emerald Room for the past week, not wanting to leave Sammy and Tina with only police surrounding them. He was speaking with his father on his cell phone in the bedroom when he heard a gunshot downstairs.

"Call the cops, Dad," Matt said, his voice low. "Get them here now." Then, Matt hung up the phone.

He knew the only reason he was still alive was because he wasn't in the kitchen with Sammy and Tina. It was likely nobody knew he was up here.

Matt took the safety off the gun he'd been wearing in his shoulder holster for the past week. Slowly, he moved down the stairs to position himself in a place he felt he could defend the women. He prepared to shoot.

But Matt froze on the lowest step of the second floor staircase when he heard the next shot and Ruiz's voice. Then another.

A few heartbeats later, Matt watched Sammy creep toward the front door. She was clutching her shoulder. Was she hurt? He had to assume Ruiz had shot her. *Look toward me, darling,* Matt thought. *I'm here. I love you, Sammy. I'm going to protect her for you.*

Her head turned. She saw Matt near the stair rail, and he watched in agony as the fear and pain spread across her face. Matt motioned her out the door with his gun, and she nodded.

Sammy scooted out the front door, and swiftly and silently, Matt scaled the steps back up to the third floor.

Now his only job was to protect Tina.

Chapter 32

End Game

S ammy stumbled her way out the door to the waiting police cars, blood pouring down her arm and chest.

"He has my niece!" she screamed. "Ruiz has my niece, and he killed Owen Donaldson and that girl Angela. Matt is upstairs with his service revolver. Ruiz doesn't know that Matt is in the house. Listen to me, listen to me, please!"

The words poured out of Sammy's mouth. Her hands were shaking, and the pain was a red-hot poker in her shoulder, but she ignored it.

"Please do something. He wants the diamonds, and he's going to kill her. HE'S GOING TO KILL THEM BOTH! Do you hear me? Tina let him think she still has the diamonds. Ruiz wants you to move away from the house or he'll kill her and I don't know where Matt went."

"Ma'am—" a young EMT said.

"Do something, do something!" Sammy begged, her voice breaking as she looked up at the man.

"Ma'am, please come with me so I can treat your shoulder, okay? The officers will do their jobs."

Simultaneously numb and hysterical, Sammy let the EMT lead her to a nearby ambulance. A few moments later, a police lieutenant walked Sammy through the information she had thus far. Detectives Amato and Coleman were dead, and Ruiz killed Donaldson. Four more deaths. The cops already knew about Angela, having found her throat slit. The baby was safe, found screaming in his crib. Police were already taking steps to remove neighbors within a two-block radius, and the SWAT team had just arrived.

Please be safe, Tina, Sammy thought as the EMT started treating her bullet wound. *Please be safe, Matt. I love you both.*

Ruiz grabbed Tina by the arm and aimed the gun just inches from her head. Her legs were shaking, but she resigned herself to her fate and managed to stand strong.

"Let go of me, you fucking bastard, or you can kill me here," she spat. "You'll never find what you're looking for. I know how to hide my treasures well. How do you think I ever survived my husband all those years? You think you're the only one who can play this game?"

"Courage is a good thing, lady, and you've already displayed plenty," Ruiz said. "I've already had a taste of your disrespect in the store, señora, so don't tempt me to teach you a lesson here." He tapped her with the Glock to make sure she understood her fate if she didn't keep her mouth shut.

"I've had more life lessons living with Jarrod than you could ever hope to duplicate."

She pulled away from Ruiz and watched him shift the gun in his hand. Ignoring the deep and frozen fear in her heart, she concentrated on the anger roiling up in her belly from ten years of hatred. *To die like this after the last three months of learning what love is all about is so unjust,* she thought as she slowly walked out of the kitchen, past the registration desk, and toward the stairs.

"Thank you for letting my aunt live," Tina said, "It shows you have some respect left for innocent persons."

"I have respect for you, though you don't know it." Ruiz's voice was steady, but for once, not angry. "You're not at fault for what happened to you in your marriage, Tina. You were a faithful wife to Oliver. Neither he nor my wife were faithful at all. It gave me pleasure to kill them. However, although you are faithful, you are also stupid." His voice turned cold again, and Tina fought to stay calm. "Playing games with me, hiding from me was stupid. It caused us both time and loss. You should have known to give me my money and the diamonds when I warned you not once, but twice. It's your fault I had to kill your friend Angela and probably you as well."

"I see," Tina said flatly, deliberately slowing her pace as they passed the registration desk. "Of course, you must be right. Everything is eventually always my fault. If you hear that often enough, you begin to believe it. Well, Jarrod would most certainly have agreed with you. You and he are two of a kind.

You're not to blame for killing Angela at all, are you? You're just an innocent bystander, just wanting what was stolen, just murdering people to have it returned to you."

"Innocent bystander? No, you bitch. I've never been innocent and never a bystander. Your husband stole from my wife when he fucked her. I killed them both—for you and for me. You're lucky I killed him. And now, I take back my property from you. It's a good thing you were always a faithful cow, or you'd already be dead as well. Fair is fair, don't you think?" Ruiz nudged the side of Tina's head with his automatic and laughed as she shuddered. "Where are the diamonds?"

"The diamonds are in my room," Tina said, stopping at the bottom of the stairs. "Too bad for you I had to give the money back to the police. They never would've protected my family from you otherwise, and I'd be in jail already. If I live to tell the police about this, I'll go to jail anyway, so back off, compadre. I don't want your stale breath in my face."

"Start moving, señora, before I carve you with my knife just to remind you of that respect you seem to be lacking. I hear the sirens as well as you, and I'm sure the police won't give up too quickly. You'll just have to make sure they believe your life is worth it."

Feet dragging as much as possible, Tina started up the staircase. She didn't think much of her chances for staying alive, but for once in her life, she was going to fight back. Perhaps she could throw him off balance. She was 195 pounds compared to his scrawny frame, but she'd seen him fight and he was known to kill three—no, four times—now.

Tina shivered and climbed up to the second floor. As she glanced around, she realized something wasn't right. Why would Matt's gray sweater be on the arm of the settee? She took a deep breath and tried to remember when she last saw him.

After the police took off for Angela's house, Matt stayed with Sammy and her in the kitchen until he went upstairs for a brief call to his father. Now, she admitted to herself that he could be dead. She hoped he made it outside to be with Sammy.

Resolved to get this over with, Tina started up to the third floor and then stopped. "Are you planning to kill me too, Ruiz? How will you get away? I could help you drive," she offered. "I can get the keys to my aunt's car and help you escape."

"Just keep going," Ruiz snarled at her.

Tina stepped into her room, two steps in front of Ruiz, and stumbled over the ottoman. In slow motion, her mind accepted the sounds of two guns shooting almost simultaneously. She whirled and saw Matt falling to the ground, blood gushing from his chest.

"No!" she screamed.

Drawing her gun out of her pocket, she aimed at Ruiz, shooting him in the forearm, sending his gun flying through the air. Tina stared at her own gun and dropped it behind her, forgetting about Ruiz, who was still standing.

Swearing savagely, Ruiz grabbed Tina with his bloody hand, slashing his knife across her cheek. Tina fell to the floor, hitting her head hard. Stars swam in her vision as she tried to stay conscious.

I tried. I tried so hard to be brave. Am I going to die? I'm so afraid. Was this really how it was going to end? After everything she'd done, after all the wrongs she'd tried to right, and she was going to die on the floor of her own room?

Tina blinked rapidly as she tried to sit up. A shadow loomed behind Ruiz. Tina's eyes opened wide, even as Ruiz grabbed her body for the final cut. Miguel, avenging angel, smashed his shovel down on Ruiz's head again and again and yet again.

Tina pulled away from Ruiz, trying to get her rescuer to hear her voice. "Stop, Miguel! Stop! Don't kill him," Tina yelled as she tried to pull herself up to stop him. "He can't hurt me any longer."

Tina put her hand on Miguel's arm. He dropped the shovel, grabbing her in his arms. She held on tight, crying with relief.

"It's okay, Tina," Miguel said, clutching her tight. "You're safe."

"Ow, ow, oh, my God, that stings so bad." Tina's eyes were watering as she tried to hold still. Did the EMTs really need to swab more antiseptic on her face?

"Seven stitches, ma'am, it will probably scar," the emergency technician told her as he examined the wound across her cheek.

She gave a half-laugh, half-cry, wondering how she managed to evade face scars for the previous ten years of her life. *This is the most important one,* she realized. *This scar will be my badge of bravery, my badge of freedom, thanks to Miguel, thanks to God, thanks to Matt and everyone who believes in me. This scar will serve as a memory of foolish choices for the rest of my life.*

Tina had watched as Ruiz was loaded into an ambulance, with blood still gushing out of his head wounds and an oxygen mask over his face.

Sammy, arm and shoulder freshly bandaged and in a sling, sat next to Tina on the gurney. "You're ok, Teensy, we're going to be ok now."

Tina put her arm around Sammy, trying to comfort her aunt, who kept her eyes trained on the emergency room doors. Matt was still in emergency surgery, and they were all anxiously waiting to hear that his surgery to remove the bullet from his chest was successful.

Tina had never seen her aunt so distraught before.

"Sammy, you're in love with him, aren't you?" Tina asked, the realization washing over her.

"I am," Sammy answered quietly.

"He'll be okay," Tina whispered, slipping her hand into Sammy's as they waited for the news together.

Chapter 33

Tina

The trauma to Ruiz's head from Miguel's shovel left bones shattered, and the EMT said it was very likely he would have brain and nerve damage. In any case, he would spend the rest of his life in prison, where they could determine if he would be well enough to stand trial for the deaths of at least four persons: his wife, Jarrod, Angela, and Owen Donaldson. Police were amassing additional charges of attempted murder, smuggling, and other drug-related charges. They were also checking the ballistic records for all four guns belonging to Jarrod Oliver, Raymond Ruiz, and Owen Donaldson, searching for additional offenses.

Tina was charged with obstruction of justice in the matter of withholding information and stolen property, but the charge was dropped due to Tina's additional statements of locations for drug hideouts and naming additional drug runners known to be associates of Jarrod Oliver. The money and diamonds were also turned over for the state's evidence.

As September ended and October leaves began to turn color, Tina stepped outdoors once again in the chilly morning, the sun's rays just beginning to shine on a side garden full of herbs, citrus trees, and fresh vegetables.

"Thank you," the woman briefly whispered to the heavens. "Thank you."

Sammy crossed the doorstep and placed her hand on Tina's shoulder. "Who are you thanking?" she asked.

Tina whirled around, throwing her arms around her aunt. "I'm not sure. I've never been sure. God? The universe? The heavens? I'm giving thanks for my life. Whoever it is, I need to thank them for my new life."

So much had changed since she arrived at Gable House. And so much had changed since Ruiz was finally taken into custody.

"Sammy, you're going to be the most beautiful bride," Tina teased. "The wedding will be absolutely perfect in Napa with Miss Ginny and Geri as witnesses. I'm so happy for you and Matt. I promise to take excellent care of Gable House until you return."

Sammy nodded and smiled. "Well, Matt is still recovering, and the doctor doesn't want him to try to work till the new year, so it seems like the perfect time for a honeymoon, Ms. Assistant Manager. Besides, I'm as close as a phone call, and Uncle Ben and Aunt Susan will be here if you need anything."

"You won't have to worry about a thing, Sammy," Tina assured her aunt.

"How do you like your college courses so far?"

After the charges against her were dropped, Tina had

called Ben and Susan to take them up on their offer of putting her through college. If she'd learned anything from the last few months, it was that waiting wasn't the answer.

"The classes are a little hard," she admitted, "but I'm getting the hang of it again after all these years. I can't believe Aunt Susan and Uncle Ben are going to help me pay for my classes. After I finish with my AA degree, I can major in Hotel and Restaurant management." Tina's eyes sparkled with joy. "The women's shelter downtown told me that they can use another volunteer to work with the residents if I want to try it. I'm not sure yet, but maybe after you and Uncle Matt come back from your honeymoon, I will. I'll have more free time then."

"That sounds fantastic," Sammy said. "I know you'll be great at it."

"Sammy, most of all, I want to, I *have* to thank you for saving me from myself."

"Tina—" Sammy started, but Tina cut her off.

"You've been my saving grace through this entire ordeal, and I believe I've come out the other side a better person, a new and hopefully happier me." Tina chuckled a bit hysterically. "Grace. I always wondered why Momma gave me that name, but I think it is forevermore appropriate. I will be Grace. No more Tina, Teensy, Christina, I don't need to answer to that name anymore. I am Grace—period."

Sammy nodded, agreeing with the rightness of the simple and peaceful name.

For just a minute more, Sammy and the thankful woman

newly named Grace stood outside the door of Gable House, enjoying the caress of the early morning breeze before they walked back inside to start another day of innkeeping.

Epilogue

A few weeks later, Grace was kneeling in the flower beds, pulling weeds, while Miguel mowed the sweeping green lawns of the manor house. She enjoyed watching him sit proudly on the mower, uniformly going up one aisle, turning to proceed down the next. He was a methodical man, not given to hasty movement unless necessary. Grace admired that.

She stood up and dusted her hands off, walking inside the newly renovated kitchen with its new baking tables, island, and floors. The quiet woman set a tray with a pitcher of fresh lemonade, two ice-filled glasses, and sugar cookies made that morning. Carrying it to the gazebo, she called Miguel to join her in a well-deserved break. Shyly she handed him his glass, then looked into his eyes.

"I still wear the baseball cap you gave me, Miguel," she said, touching the worn-out brim of the cap that always perched on her head when she worked in the gardens. "It's protected me from the sun, and you've protected me from myself."

Taking his work-worn hand in hers, she leaned in and kissed him quickly on the cheek.

"You were right. Time heals." Grace smiled, a warm and welcoming radiant smile, and basked in the warmth of the sun with her true friend.

Acknowledgments

Thank you to my family and friends who read and re-read this story's drafts, reassuring me with their comments, thoughts, and confidence. You are the center of my world. Thanks to the Foothill Ranch Library Writers Support & Critique Group for their subtle suggestions for more substantial content.

Thanks to my editor Hannah Bauman of Between the Lines Editing (btleditorial.com). Your thoughtful edits helped make this story clearer. And to Melinda Martin of Martin Publishing Services (martinpublishingservices.com) for fabulous cover design and interior layout.

About the Author

Mari-Lynne Infantino

Mari-Lynne has been scribbling stories and poetry since she was able to hold a pencil. Blessed with seven siblings, two children, five grandchildren, and eight great-grandchildren, she has always found her life to be filled with imagination, laughter, love, and sometimes tears—the perfect combination for storytelling.

Retired, after more than fifty years in administration, she is ready to make her dream of being an author a reality.

Connect with Author

You can find Mari-Lynne at marilynneinfantino.com.

The Sum of Her Love

Sustained by deep friendship and consuming love affair, Ariana, a children's book writer, and Gabriel, her illustrator, have been together for more than forty years. Now in their mid-eighties, Gabriel is in a nursing home with end-stage Alzheimer's Disease.

Devastated, Ariana must find the will to bring their chapter to a loving close. When not physically at his side, Ariana breathes their love story to life through her memories replete with laughter, tears, and sometimes exasperation. Ever watchful, Ariana's extended family wrap their arms around their beloved matriarch, determined that she doesn't slip away from a broken heart.

Gabriel's daughter has never understood her father's love for Ariana. Together, stepmother and stepdaughter struggle for acceptance before Gabriel's passing.

The Sum Of Her Love is a beautiful story of enduring love, family, and forgiveness.

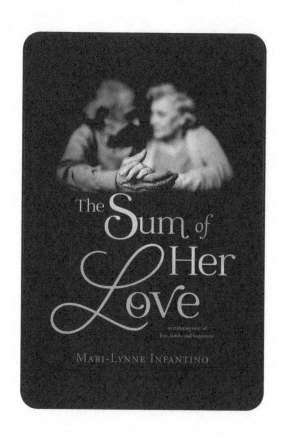

Download for free at

marilynneinfantino.com/books

Made in USA - Kendallville, IN
1219380_9781736083413
12.30.2020 0859